THE THREE BROTHERS

Other books by Michael McLaverty published by
Poolbeg Press:

Novels
Call My Brother Back
Lost Fields
In This Thy Day

Short stories
The Road to the Shore
Collected Short Stories

The Three Brothers

MICHAEL McLAVERTY

poolbeg press

First published 1948 by
Jonathan Cape Ltd.,

This edition published 1982 by
Poolbeg Press Ltd.
Knocksedan House,
Swords, Co. Dublin, Ireland.

The generous assistance of the Arts Council
of Northern Ireland in the publication of this
book is gratefully acknowledged

Cover by Robert Ballagh
Design by Steven Hope

Printed by Cahill Printers Ltd.,
East Wall Road, Dublin 3.

"Sorrow and suffering and joy are three strands in the tether of God; sorrow and suffering strengthen fervour, and joy strengthens hope. Without fervour and without hope the spirit breaks loose, and when the spirit breaks loose from the tethering Man roams like an animal without a home." — Anonymous.

To Denis Ireland

THE THREE BROTHERS

CHAPTER ONE

WHEN he was half-way up the street after getting off the tram he saw a light in his own parlour window. His two sons would be studying, he thought, or maybe Eileen practising at the piano. He stood for a minute in the cold silence of the street and inclined his ear towards the house, but nothing came to him except the receding hum of the tram as it sped towards the terminus. Hm! he said, those fellows aren't in so great a hurry to get you to your business in the mornings: sitting parked at the terminus and drinking tea out of thermos flasks till you'd think they had taken root; and then at this time of the night they'd drive you past your stop if you weren't careful. Please God, when he'd have Frank finished at the university he'd buy a little car and make himself independent of trams. That's what he'd do – he could afford a little car then, and Mary and himself could go off by themselves on a Sunday down to the sea, or maybe drive out into the country to see his brother Bob and his half-sister Nelly. It was good for a man to get out of the city, once in a while, and it was good for a woman, too, to get away from the same old sink and the hot fumes of the cooker. He braced his shoulders and fumbled in his pocket for the latch-key. His foot crunched on a bit of coal at the gate of the garden. 'So the coal has come at last,' he said to himself. 'I hope Mary has counted the bags, for those coalmen would do you up to your very eyes – nothing in their heads only trickery and dishonesty! Nothing but dishonesty in the world! Charwomen and washerwomen with high recommendations we've had and when they had cleaned up and gone off there was always something missing: sheets and blankets, and only last week a case of silver spoons had disappeared. Disappeared! – yes, there's nothing but dishonesty growing up around you.'

He turned the key in the lock and let himself into the dark hallway: a line of light shone under the parlour door and one from under the door of the kitchen. They were using plenty of light anyway, but there was nothing you could do about it when you've a family to rear and educate; you can't expect your children to concentrate on their studies when everybody's gabbling and foostering around them; and there's Anne and her tongue always going like a handbell—upon my word she'd talk the handle off a jug!

In the darkness he took off his hat and hung it on the hallstand. Quietly he opened the parlour door and looked inside. Anne was seated at the table correcting exercise books and Brendan was reading beside the fire.

'Where's Frank?' the father asked, standing with his hand on the door-knob.

Brendan glanced at Anne, but Anne, ignoring his questioning look, continued to correct her exercise books with evident impatience. 'Their compositions are as alike as penny tram-tickets,' she said aloud. 'The same old phrases in them all . . . a carpet of leaves . . . in autumn the farmers gather in the crops . . . in autumn we get apples. They're unteachable! The teacher who handed that class on to me had no faith in the individual. I've no luck to be stuck in a school like that.'

'You're fortunate, girl, to get into any school and you just out of the training college.'

'I wish, Father, I had failed my examination outright. I haven't the patience! I haven't the temperament!'

'That's not what Miss Mallon told me this morning when I met her and her brother on the way to their school. She told me you were shaping most promisingly and had excellent control of your class. She said you would make a very efficient teacher when you have a few years' experience.'

'I wish, Father, you wouldn't discuss me with the Mallons. A school inspector is due any time now, and today Miss Mallon came into my room and threatened the children with the cane if they didn't do well for me in the examination The children were frightened out of their wits, and when I told Miss Mallon we were taught in the training college to fill our pupils with joy before an exam she laughed scornfully. "Listen to me, Miss Caffrey," she said, "forget all you ever learnt about psychology when you stand in front of a class. The children in this town don't respond to kindness," – those are her very words.'

Anne lifted an exercise book from the pile in front of her. 'Look, Father, at the handwriting in these exercises – if a child's handwriting takes on a characteristic of its own Miss Mallon condemns it. The handwriting must be uniform throughout the school. Education and uniformity – that's what it is. The children are treated as a group: their compositions must be begun in the same way, must contain the same ideas, and must have the same handwriting. It's deadening, Father, I tell you. She even told me that poetry was a waste of time and that the new inspector does not ask for poetry. There's no life in the teaching – it's all rattled up for exams. If I continue at teaching I shall try to get away to a small school in the country where I can work out my belief in individuals as individuals. I will teach for life and not for school. I'll teach poetry and music and singing and drawing, for without that we are only half alive.'

'All I can say is that Miss Mallon has done well for her own nephews: one out a doctor, one doing Arts, and another away to be a Christian Brother.'

'I wouldn't give that for the whole lot of them,' and she snapped her fingers in the air. 'They're all a spineless, cautious lot – afraid to give an opinion about anything in case they'd be in the wrong.'

'Don't be so bitter, Anne. It only poisons and sours your nature. Be obedient to Miss Mallon while you're in her school.'

'Obedience and silence when you know in your heart and soul that it is wrong.'

15

'Maybe at the end of your days you'll find your ideas are not one whit better than Miss Mallon's.'

She lifted another book from the pile, and seeing that he had annoyed her he asked again if Frank were in.

'I don't think he is,' she said, and then turned to Brendan. 'Do you know where he is?'

'Indeed I don't. Frank doesn't announce to me about his goings and comings.'

'I hope he did some studying today,' added the father, and he closed the door gently and went into the warm kitchen where his wife and Eileen were folding the clothes they had just smoothed.

He rubbed his hands together and held them to the heat of the range: 'There's a frosty edge on that night. It's a pity of anyone without a fire a night like that.'

Mary, his wife, rumpled the cushion on his armchair and handed him his slippers that were warming on the plate-rack, and when he had them on, Eileen took his boots and began to polish them over the sink in the scullery.

'How was business today?' said his wife, offering him a bowl of porridge with a thick layer of cream on it.

'Slack enough, Mary, considering the time of the year. With the cold weather setting in you'd think there'd be a run on boys' overcoats. I only sold three in that line today. I'm afraid there'll not be much money floating about this Christmas.' He paused as if listening to the hum of the range and as he did so the milk dribbled from his spoon, and his wife gave him a serviette to spread on his knees. Presently he handed her the empty bowl: 'There's nothing like porridge and milk — I owe my health to that. But the young nowadays turn up their noses at it. Frank, for instance — and well seen on him. His bread and tea won't stand by him when he gets into the race of his studies. He's very late tonight, and if he misses the last tram, a walk home in that raw air won't answer him. I wonder where he'd be.'

'Maybe in the Reference Library looking up something important.'

'The libraries are closed long ago. Brendan could tell you that.'

'Don't be upsetting yourself about him. He'll be in fresh as Larry before you're half-way up the stairs.'

'If his brain were only half as fresh I'd not be worrying. The Mallons didn't get their exams by walking and gallivanting all night about the streets. If he doesn't get the bulk of his work done in the winter he'll not get it done when the days brighten.'

'During the daytime Frank does his studying. He thinks he can work better in daylight than in gaslight.'

'If he were interested in his studies he could work in any light. What kind of an almanac has he been reading to put that nonsense in his head.' He took his pipe and filled it, for it was only in the evenings he could enjoy a smoke, it never occurring to him to have a draw at it during the day, to steal off to the lavatory like the rest of the staff and have a quiet smoke to himself. He took an old envelope from his pocket, tore a strip off it and lit his pipe.

'Oh, that reminds me,' said Mary and she took a letter from the mantelpiece. 'That came on the evening's post.' He scrutinized the handwriting on the envelope and then looked at the back where there was an embossed address in blue: R. Caffrey, High Class Draper, Monabeg, Co. Antrim. It was from his brother Bob and he supposed he was wanting another consignment of red flannel or blankets – the country people at any rate won't let the wind whistle through them. He put the letter unread into his pocket, glanced at the clock, and said with sudden anger: 'Well, if Frank thinks I'll spend my hard-earned money on a wastrel he's making a sad mistake.'

'Don't excite yourself, John,' placated his wife. 'I'm sure the boy will get his second medical as easily as he got his first.'

'We'll see.'

'And anyway too much studying would ruin the boy's health. There are times when I think it would be better for us all to live in a small way and be content with it – just like Bob and Nelly, happy and unworried, in their little drapery store. And poor Frank – when he's finished he'll probably be ready for export, leaving the land that made him and seeking his living in a country where he'll be a perfect stranger. My mind is in a confusion about him; and when I kneel at Mass in the mornings I often wonder if I did right in urging him to do medicine. I would love him to be a doctor so that I could talk about my boy to strangers. But it's pride, I know, and when I see his pale face and his thin hands with the blue veins showing through them I feel in my heart I've wronged him.'

He took the pipe from his lips and gave her an uncomprehending look. 'Do you want me not to do my duty by my children? I want to give them all a good start in life – better than I ever got. To give them all a respectable profession and bring security into their lives.'

'If they haven't their health what'd be the use of it all? You made Brendan go for the library when he wanted to go on for the bank.'

Eileen came from the scullery and he told her to go into the parlour and play a few sprightly tunes on the piano, and when she had gone and his wife and himself were alone in the kitchen he stared at her with a hard look of disapproval: 'Time and time again I've told you why I kept Brendan from the bank. Since the day his Uncle D. J. embezzled a hundred pounds when he was a young railway clerk in Monabeg Brendan's chances of being appointed to a position in any bank were ruined.'

'That's years ago now. And didn't you yourself repay every penny of it? And didn't Father Delaney use his influence to hush it up and not allow it to reach the law or the newspapers?'

'He did, but though he has forgotten it the people never do. They hold an evil thing in their minds as easily as they remember their prayers. And so, before a lad would be selected for the bank his pedigree is inquired into as if he were a Derby racehorse. And take Frank: he wanted to do medicine and you encouraged him and I allowed him, though it will take me busy to meet his fees. And since Anne didn't know what she wanted I pushed her on for the teaching.'

'She doesn't like it she tells me.'

'If she doesn't, she should learn to like it. "There's nothing either good or bad but thinking makes it so." If she were in some other profession she'd dislike that too. Let her be content with what she has and the sun will shine on her. Being with the young all day will keep her young – and there's nothing more you could wish for your daughter!'

'That's what you think it should be, John. But if you look around you at the lady teachers at Mass on a Sunday you'd see the strained look on their faces.'

'I go to Mass to pray not to look around me,' and he got up from the armchair; and thinking that he was going to bed she remained silent. She lifted an unfinished scarf with the university colours, and as her needles clicked she watched her husband covertly as he unlocked a drawer in the sideboard and took out a fat notebook. She sighed and glanced furtively at the clock, and in the silence she heard the scratch of his pen as he made a note of his expenses for the day. 'There's one thing certain,' he said aloud, 'that family of ours costs me a nice penny. Listen to these few items since last June: Two Ladies' bicycles £14; two tennis rackets £4; Music fees, four guineas, and a list as long as your arm for frocks, shoes, bathing costumes, books, and examination fees. Upon my solemn word it would take me to be a millionaire to hold out to it.' He turned to the book again and at a back page under the heading 'D. J.' he totted up a column of small amounts that he had sent to his brother who was now living in England. 'Well,' he said to himself, 'he'll not get another shilling from me to fritter on racehorses – not another mouldy halfpenny.'

'What's that you say, John?'

'I was saying that that family of ours is living like royalty. It'd take a mint of money to keep up to their style,' and he closed the notebook and stowed it safely away in a locked drawer.

'You should thank God,' she commented, 'we've got them so far without a penny of debt. Where there's debt there's always danger.'

He was ready to call his family for the rosary when there was a knock at the door and Frank came in, a high flush on his cheeks, and his hair flat with sweat.

'I nearly missed the last tram,' he panted. 'I was over at a friend's copying the few lectures I missed the week I was off with the 'flu.'

'You did well to get them,' his father said, unable to conceal his pleasure. 'You never know but you might get an exam question on those very lectures.'

Frank sat at the table while his mother prepared a meal for him, and as he scanned a notebook with a show of pleasurable concentration his father sat quite still, refilled his pipe and drew forth the letter that had come from his brother in the country.

Dear John: It's possible that I may get a run up to town to see you all before Christmas. Although it's the busy time of the year with me, yet a few things have happened that make it urgent that I go soon. Dr. O'Neill is not fully satisfied with the way my stomach is reacting to his treatment and he advises me to go up to St. Jude's Private Hospital for a few days and have an X-ray and a thorough examination by a specialist. He doesn't think there is anything seriously wrong with me but just to make sure that he is acting on the right lines he would like to hear the result of an X-ray as soon as possible. It may be a duodenal ulcer, he says, and if that were the case he advises me to undergo an operation; it would have to be done some time, and since his powders and bottles have no effect on me things would grow worse instead of better. My insides I may tell you have cost me a pile of money and when Dr. O'Neill sends in his quarterly account it almost staggers me. I wish I could carry on without the operation for that, too, I believe is a costly business. I hate leaving the shop even for a whole day, and it just occurs to me that I have stood behind the counter for forty years without a day's serious illness. Nelly, as you know, is not of much help to me in the shop, for somehow she hasn't the pleasing and patient way with customers that I have, and so if I have to lie up in hospital for any length of time some of my best paying customers might take themselves off to Daly's across the street, and once you lose them they'd never return even if my prices were lower.

The Dalys have got their shop decorated recently and I am thinking of renovating my own in the spring of the year. I would like the window enlarged in the front and an awning over it with my name in big black letters on top of the canvas. Only the other day the sun faded a suit I had in the window; it seemed to me to be in perfect health until the buyer lifted up one of the lapels and showed the unfaded material – our country people are as cute as pet foxes! When I have the window in they'll have no more complaints. But it will cost me a heap; I had estimates from many builders and after much thought I've decided to give it to the local lad, Philip Doran – he's an honest careful workman – and, after all, there's nothing like giving it to your own neighbour.

I had a letter from D. J. recently with the Liverpool postmark on it and asking me for the loan of three pounds. I laughed outright at the word 'loan' – he's an artful dodger! Of course I squeezed his letter into a ball and tossed it into the fire. 'If a man will not work do not let him eat', said St. Paul, and he knew a thing or two about human nature; he had his head screwed on in the right place. I hope the playboy is not pestering you for money.

You must be a happy man now with Brendan installed in the library and Anne teaching in a school in the city. Myself and Nelly always remember you in our prayers. And then to think you'll have Frank finished within a few years – Doctor Frank Caffrey: there's something aristocratic the way those words run together, like old playmates you may say.

Before I close I am wondering if, with all this expense staring me in the face, you could repay me before Christmas the two hundred pounds I lent you. You know, John, I wouldn't ask you for it so soon only I know things are much easier with you since your two children are now in good sound positions – God spare them their health to enjoy it.

And by the way if I go up to the hospital I am sure the missus and yourself would allow Eileen to come and stay with Nelly and help her in the shop. Nelly and she get on well together. I could get local help but you know yourself how hard it is to get a girl you could trust – there's nobody like your own when all is said and done.

I will be sending your firm an order after Christmas for some boys' suits and children's frocks.

My blessings to you all for Christmas and the New Year. Your affectionate brother, BOB

His face flushed as he ended the letter, and he felt a heavy hurried throbbing in his temples. He tried to control himself as he stood up and put the letter in the fire. From the parlour came the heavy notes of the piano and Brendan singing.

'Hasn't Brendan a lovely baritone voice?' said Mrs. Caffrey. 'It reminds me for all the world like his Uncle D. J.'s. But he'll never have that deep richness of tone that his uncle has – never. Poor D. J. many a lovely song he sang for us in our young days.'

'Och, tell them to stop that singing and playing,' he said

with rising anger. 'Nobody could study with that randybooze. Two fires and gaslight in every room – expense at every turn. We'll say the rosary and let me get to bed.'

And when they were all kneeling around him he gave out the prayers in a heedless disjointed manner: sometimes saying twelve Hail Marys to a decade and sometimes eight, and finally when he had finished he told them all to hurry to bed; and then without a word he wearily climbed the stairs to the cold darkness of his room. In the dim light from the window he began to undress, pausing now and again to settle his thoughts and change his attitude to the letter he had just read. But the more he thought of it the more his mind clenched on individual lines, and the more he accused his brother of hardness and meanness of heart. A man that could buy up all Monabeg – lock, stock and barrel – and not feel the pinch of it! Stood for forty years at the counter – that's an item to boast of: a man that never took a holiday in his life for fear he'd lose a penny. A man that opened his shop in the mornings an hour before all the others and shut it last in the evenings. With money rotten in the bank and afraid to touch it. A man without chick or child and responsible to no one. No, I'll not pay him yet! And didn't I tell him that as soon as Frank was finished I'd pay back every single penny he lent me. And what under God does he think Brendan is earning in the library and Anne in the school and she only appointed? I couldn't do it; I'll write to him in the morning and explain everything and hide nothing.

He got into bed, and he lay on his back so that he wouldn't hear the heavy insistent pulse at the side of his head. He tried to dismiss his brother from his mind but he came up all the more vividly before him, standing as he always did behind the counter in Monabeg, his hat on his head, and his eyes now on a customer and now at the window where he could see everyone who passed in and out of Daly's drapery on the other side of the street. A nice way for anyone to live one's life! Hoping day after day that a time would come when he could drive Peter Daly and his family from Monabeg. It's somebody's blessing Bob needed and not money. But when all was said and done one had to admit that he had built up a good business for himself – better than poor D. J. could have done: a man that'd have gambled every shirt and sock in the place. When he did get a haul from the racehorses many's the treat he gave the children when they were young, rigging them out in new clothes and taking them on a trip to the seaside where he made them sick with ice-cream and sweets. Money would burn a hole in his pocket. It's always the big-hearted that have usually nothing to give. And there was some truth in what D. J. said of Bob: 'Bob has the Midas touch. Whatever he touches turns to gold. Upon my word he would make money where many a Jew would die of starvation.' He smiled at that in the darkness, turned on the pillow and became aware of the voices from downstairs. He could hear Anne's voice and then Frank's sharp in protest. He leaned out of bed and hammered on the floor with his slipper, and presently his wife came into the room with a lighted candlestick in her hand, and her hair down her back like a young girl.

'Did you tell them to go to bed?' he asked.

'I did; they're getting ready now. Don't be upsetting yourself, John. They're getting big now and you can't treat them like little children all the time.'

'Sure what have they to talk about at this time of night. Burning coal and gas to no purpose. If they were studying I wouldn't mind.'

She had blown out the candle and was standing at the window unbuttoning her dress. The light from the kitchen shone into the garden and she noticed a white frost on the ground. 'It's beginning to freeze,' she said, and then the light left the garden, quenching it in darkness. 'They're coming now ... You wouldn't like a hot jar for your feet,

John? I didn't know it was so cold till I saw the mist gathering at the window.'

'I don't feel the cold one bit,' he said, and when she got in beside him he knew it would be a long time before sleep would come to him. 'It's a pity, Mary, we didn't move to a bigger house long ago – a house with one extra room in it. And it's not myself I'm thinking of – it's you. You would sleep better if you had a room and a bed to yourself. I keep you awake.'

'What nonsense, John! A woman can do with very little sleep.'

'But there'll be a good time coming, never you fear. Please God, when Frank's finished we'll be able to buy a little car and the two of us could drive off after Mass on Sunday, or maybe the children would like to come with us and we could have a picnic down at Inch Abbey and Anne could tell us about the old monks that lived in the twelfth century: it must have been a lovely age to live in – not as fretful or worried as our own.' He tried to think of Inch as he had seen it one day long ago in June with the trees heavy with cool leaves, the stones of the old ruins warm to the touch, the river as quiet as a lake, and the roach sunning themselves in the shallow edges. The peaceful rhythm of that memory was slowly swaying and settling in his mind when suddenly it was shattered by the noise of his sons in the room above his head.

'Listen to that, Mary, for the love of God. Wouldn't you think they were trying to put their feet through the ceiling?'

'Go to sleep and don't heed them.'

There was another thunder of a noise.

'Upon my word you'd think we stabled a couple of horses up in that attic,' and when he saw Mary rising to speak to them he called her back and shouted up at the ceiling: 'Will you get into bed there and go to sleep?'

'There you are,' said Frank who was locking a suitcase

and pushing it below the bed with his toe. 'You've wakened father with your talk.'

'I'm sure you're greatly perturbed about father's sleep,' Brendan answered from his side of the room as he glared at Frank hopping into bed with a lighted cigarette and a book. He watched him as Frank inhaled the cigarette, holding the smoke till you'd have thought it was absorbed inside him, and then exhaling it with a slow and leisurely reluctance. 'Are you ever going to give up that disgusting habit of smoking in bed?' he shouted across to him.

'Keep quiet sometime,' Frank said. 'You'd drive a fellow to drink with your chandering.'

'From what I hear it wouldn't take much to drive you.'

Frank ignored him, and then as he turned a page in his book he looked up and saw the smoke disappearing rapidly through the open skylight. He shrugged his shoulders from the cold and stood up on the bed to close the window.

'Leave that open!' said Brendan.

'I'll not. Do you want me foundered?' He closed it with a bang and went on smoking. Brendan watched the smoke billowing up to the sloping ceiling and pressing against the dark pane. Without a word he stood up on his own bed and reopened the window.

'Open the door if you're so fond of fresh air,' said Frank.

'I will not! My father's stale tobacco floating in and yours wanting to get out. I will not – fresh air never killed anyone,' and he settled down in bed again, his arms under his head, and his eyes fixed on the gaslight above the mantelpiece.

Frank coughed and threw the butt of his cigarette in the empty fire grate. 'I tell you there's a frost tonight and a vicious draught from that skylight. I'm going to close it and if you interfere I'll give you this,' and he raised his fist. 'There's a rush of air up that chimney that'd cut the ankles of you. You'd think a medical student knew nothing about ventilation,' and he lifted his book again.

26

'Some medical student!' said Brendan, losing his temper. 'We're not all as blind as you think.'

'What are you driving at?' Frank said in a subdued voice.

'I'll tell you if you want to know. You're not enrolled as a second medical. You were supposed to enrol last October but you and another of your so-called friends – I'll not mention his name – stuck to the fees and squandered them. And what's more all the money you got from father for medical books went the same way.'

'It's not true,' Frank said lamely. 'It's not true. . . .'

'I wish to God it were not true! But it's too true! And if father or mother gets to hear of it it would break their hearts.'

'And you'll tell them?'

'I wouldn't be so unkind to them. All I hope is that you'll work now in isolation, and that next year you'll enrol and work with some speck of honesty in you. You're a fool, an irresponsible idiot – that's what you are.'

'It's well there's only one of my species in the family. You are free to reveal all to father anytime you're in the mood. Do you hear that? – my library detective!'

'I'm never in the mood to bring despair to those who tried to rear me decently.'

Frank closed his book and turned out the light. 'Good night,' he said without enthusiasm, and for a few minutes Brendan remained silent before he answered 'good night' in return.

CHAPTER TWO

THE following morning when Eileen rapped her father's door he was lying awake. His wife had already risen an hour ago and gone to an early Mass and since then he had been concentrating on the resolution he had come to during the sleepless hours of the night. He had decided to pay the debt he owed his brother. He had an endowment insurance policy of five hundred pounds which was due in another six years and he resolved to surrender it now. He detested touching it before its completion for he had often looked forward to the full payment of the policy and often imagined himself presenting it to his eldest son when he had passed his final medical: 'There's a little present, Frank, to help you to make a start in your own town,' he would have said. Now all that was gone and he realized Frank would have to go abroad for a while before settling down in his own country. It wouldn't do him any harm though – it would give him experience and confidence and enlargement of mind. There was nothing like a bit of travel for a young doctor when you came to think of it.

He rose and went into the bathroom, and whilst shaving he became aware, with a baffled sense of surprise, that nothing would make him falter or waver in his decision – he would surrender the insurance policy and that was the end of that. He came downstairs and went straight to his private drawer and drew forth the insurance policy and a few pounds from what he called 'the reserve fund'. Years ago he had kept a banking account but when the children's education had become expensive he found he could keep a better check on his money by handling it directly.

He had almost finished his breakfast when Frank and Anne sat down to theirs and he handed Frank a ten-shilling note for himself. 'Work hard, my lad,' he said expansively. 'The more you keep at it the sooner you'll be out in the world as your own boss. Take the Mallons up the street – not a teaspoonful of brains amongst the lot of them – and yet they have all got on, more power to them.'

Anne raised her eyes from her cup: 'One out a doctor, one doing arts.'

'Now, Anne, I'm not in the mood to hear you slight your

decent neighbours. Only for Miss Mallon you might be stuck in some mountainy school with heather up to your eyebrows — a school that you'd have to sweep out with a bit of a furze bush. What I want to say to Frank is this: apply yourself and you'll pass any examination. Mind you, I don't want you to flog yourself to death. Just do a little every day and it'll keep the mind up to scratch — that's the card to play.'

Eileen helped him into his heavy coat and handed him his umbrella; and at the hall door he stood and called back: 'Mind what I said, Frank.' He put up his umbrella and hurried into the street that was slippery with sleet and melted frost. Half way to the tram-stop he overtook Mr. Mallon and he was glad to see that his sister wasn't with him for he wished to avoid any discussion of Anne's teaching.

'Wet as usual, Mr. Mallon.'

'A wretched climate, Mr. Caffrey. It's weather like that that ruins our school attendances — I'll have a small class before me today, I'm thinking.'

'Those new-fangled wireless sets wouldn't be upsetting the air, would you think?'

'Not at all,' said Mr. Mallon. 'That's old women's talk — it has so many ludicrous errors that I wouldn't countenance one of them for one fraction of a second. It's like this,' and he held erect the fingers of his left hand as if he were demonstrating the multiplication table. 'You see, Mr. Caffrey, the rain is in liquid particles like the formation of a cloud and these are in the air but not of it. But a wireless wave is not in the air — it's in what is termed the ether and the ether is everywhere. Wireless waves, Mr. Caffrey, are speeding through your umbrella and racing through every bone in your body this very instant.'

Mr. Caffrey cast a dubious glance at the fabric of his umbrella upon which the rain was thubbing with rhythmic persistence. 'Upon my word, Mr. Mallon, we're living in a wonderful age.'

'If your eyes were made differently we might be able to see the ether and thousands of waves bursting through it.'

'That's an extraordinary thought. A thought like that would stupefy an ordinary mortal like myself. I can't comprehend it.'

Mr. Mallon avoided the puddles on the road by striding across them' and Mr. Caffrey had to give a little run now and again to keep pace with him.

'We'll not live to see it, Mr. Caffrey, but a time will come when we'll put a gadget to our ears and tune in to a man's inmost thoughts. It's my belief that when a man is engaged in thought his brain is continually sending out little pulsations into the ether.'

'You don't say so!'

'I do indeed. Mark my words, as sure as there is rain in Ireland, a time will come when you'll be able to tune in to what a man is thinking.'

'It'd be rather embarrassing to say the least of it. But if it would make people truthful and sincere you wouldn't mind using the little gadget once in a while. A polite kind of eavesdropping it would be. I suppose the moral theologians, in a case like that, would have to come together to keep us within reasonable bounds. That'd be a new temptation we'd have to avoid. I think, Mr. Mallon, we have enough temptations to cope with as it is without new ones coming our way.'

'I'm not well versed in moral theology, and I wouldn't venture an opinion. The new science of wireless is my line.'

'As well as slapping a lad for bad handwriting, eh?' smiled Mr. Caffrey, but noticing a cold affront on the teacher's face he added flatteringly: 'It's a marvellous gift to be able to build a wireless like the one you showed me the other night. And to think that that little cat's whisker, as you called it, is so important.'

A motor car whizzed past with a schoolboy in the back of it, smiling out at them. The teacher launched into a technical account of a new wireless he was building, but Mr. Caffrey had already lost interest in him. His mind was following the track of the car: it was Mr. Smith's car and his whole family in it – one son. These Protestants and their tiny families! They must have a poor opinion of themselves, he thought, when they have no desire to bring children into the world. And the more intelligent the parents the less the number in the family – it's a crime and a disservice to their religion and their country. For himself he could say that he had four fine children and the two infants that were lying in the graveyard of Monabeg would have been six. He could say with truth that he had much joy in the rearing of them and much sorrow, too. Life was certainly no picnic; and the sorrow, he thought, was as necessary to its fulfilment as winter was to the trees. Sorrow was God's tether he had often heard his old father say – God rest his soul.

'. . . that method would improve the reception,' Mr. Mallon's voice broke in. 'What would you think?'

'I'm sure it would,' Mr. Caffrey said meekly, not knowing what he was endorsing, and not knowing what Mr. Mallon had been saying previously.

A tram came forward and Mr. Caffrey folded his umbrella and shook the rain off it. The inside of the tram was cold, and muddied tickets lay in the wet runnels of the corrugated floor. The passengers, hunched in heavy coats, sat in morose silence, and scowled when the tram lurched at a stop and fresh passengers, cold and wet, stamped their feet on the floor and squeezed themselves on to the already crowded seats. But to all this Mr. Caffrey kept smiling to himself, his soul overflowing with a sweet joy that he wished to share if only there was a way of doing so. And to think that last night he had tortured his mind through long stretches of the night. A man must move away from himself to win freedom for his mind. There was nothing like deciding at

31

once and having done with it; and there was great relief to know that at the end of this day his debt would be paid – he would be a free man, for to be in debt was to be enslaved. The manager of the insurance would try to dissuade him from surrendering the policy but he wouldn't listen to him. His mind was made up; and what if he had died and this secret debt to come out when he was under the sod – Mary would never have forgiven him!

He smoothed the top of his umbrella, blew out his breath with a sigh of satisfaction, and smiled at a little boy who was drawing with his finger on the misty window. Father Christmas he was drawing! And what was he printing? . . . A –Meery – Xmas.

'Look at the size of him and he can't spell Merry,' said Mr. Mallon, and relapsed again into a contemptuous silence, and then suddenly sprang to his feet, and as he was pushing his way out of the tram Mr. Caffrey swept a clean patch in the window with his tram-ticket and watched him stride across the road to his school. A few little girls with coats over their heads were running to the Girls' entrance and he looked at his watch and hoped that Anne would not be late. Anyway he was sure Miss Mallon would not be too strict with her – they were good neighbours, when all was said and done.

At the centre of the city he alighted and hurried up Bank Street to nine o'clock Mass in St. Mary's and there in the heat and quiet of the church he followed the Mass with an unaccustomed and concentrated fervour that surprised him, and when the priest turned to give the final blessing: Benedicat vos omnipotens Deus, Pater, et Filius, et Spiritus Sanctus, Mr. Caffrey humbly answered 'Amen', and left the church.

When he reached the shop his two assistants were already behind the counter, one taking the canvas covers from the shelves, and the other dusting bales of suiting with a stiff handbrush. He bade them good morning and when he had taken off his coat and smoothed his thin hair a lady with a young boy entered the shop and he went to attend her. She wanted a warm overcoat for the boy, and as Mr. Caffrey fitted him into one and then another, bringing the boy to the open door where the original fabric could be plainly seen, he kept up a continual chat with the lady and praised the boy warmly when he heard how far advanced he was in his school. 'Nothing like a bit of education, Madame,' he said as he parcelled up the coat in brown paper and snipped the twine with his tiny scissors. And he began to tell the lady about his own family and the boy he had at Queen's University doing medicine. 'It'll be no time at all, Madame, until your own lad is at the university. There's nothing like giving a lad a chance if he has ability.' He opened the door for them and with a hearty 'good morning' he shook hands with the boy and wished him health and strength to wear out the new coat. At the door he stood for a minute gazing at the cold-looking sky in which there was a hint of unreleased snow. 'It can't make up its mind what to do – snow or sleet,' he said to himself, and with the sky in such a peevish mood business would be slack. He looked at his windows which were swept bare and made ready for the Christmas display. There was nothing like grasping the opportunity and getting them into trim immediately – and although he could have taken an easy day to himself he worked as diligently as if the shop and its contents belonged to himself. 'Lads,' he said, rubbing his hands and addressing his two assistants, 'we'll give the Christmas tiff to the windows. By the grudging look of that sky we won't be too busy at the counters. Give me a lift in with the dummies.' He had names for them all. 'Hector' – the boy with the pink cheeks; 'Stevie' – the youth with the thin face and the chip knocked out of his left eye; and 'Venus' – the tall dummy that had lost a hand. They were already dressed and standing rigidly in corners of the department. He straightened their ties, fixed the flaps of their pockets when he had them installed in the window, and to conceal the loss of Venus's hand he had a large price-ticket pinned on the cuff. 'When I'm retired you'll remember that trick,' he said to his assistants proudly. 'Venus is a faithful old warrior and to cast him out would be like destroying part of the building.'

'But Mr. Caffrey,' said one of the assistants, with a furtive wink at his companion, 'you're mixing your genders, I think. Wasn't Venus a woman?'

'I know as well as you do that Venus was a beautiful lady with some part of her anatomy missing. There's one hand off our Venus, and Venus he has been called since I stepped in here from the country forty years ago. When I retire you can rechristen him Cuchualain or whatever fancy name you like.' And he put his hands in his pockets and stood back to survey the window, sometimes moving a dummy a bit to the right and then moving it back again, believing that he had produced an essential alteration. His assistants carried in shirts, pullovers, hats, and ties and arranged them on the brackets indicated by Mr. Caffrey. And finally when he had sent one of them for a few boxes of powdered frost to sprinkle on the floor he became aware of someone staring at him through the window. He gave a polite sideways glance, and in that instant recognized his brother D. J. in an oil-stained raincoat, a week's growth of beard, and a cigarette in his mouth. D. J. smiled at him but Mr. Caffrey neither smiled back nor nodded in recognition. But somehow his fingers had lost their nimbleness as he went to and fro across the window, adjusting a bracket or a tie or the slant of a hat. Now and again he paused with his back to the window and scrutinized his brother's reflection in one of the polished brackets.

'There's an old fella staring at us, Mr. Caffrey,' ventured one of the assistants.

'Well, let him stare away – that's what we are decorating the window for: to attract buyers.'

'By the cut of him he's hardly likely to buy a shoelace.'

Mr. Caffrey reddened and turned to the assistants: 'It's

how a man's mind is dressed that matters – not the clothes he wears. Remember that my young dandelions.' Then he faced the window and with a cold, forbidding stare tried to drive away his brother, but his brother winked back and smoked his cigarette with unflinching indifference.

'I believe he's coming in.'

'I'll attend to him. Each of you sprinkle the silver frost and be careful you don't sprinkle it on the hats or shirts – the floor's the place for the frost,' and he was going to tell them to watch how and where the snow was falling outside, when the sight of his brother's cap plastered with snow corrected him. He strode from the window, clapped his hands in feigned contentment, and greeted his brother with a loud: 'Good morning, Sir,' to convey the impression that he was meeting a complete stranger. 'Step this way, Sir,' and he manoeuvred his brother to a quiet corner of the department, and before D. J. had time to fake an excuse for his presence Mr. Caffrey had already flared at him: 'Now look here, D. J.! Time and again I've warned you not to call at my business premises, and here you are with an impertinent cigarette in your mouth and looking ten times shabbier than your usual,' and he surveyed the old raincoat and the melted snow dribbling from the shoulders. 'Take that cigarette out of your mouth and have some respect for this department.'

'Ah, John, for the love of God, don't be hard on me. I'm just off the Liverpool boat and I haven't eaten a bite since yesterday afternoon. I'm down and out.'

'Were you ever anything else? And how did you get the money for cigarettes?'

D. J. explained that he had helped a passenger that was seasick and the passenger had given him a packet of twenty cigarettes.

'And what do you want off me?' and he glanced at the tired, unwashed face of his brother.

'John, if you could lend me a pound or two. As God's my

judge I wouldn't come here only my present circumstances have driven me to it.'

A gentleman entered and Mr. Caffrey bowed to him and tapped with his pencil at the window partition for one of the assistants. He continued to talk to his brother, and in a quiet voice recited the number of times he had used his influence in getting him a respectable job, the number of times he had lent him money, and the number of times he had offered to pay his fare to Australia if only he had the decency and courage to go there and make a new start in life. 'And here like a bad penny you turn up again from England to torment and nag and badger the soul out of me. And wouldn't I give you money if I knew you'd spend it decently? – but off you'll go and spend it on drink or gamble it on horses. I'm tired of you and your selfishness.' Another customer, a fat little man, entered the department and Mr. Caffrey went to attend him, glancing now and again at his brother who was standing abjectly in a corner, a dark patch of wet gathering at his feet. He'd show him, this time, that money wasn't come easy, go easy; he'd let him cool his heels in the corner for a while before handing him a pound or two to fritter away on racehorses.

He lifted down a bundle of suits from the shelves and displayed them leisurely before the customer, and all the time his brother yawned or half-closed his eyes as if there was nothing of interest in the world but sleep. And the fat little customer would try on one coat and then another, and each time survey his back and front in the two folding mirrors while Mr. Caffrey would unsling the yellow tape from his shoulders and measure and remeasure the man's waist and each time conclude: 'The coat's a grand fit but I'm afraid a slight alteration would have to be made in the waistband of the trousers. Just raise your arms again, Sir, till I make certain of my measurement. Would you like them a tight fit around the waist, Sir, or would you like me to allow a

36

half inch or so for your winter woollens?' and the slow and cautious way he drawled the words irritated D. J. till suddenly he whisked from his corner, and so quickly did he disappear through the glass door that it swung to and fro emitting the cold snowy air from outside. 'Maybe he was hungry after all,' Mr. Caffrey said regretfully to himself, and as he opened the door to usher the fat little man off the premises he heard the unmistakable voice of his brother singing 'The Last Rose of Summer'. He closed the door quickly and through the glass panels eyed his brother walking up and down at the kerb, the snow falling on him in big heavy flakes, and his cap held out to the passers-by – all of them too uncomfortable to pay any heed to him. Mr. Caffrey withdrew to the seclusion of his counter but even there he could hear the words of the song distinctly '. . . all her lovely companions have faded and gone . . .'. He glanced at his assistants but they were bent over their account books, and he stood irresolute, wondering if he should send one of them out to him with a shilling or threaten him with the police for obstructing the traffic. The song came to an end, and in the halted stillness that followed Mr. Caffrey bowed his head and made meaningless squiggles on the counter with his pencil. 'In God's name let him come in again,' he adjured himself, but at that moment his brother burst into 'Adieu to Inisfail' and unable to endure the agony of irresolution any longer he went to the door and beckoned D. J. out of the snow. He led him into a private fitting-room and when he had shot the bolt in the door he quelled his anger by silently staring at his brother and at the snow lying like grains of salt in his hair. D. J. held his head like a culpable schoolboy and felt the unseen eyes of his brother penetrate him like a stinging pain.

'Well?' John said.

D. J. twisted the cap in his hand and dirty drops of water fell on to the carpet.

'In the name of God, what do you want from me D. J.?'

'It's hunger, John, that's left me the way I am.'

'And why didn't you tell me that at first?'

D. J. shook his head. 'I did but you didn't believe me.'

'Is it any wonder I didn't? – you tell the truth so seldom.'

D. J. opened his oil-stained coat and turned out the pockets of his old flannel trousers. 'There you are – empty. Nothing in them only a few pickles of corn.' He lifted up his right boot and through the broken sole could be seen his bare foot, pink and wet with the cold.

'You're derelict, man,' said John. 'You're a wreck. You've lost your self-respect to fall into such misery. Take off your clothes and I'll get you a suit and a pair of shoes. Let this be the last of it. I have what you haven't – the responsibility of a family.'

'I'm a burden to you. But I'll not forget you – never fear. When my ship comes home I'll not forget the hand that befriended me,' and he looked up with watery eyes.

'You've been talking about that ship for a long time. She has foundered too often on the racecourses. Give up the gambling and drag yourself together or it's an early grave you'll be sailing for,' and he noticed the pale flesh on his arms and the scrawny look of his neck. But maybe if he had a shave and a wash his face wouldn't look so gaunt; and he reflected that though his brother was now fifty-five his long black hair had few grey streaks in it; his own, he must confess, had gone grey years ago and he felt it was all the worrying over this brother that had caused him to age so quickly. D. J. took off his trousers and stood before his brother clad only in his shirt; and with his long thin legs, his eyes dark and astonished, he looked as Lazarus must have looked when he emerged from the tomb.

Mr. Caffrey sent one of his assistants to the shoe department for a few size tens of narrow width, and when he had his brother fitted out from head to heels and a new raincoat on him to protect his suit, he bundled up the old garments in

38

brown paper and commanded D. J. not to take them with him. He gave him six or seven shillings for his pocket, told him to get a shave and to go up to the house where Mary would make him welcome. He unlocked the door of the private fitting-room and after releasing his brother he rested on a chair for a while, waiting for the bewilderment to subside in his mind. But when he opened his eyes he was confronted by the bundle on the floor and it set him wondering how he would dispose of it. He thought of dumping it in the River Lagan but dismissed that thought immediately for he was aware he might have the police stalking him all day and pestering him with questions that he'd have been unable to answer with any calm orderliness. 'I should have let him take them even he did pawn them,' he said with reproachful consolation. 'And the boots – they were worthless!' and he lifted them from the carpet and wrapped them up carelessly in brown paper. Then he hid the larger bundle, and taking the parcel of wet boots under his arm he put on his hat and coat and walked through the snow to the insurance office where, with a stubborn and almost insolent silence, he refused to listen to the persuasive manager who advised him not to act rashly. He asked for his cheque but the manager politely told him that his claim would have to be presented to a Board of Directors and the money would be paid in due course. 'Look here!' said John with evident annoyance. 'Let them send me no letters begging me to reconsider this intention of mine. My mind is firmly and finally made up. Make a note of that!' He swung out of the office and making his way to a bank manager whom he knew he explained his plight and got the loan of two hundred pounds on condition it would be paid within one month. He set off for the General Post Office and there he dumped the parcel of wet boots in the waste-paper basket, dispatched the debt to his brother Bob, mentioning nothing about D. J. in the accompanying letter and in the fogged distortion of his mind, forgot to refer to Bob's illness and his intended visit to the city for the X-ray. When the letter had fallen from his hands into the post-box he remembered then what he should have written and though he hurried out of the post office he knew that that omission and his failure to amend it would harass him throughout the day. At the entrance to the shop he shook the snow off his coat and when he came inside he was surprised to see his daughter Eileen awaiting him.

'Oh, Father,' she said brightly, her cheeks flushed with the cold air, 'mother sent me down with your spats,' and she placed her basket on the counter. 'And you could never guess who's here,' she went on. 'Uncle D. J.! He arrived off the boat this morning and he told us somebody stole his portmanteau. But mother has persuaded him to stay the night with us and we've asked the Mallons down for the evening to hear him sing. Mother is terribly proud of uncle's lovely baritone voice – she says it has great charm.'

'One can get very tired of it,' he said wanly. She noticed that he was paler than usual: the cold, she thought, and she tried to make him come out with her for a cup of coffee.

'Not now, Eileen, I am expecting a few travellers, and these clumsy assistants wouldn't know what to do with them.' She glanced round at the assistants and caught them staring at her legs, and she hoped they weren't exchanging remarks about the streaks of mud on her stockings. She walked over to the long mirror, put up the green hood of her coat and arranged her hair. Her father was proud of her appearance and regretted that she was so easily deceived by D. J. a man that would tell a lie as easily as he drew his breath. But God had ordained him to be his brother, and his brother and her uncle he would remain *per omnia saecula saeculorum*. Of his two boys, Frank and Brendan, neither of them, he thought, was like D. J. – Brendan had his voice but not his unsteadiness, and Frank was thin and lanky like him, and a bit on the lazy side but that was all.

'You'll be home early to greet uncle – won't you, Father?'
and she blew her warm breath into her gloves before putting
them on.

'I'll try.'

'Do, Father! He's staying overnight at great inconvenience
to himself. He had arranged to go to Uncle Bob's in the country but mother asked him to send a telegram to say he needn't
be expected for a day or two.'

'It was wrong of your mother to interfere like that . . . to be
upsetting your uncle's programme whatever that might be.'

She lifted her basket from the counter somewhat abashed.
'Oh, Father, it was so kind of him to agree to stay. After all it
was four years since his last visit and even that was short.'

'Your Uncle D. J. is as restless as the wind and if your Uncle
Bob was expecting him it was a bit selfish of your mother and
you to break his arrangements.'

'But we've only asked him to stay one night,' she pleaded.
'We want to show him off to the Mallons . . . Be home early?'
and she held her head coaxingly to the side.

He nodded without any enthusiasm and as he watched her
swing through the door he knew that some day he would have
to tell them the truth about their Uncle D. J.

CHAPTER THREE

THAT evening he left the shop later than usual. The
snow had ceased falling, and it lay crusted on the ground
and put a sharp edge on the night wind. He made his way up
Bank Street carrying the parcel in which the clothes were already
pressing their way through a sodden corner of the paper.
Outside a pub he saw the man he was looking for – an old
beggar whose bare chest was exposed to the cold. He thrust the
bundle into his hand, gave him sixpence, and continued his

way to St. Mary's chapel where he took his place in the shadowy quiet of a side altar. The church was almost empty and the only light came from the candelabra, the pointed flames tilting and swaying in every draught that stole around them. Mr. Caffrey knelt with his hands joined and fixed his gaze on the tabernacle. His mind was confused and unsettled, and he recalled, as if from the past, the buoyancy of mood with which he left his house in the morning, and how in the tram-car with Mr. Mallon the congested group of gloom failed to quell the sharp spirit of his hope. That was life, he reasoned with himself with an air of detached discovery it was full of peaks of joy and clefts of unrelieved depression: and he thought of the old beggar out in the night, and supposed that that shivering man had followed him with his eyes, envying him his footwear but not his spats, his heavy overcoat but not his umbrella – envying the thin surface of his outside life and seeing nothing of the rough spaces of his inward mind. A candle falling from its socket brought him back with a start and he addressed himself to his usual routine of evening prayers, usually prayers of praise, for it was those that afforded his soul its greatest refreshment, and he recited the Divine Praises, the Magnificat, and with a reserved feeling of slight conceit he raised a prayer of praise to the Holy Ghost whom, he thought, was innocently outcast from the lips of the laity. God knows he had a lot to be thankful for: he had his health, he had his wife, and God had preserved him until his children were of an age when they could fend for themselves – and what if D. J. should arrive now and again to torment his mind with his trickery, dishonesty, and indolence: he suffered little or nothing from him when compared with lives he had read about in books or in papers, or what he had heard from friends – it had all, perhaps, a hidden meaning, composing the substance of his life, a rope of God's by which he was held fast to the realities of life now and to come. Suffering in some form was necessary to the growth of his soul, he told himself: without it he could have fallen into selfish ways, stamping on everything that tended to gnaw at his own comfort; after all, the pain that others brought to you was, perhaps, to the soul what rain was to the hardened earth, and the pain that one inflicted on oneself by impatience and unkindness was like a frost on growing things.

Before he rose he said a prayer for the success of Bob's X-ray, then he dusted his knees with his handkerchief and made his way slowly down the aisle. At the open door he saw the snow falling again and he remembered with a jerk that he had left his umbrella behind him on the seat. He hurried back for it, and all the way home in the tram he reflected on that mistake – it had never happened to him before, it was a misfortune that Mary continually suffered from – forgetting parcels and umbrellas till he was sick, sore, and tired calling at the tramways' Lost Property Office. He must be getting old – forgetfulness, he had read, was one of the signs of it. Yes, he was getting old, there was no doubt about that: in a few years he would have to retire and he only hoped that he'd live to see Frank finished at the university, Brendan securely placed in the library, Anne in love with her school, and Eileen, he hoped, married to a decent young man that could give her a home and a family of her own. There was nothing more he could wish or hope for – he was content.

Half-way up the street he saw the familiar light in the parlour window and he knew that within D. J. would be holding forth, discoursing at length between each song, and smoking somebody else's cigarettes. What anyone saw in D. J. he could never really understand. Maybe, after all, it was only on himself that he played his meanness. Anyhow the children liked him, and for that reason he'd try to hide from them the warped part of D. J.'s nature.

At the gate he heard Brendan finishing 'The Minstrel Boy'; there was silence for a minute, then a gentle clapping of hands and finally D. J.'s voice loud and hearty above the rest: 'The makings of a John MacCormack – I must speak to your father about getting your voice trained.'

'Must he, indeed!' said Mr. Caffrey to himself as he turned the key in the door and let himself into the hallway; he can keep his runaway notions to himself – let Brendan stick to his library and he can John MacCormack to his heart's content at some ceilidhe or at a family gathering like the one this evening. If D. J. thinks I'll allow him to ruin my children with his mad ideas he's making a sad mistake – a sad mistake!

Eileen heard him in the hall and came out. 'Oh, Father, you've missed the best part of the evening! Uncle has been singing for nearly an hour for us. Mr. Mallon is inside and he thinks there's a great future for uncle when the wireless sets are improved – everybody will have an opportunity of hearing him then.' She followed her father into the kitchen, talking all the time as she ladled out for him his usual supper of porridge and cream. He inquired about Frank, about Anne, and she told him they were all in the parlour welcoming uncle.

'Your uncle's singing won't get Frank through his examinations, I'm thinking.'

'Oh, Father, you're very hard,' and she fidgeted, eager to be back to the company again. 'Sure it will only be for one night or two.' There was a burst of laughter from the parlour.

'Father, hurry – you're missing all the fun.'

'Run you on, Eileen; I'll be in in my own good time.'

He sat alone at the table. The whole house had gone crazy over an uncle that was hardly worth a spent match. He'd have to confide in his family – there was no doubt about that. He should have warned them long ago that Uncle D. J. was a low, good-for-nothing wastrel – spending more than he ever earned, and borrowing more than he could ever pay back: that he would stick at no job, and that he was even twice in jail in England for defrauding landladies of their just earnings. He was a lovely uncle, he must say – a lovely specimen to have near his growing children! And even if he could sing a song or two, what of that? – if it came to the bit he might be able to do as well himself if he tried! Tonight or tomorrow he'd have to put his cards on the table and reel off the evil twists in his brother's nature; he'd have to get rid of him – there were no two ways about that! And look at that performance in the snow this morning – singing 'The Last Rose of Summer' and holding out his cap like a penny-farthing tramp. What would they say to that! It was no laughing matter especially when you're related to the chief performer. Upon my word, if you heard that story about somebody else's brother you'd laugh yourself sick, but when it's your own kith and kin it's a different morsel entirely!

He pushed the empty plate away from him as if he had a grudge against it, filled his pipe, and entered the company as quietly as he could. They began to rise from their chairs to make room, and their confused cries of: 'Sit here, Father . . . Sit here, Mr. Caffrey,' embarrassed him.

'Don't stir now, I only dropped in for a minute,' and he smiled warmly at Miss Mallon and her brother.

The room was filled with smoke, and D. J. was standing with one elbow resting on top of the piano. Frank was offering him a cigarette. 'You positively disgrace me, Frank; I'm smoking all yours . . . and me with a full box or two in my overcoat pocket,' and as he made a move to go for them, they all with one voice told him not to trouble himself. He'd have some trouble finding them, thought Mr. Caffrey, they'd be lost like his portmanteau.

'I was telling Anne and Mr. and Miss Mallon about our old teacher Master Cullen in the country,' D. J. announced with a theatrical bow towards his brother, 'and they don't believe a word of what I say. You can vouch for the truth.' He pouted his lips and blew a few dexterous smoke rings into the air. 'They didn't believe me when I told them how he drank a can of buttermilk in the June afternoons in the class-room and fell asleep after it; and how one night in Lynch's

45

pub he screwed a man's wooden leg to the partition of the snug. And I was just getting ready to tell them about the trout when you came in,' and he bowed to his brother again. 'It was like this, ladies and gentlemen and medical students and librarians, Master Cullen was the devil of a man for fishing. There was a river flowed through the fields at the back of the school and in May when the trout were rising the Master couldn't contain himself. He had his fishing-rod rolled up in a map in the corner and many a time he left us to our work and went out to cast a fly or two. He was out one day fishing irregularly and not according to the official curriculum when Father Delaney came in, a big man as slow on his feet as a circus elephant. He asked for Master Cullen and your father here went out for him, and while he was out Father Delaney was standing at the window laughing at Cullen flinging down his rod. "He's caught this time," said I to myself, "there'll be unholy ructions in this school in a minute." In came the Master with a live trout hanging from his forefinger but no rod to be seen. "Are they biting well, Master?" asked Father Delaney, and he slumped down on a chair with his feet wide apart. "Deed if I could answer you aright, Father," said Cullen. "I saw a few rings in the water, and since I had to give an object lesson on a fish today I thought there'd be nothing like the genuine article for demonstrating."

'"Quite so," said Father Delaney, and he took out his spectacle case to show he was in no mood for leaving. "There's nothing like going from the particular to the general, from the concrete to the abstract — the hall-mark of good teaching, I may say. But don't let me interrupt your lesson," he added, and he placed his hat on the floor below his chair and spread his huge hands on each knee.

'But Master Cullen wasn't balked one bit or put off his course and he never knew whether the priest was taking a hand out of him or not. But there and then he held the trout horizontally between his hands — the poor thing gasping for breath and an awe-stricken look in its eyes. "Now, boys," said Cullen; and we couldn't keep our faces straight. "You hear people saying — ignorant and vulgar people, of course — saying that So-and-so drinks like a fish. Now, boys, a fish when it's opening its gills is not drinking — it's breathing," and he pointed his pencil at the gills of the trout. "These gills at the side of its face form the same physical purpose as your nose in the middle of your face; it's its breathing compendium and the fish extracts air out of the water in the same way as your nose extracts perfume from the wind. And some of you bad boys when you're in the turf-bog often stir the bog water with a spade and when the water becomes thick with mud you delight in seeing the pike rising to the top where you can strike at them with a stick or your spade — it's a very cruel pastime . . . Now look at my little trout. Do you see him gasping now? What is happening?"

'"He's breathing," we all answered.

' "He's not!" rapped out Master Cullen, and the priest who was flicking through a composition book looked up at him puzzledly.

' "He's choking, the poor fellow. He's choking — that's what's wrong with him. He's getting too much air and the gills can't cope with it. These sensitive gills are fashioned for water in the same delicate way as the Almighty made your nose for air. If you boys were below the water you would choke although if you had gills like this tiny fish you would live."

' "Just like the mermaids, Sir," your father answered, for he was the brightest lad in the school.

'The trout went on choking and breathing, and all the time we were watching the wet gleam fade from its skin and the spotted fins close up like a fan. The Master soon turned to describe the function of its tail and its fins, and when he had finished and questioned us he pinned the trout by the fins to the board with a few drawing-pins and asked us to make a sketch of it in our books and to colour them with our crayons.

' "Very informative lesson indeed," said Father Delaney and he put his spectacles in his case.

' "They'll remember that till the day they die," said Master Cullen.

' "And so will I," said the priest with a smile. And when the priest was gone from the school Cullen was out at the back like a hare, and in with his rod again, and the rest of his catch wrapped in rushes. And all that month of May, even after rain, we saw him standing at the window with a long look on his face, and during the remainder of my days at school he never ventured out again during school hours. What do you think of that for a teacher?' D. J. concluded with a nod to Mister Mallon.

Anne laughed. 'We wouldn't drink much buttermilk or go out of doors in our city schools. Sure we wouldn't, Miss Mallon?'

'Indeed we would not, Anne. You would never know the minute some official would drop in unannounced. But I never liked buttermilk myself – it doesn't agree with me,' said Miss Mallon, and the serious tone of her voice checked the smile that Anne directed at her.

'What kind of people did he turn out, Uncle?'

'Well,' said Uncle D. J. with a spectacular flourish of his arm. 'I'm one of his produce; your father is another and your Uncle Bob in Monabeg is another. But you can't condemn the man's teaching by regarding us. Your father was his pride: he was a Mass-server when he wasn't the size of two turf. Of course I was an altar boy myself till one day Father Delaney caught me and my partner rolling a glass marble to one another on the altar steps and both of us were unfrocked there and then.'

Mr. Caffrey yawned, suffering his brother in patience, and yearning for the night to come to an end.

'He sent your father to St. Malachy's College hoping he'd become a priest but your father left after three years and there

48

he is before your eyes: a good honest citizen. On some days he had us doing scenes from *Macbeth* and declaiming speeches from *Hamlet* when we had little knowledge of what we were saying. Poor old Cullen, he was very close to us all; he was never sarcastic and always had time to listen to you. He was in many ways a gentleman.'

'I wish I had met him,' said Anne.

'He was what I would call "a character",' said Mr. Mallon, 'and I must say I'd have no room for a character in my school. He was a misfit.'

'I suppose he didn't conform to type,' said Anne. 'HE wasn't uniform! Indeed the world would be a very unhappy and boring place if we hadn't a character or two to enliven it.'

There was an awkward silence. That was Anne for all the world, thought Mr. Caffrey, always argumentative – why couldn't she let Mr. Mallon have his opinion without disputing with him. 'Mr. Cullen was a great one for choral singing,' put in Mr. Caffrey, and smiled benignly at the Mallons. 'There were afternoons when we did nothing but sing and sing as if there was nothing else of importance in the world but to sing.'

The silence continued. Mr. Mallon fidgeted, and then Miss Mallon rose to her feet, said it was time they were leaving, and thanked them all for the enjoyable evening. And when they were gone Mrs. Caffrey announced that Uncle D. J. must surely be exhausted and ready for his bed, and she told Brendan to go upstairs along with him.

Brendan escorted him to the attic where a stretcher-bed was already prepared for him.

'A nice comfortable room,' said D. J., and as they undressed he asked Brendan how he liked his job in the library and inquired if he backed horses at all.

'To tell you the truth, Uncle, I wouldn't know a racehorse from a dray-horse.'

'Too bad, too bad,' he said, and in doleful tones told how he had lost his cheque book with his portmanteau and wondered if it were possible for him to get the loan of a pound or two till the portmanteau was discovered or until he could get in touch with his Liverpool bank.

'You see, Brendan son, an old horse of mine, Old Orkney, is running tomorrow in the Manchester November Handicap and I don't want it to run without having a little flutter on it. A pound or ten shillings would be enough to lend me if you could spare it.'

'But, Uncle, I haven't got ten shillings but I'll ask father for you.'

'My boy, my boy, don't ever do the like of that,' and he sat on the edge of the bed and stared in silence at a burnt stain on the oil-cloth. 'No, Brendan,' he said after a pause, 'it would never do to ask your father. I want everything to pass quietly. Everyone has lavished so much sympathy on me over the loss of my traps that it is – how shall I put it? – embarrassing and degrading for a man of my independence.'

'Oh, I'll not do it since you have warned me. I could give you three shillings if that would be of any use to you,' and as he thrust his hand into his pocket Uncle D. J. raised a silent, protesting hand.

'But you must take it, Uncle; you may find some use for it.'

D. J. fingered his chin for a moment, and then hearing a step on the stairs he said: 'Since you insist I may as well please you by taking it,' and he had it stowed safely in his waist-coat pocket when Frank entered the room. Frank offered him a cigarette, and when they were lying in bed and the skylight open to the first hole Frank asked his uncle politely if he desired the window full open, partially open, or totally closed.

'On account of my sleepless night on the boat I feel rather shivery and, if you don't mind, I would prefer it closed . . . I leave myself entirely in your hands, of course.'

'We always try to please our guests,' said Frank, and he smiled mockingly at Brendan, 'and we shall close it.'

'Passed unanimously,' said Uncle D. J. and blew a few smoke rings towards the gas-mantle.

Brendan lay still, and hoped that by shutting his eyes he could swerve his mind from the layers of smoke that were exploring the boxed-up room. The smoke came to him, sharp and keen, over his blankets and he opened his eyes and tried to ward it off by blowing inaudibly at it. If only they'd cease talking.

'Maybe, Frank my lad, you'll be attending me in my last illness, seeing me comfortably off this mortal bit of turf. You'll make a great doctor – there's no mistake about that. A grand doctor – one of the old brigade: slow and cautious and full of everything but brains!' and he laughed so loudly at his own joke that the springs of his bed whirred under his weight. 'One of the old brigade! – that's a bloody good one.'

At last Frank and he had ceased talking, the gas was turned out, and in the darkness Brendan swirled his hand in the air, hoping to create sufficient circulation to draw the noxious smell up the chimney. Soon his uncle was snoring. On the skylight sleet or snow was falling; and thinking of the coldness of the outside air and how lean it would grow during the night Brendan felt that the sour air of the room would contract and disappear with the encroaching frost. And soothed by that thought he, too, slept.

CHAPTER FOUR

THE stuffy air of the room seemed to have teased Brendan's mind and he awoke when it was still dark and lay wide awake until he heard the clock in the parlour strike six. He got up quietly and went downstairs and lit the fire in the range for Eileen. He spread the cloth on the breakfast table and laid out the knives and forks, the cups and saucers. The sight of the brightly lit fire and the clean-swept kitchen put Eileen in good form and she thanked him and began preparing the breakfast. He borrowed five shillings from her and, on hearing Frank go into the bathroom, he slipped upstairs and handed them royally to his uncle.

'You are a fine boy,' said Uncle D. J. with affected reverence, 'and you'll go far in your job. Always ascend – life is like a ladder, ascend always, ascend,' and he raised his hand slowly to the skylight. He inquired where his library was situated and told him he'd call to inspect the establishment which he was sure, some day, his nephew would have the honour of adorning as head librarian, and his name printed in gold on those black mortuary-looking regulations that were boarded outside the municipal libraries. 'They always remind me of a presbyterian church,' he laughed.

'It'll be a long time before I'm head,' said Brendan feeling shy now before his unshaven uncle. 'And I don't know if I'd like it for it has made the head librarian like a machine and he smacks out his orders like the keys of a typewriter.'

Uncle D. J. shut one eye portentously. 'Young boy, let your uncle give you a word or two of valuable advice: with a boss of that ilk – exchange few words, listen with deference, and then do what you yourself think is best. Am I right?'

Brendan smiled. 'I couldn't act like that, Uncle. I'd rather obey him, for it would mean in the long run that my stay under him would be happier. And since he is responsible for all mistakes it would be scurvy of me to allow my mistakes to be levelled at him.'

'Ah, my boy, don't take life so seriously. Go in late occasionally, take plenty of sick-leave, and have a smoke or two on the q.t.'

At the word 'late' Brendan glanced at his watch and bowed himself politely from the room.

He was always the first to arrive at the library, usually when the dwarfish janitor was pushing back the fold-up iron gate in front of the oak door, or when the charwomen were finishing their cleaning and exchanging gossip in voices loud enough to seem sacrilegious in the church-like atmosphere of the library. This morning the door was wide open and the tiled vestibule was still damp from the cleaners' cloths. He took wide steps across the damp floor, hung up his coat in the staff room, and came to help the janitor to black-out with an inked roller the sporting columns in the morning's papers prior to screwing them into their jackets in the public newsroom.

It mystified him, at first, this black mourning that was plastered on the newspapers, and on the day he had asked the janitor the reason for it, the tiny little man smiled at him somewhat patronizingly: 'Mr. Caffrey, my lad, you don't know the meanness of the public the way I do. If the racing columns were exposed to all and sundry that newsroom would be like a bookmaker's office and instead of a parquet floor we'd have to strew it with sawdust like a butcher's shop on a wet day. There'd be no silence; the police would be in to keep order; they'd scribble horses' names on the walls, and some of the early birds would cut out the racing columns with a razor blade and make off to a quiet corner of the park. Life for me would not be worth living. It'd be a failure from the kick-off,' and he rolled the black ink once more over a corner of a paper that wasn't sufficiently obliterated.

This morning as they worked at the papers Brendan noticed one particular newspaper that had not been inked: 'Here's one has escaped the black cap,' he said.

'I give that one a reprieve,' said the janitor, drawing his sleeve across his nose. 'That's for yours truly, and when I've studied the sporting page in the boiler-house and picked out my fancies I'll instal it for the unappreciative public. There's an old fellow, an ex-schoolmaster, strides in to have a look at this paper every morning and I love to keep him waiting. He reads nothing in it only the Wanted columns and what he wants God only knows except for someone to make a cheap coffin for him.' The janitor lifted his keys and a bundle of papers. 'You don't touch the horses yourself, I suppose?'

'I don't,' said Brendan.

'You're a wise lad. It's a craze; it's dirt in the blood; it's like drink only not as satisfying. A man would pawn his suit to back a horse. It's a mug's game and that's the whole story.'

'I've got a tip for a horse,' Brendan said, and glanced furtively around. 'Old Orkney will win the Manchester November Handicap.'

The janitor sat down again and took from his pocket the untouched paper and scrutinized the list of runners. He pursed his lips and shook his head: 'It's the biggest donkey in the race. The man who tipped you that is . . .' and he tapped his forehead with his finger. 'No, it wouldn't win a three-legged race.'

'It was my uncle gave it to me.'

'Your uncle! Well, well, I thought an uncle of yours would be a man of intelligence.'

'He's a great singer.'

'Tell him from me to stick to his singing. He knows nothing about the turf except, perhaps, that the grass is green.'

'But he's just over from England on a visit.'

'From England! God above you should have told me that before – he might be a man in the know,' and he winked an eye with slow cunning and perused the paper again. He shook his head in solemn despair: 'It has as much chance as a snow-ball in hell. I really and truly tender to your uncle my deepest sympathy. It's only fools that follow horses and it's only a damned fool would follow a horse like that,' and he slowly gathered up his papers. 'We'll have a full house today. Look at the way the snow is falling and the mist is smudging the windows.'

Brendan went to his own department, and as he arranged the books that had been displaced by the careless public he dwelt on what the janitor had told him and wondered if Uncle

54

D. J. was a man that would pawn his suit to back a horse. He recalled a post-card he had sent them from England one Christmas: it was entitled *How to make Money following Horses* and depicted two little boys with a shovel and a box-cart expectantly following a coalman's horse. He smiled at that and moved from shelf to shelf, his practised eye detecting books that had strayed from their proper sections.

The two lady assistants came in, glanced at the clock, and nodded questioningly at Brendan.

'He's not in yet,' Brendan said and wondered then if the boss were ill. Presently he followed them into the staff room. They had already taken off their coats, and their goloshes were spread on a newspaper beside the gas-stove. One was hiding a bag of buns in a bookcase of censored books and announcing that if the boss wanted a bun for his tea he'd have to go and buy one. They powdered their faces quickly and hurried from the room before the head arrived.

At ten minutes past ten he fussed in, glancing at his watch. 'Clock's fast,' he said, loud enough to be heard. 'Clock's fast. Window-cleaner here yet, Dick?' he spoke to the janitor. 'No, ring him up again. Look at those outside windows – bad language scribbled on them!' He put his hand on one of the radiators. 'Keep up the heat, Dick. Go to boiler, rake out, and clean flues.' He went to his private room, and called Brendan, and was glad to hear that all books were arranged in their proper order.

'That's the way to rise in the world,' he said. 'Do things without being told. Don't await orders from headquarters,' and he rapped out his words with mechanical sharpness: 'Print that notice on a large card and hang up in the newsroom,' and he handed Brendan a slip of paper on which he had printed:

WARNING: IN BELFAST CUSTODY COURT LAST WEEK MAN FINED 10S. FOR MALICIOUS MUTILATION OF LIBRARY NEWSPAPERS.

'Your best printing. Report when done.' Brendan turned

to go and the head called him back. 'Look into the Reading Room occasionally. Radiators newly painted last week. Men lie up against them in cold weather. Dirty them with their feet – no respect. Make them sit around the tables or else leave the establishment. A library for the use of the mind not for the comforts of the body. Not a doss-house – remember!'

Brendan ascended the stairs to a quiet store-room and looked into the Reading Room as he passed. There was a smell of heat and floor-polish, and one man who daily occupied the same chair had it usually tilted on its hind legs, and there was a greasy spot on the wall where his head had rested. He always came into the library with his pockets stuffed with bread he had begged from the Redemptorist Monastery and what he couldn't eat he tossed out of sight behind the radiators. Brendan was afraid of him, and this morning when he saw him on his chair, his two feet against the radiator, a magazine open upon his lap, and his cap down over his eyes, Brendan tiptoed past the door and began to print the notice in the unventilated store-room.

Within the space of an hour he entered the head's office with the finished card and the head made him stand a few yards away from him while he critically eyed the card. 'It'll do. Letters not uniform height. Suit the public. Clip off the wide margin. It'd give them too much room to scribble on it . . . insulting references about me. Doesn't matter: Sticks and stones may break my bones but names . . . Ever hear that?'

Brendan smiled and felt that an honest innocence was hidden by the old fellow's abruptness. He hurried away from him in case he'd be asked if everything was in order in the Reading Room. He hung up the notice in a conspicuous place, his face red to the ears because of the men who gathered around him, and then he heard a commotion on the stairs and saw the head ushering the sleeping man downstairs. 'Be off now! Read a magazine by all means. But you're not allowed to sleep and scrape the radiators.'

'I wasn't sleeping! I was meditating!'

'Allow me – you were snoring!'

'I was meditating,' he persisted, and then yelled forth a collection of curses that made Mr. Dunne order Brendan to phone for the police.

'You're training that specimen well,' said the tramp, slowly buttoning his coat. 'I could wallop the two of you without drawing my breath. Do you hear that? – you scourgers of the poor.' He seized the handle of the door as if he would wrench it from its socket, and with a last malevolent look at Mr. Dunne he shouted: 'You long-necked rook with not enough breath in your gullet to make a decent cough, may the devil skin and roast you!' and fastening the collar of his coat with a safety-pin he went muttering out into the snow.

Except for a subdued whispering in the newsroom the silence once more expanded freely and Brendan was surprised to feel that a pity for the old man was ousting a momentary anger. He had to undergo a cross-examination in Mr. Dunne's office and he was informed that he had failed in his duty for it was evident from the burnt smell of leather in the Reading Room that the man had been a long time there with his feet against the radiators. 'Didn't you see him?' the head rapped out.

'I did, Mr. Dunne,' Brendan said meekly, 'but I was afraid to tell him to leave. Last week I wakened him out of his sleep and he gripped me by the throat and said he'd throttle the miserable life out of me for disturbing his meditations.'

Mr. Dunne tapped on his desk with his pencil. 'Listen! Do your duty no matter if it costs you your life! To be a success as a public librarian you must speak as one in authority. Command – never plead!'

Presently the head took his umbrella and sallied off to the Central Library, leaving Brendan in charge. The girl assistants went off to the staff room to make tea and Brendan was left alone. Two or three people stood around the shelves of

Fiction. The evening would be the busiest time, so he got a pot of paste, the library's official stamp, and proceeded to index and catalogue a bundle of new books that lay on his desk.

A voice whispered to him at the open inquiry window. It was his Uncle D. J. Brendan pressed the lever that released the swing door and allowed his uncle to enter.

'A palatial place,' said Uncle D. J. sweeping the room with a slow eye. 'A respectable and commodious establishment! As quiet and peaceful as a Benedictine monastery. Hot and wholesome as a summery day. Windows are a bit begrimed – too near the factories, I suppose.'

'Have a tour round the shelves, Uncle, and I'll join you in a few minutes. I'm my own boss, this morning. Put your hat on – nobody takes off their head-gear here except the staff: that's our privilege.'

Now and again he raised his head and watched his uncle move leisurely from section to section, pass the numerous shelves marked Fiction, and finally halt at the section labelled Biography. He was rather well educated, he thought, none of your Wild West stuff for him.

In about ten minutes Brendan had his new books numbered and stamped, and as he carried them out to their appropriate sections his uncle came over to him and announced that he was going.

'But, Uncle, you can't go so soon. Come and join me and the lady assistants in a cup of tea. The boss won't be back for another hour.'

'I would only embarrass the girls. I'll come back soon again and you can explain to me the ins and outs of the library. I only dropped in for a minute when I was passing. I've a little job to do,' and he made towards the exit. Brendan accompanied him to the door and told him what the janitor said about Old Orkney. Uncle D. J. braced his shoulders and winked an eye. 'From this day on you'll have no peace with that fellow hounding after you for another of your uncle's tips. With ignorance you always get contempt,' and he went out into the snowy street.

'He's an interesting old fella,' Brendan thought as he sauntered to the Biography section to ensure that his uncle had not disarranged any of the books from their proper order. In some shelves he noticed books lying loosely together where, an hour or so ago, they were tightly packed. *Enrico Caruso* by Pierre Key was missing and *George Frideric Handel* by Newman Flower – there was another missing, possibly *Bismarck* by Emil Ludwig which had only recently been put in circulation. He searched the daily filing cabinet to see if they had been issued to borrowers when he himself had been engaged in printing the Warning notice. Nothing had been issued except a few books of fiction. He walked around the shelves again, furtively gazing at the few people who were standing around fingering books. None of them had bulgy pockets. One, however, had an attaché case. Calmly he returned to the Biography section, hoping that he'd discover in some inappropriate corner the books he was sure were missing. He moved the books tightly together, the dark gaps as conspicuous now as the loss of front teeth. Once again he searched the files; and then he asked the lady assistants if they had issued any biography. They shook their heads and went on drinking tea without concern.

He sat down behind his desk and fixed his eye on the man with the attaché case. Eventually the man approached him, placed two books on the desk, and when Brendan had stamped them the attaché case was opened before his eyes and the two books placed inside it. The case was empty. There was no doubt about it now – Uncle D. J. had taken them, though why he took them without mentioning it God only knew! If he had wanted them on loan for a day or two all he had to do was to ask and he would have handed them to him with pleasure.

The boss came back, his face red and frozen, and seeing Brendan seated on the chair he asked sarcastically if he were

59

tired and then handed him his wet umbrella to place upright in the wash-hand basin in the staff room. He passed quickly to his office and Brendan noticing his ill-humour decided to say nothing about the missing books until he had talked it over with his father.

At lunch hour he went round to his father's clothing department, and his father listened to him in silence, his head bent over an account book.

At last he looked up and sighed. 'You'll have to report the loss.'

'But it might implicate Uncle D. J. and it would appear also that I was guilty of slackness.'

'It doesn't matter. You'll have to speak out. The greatest torment of a fault lies in its concealment.'

'Could we not wait until tonight, until we see Uncle D. J.? He may have taken the loan of them.'

'And what if he has sold them?'

'Uncle D. J.?'

'Yes, your Uncle D. J. I'm sorry to say he has done many strange things in his life and that would be one of the slightest of them.'

'But we could wait, Father. It's only at stocktaking the stolen ones are missed.'

His father hesitated for a minute. 'If your uncle has taken them we'll have to replace them. But say nothing until I see him and should he turn up this evening let me tackle him.'

They went out to a restaurant together, and when Brendan noticed the unusual flush on his father's face and a large vein bulging prominently at the side of his forehead he was sorry for what he had told him. He should have kept it to himself – God knows his father had enough worry on his mind and if he should ever hear about Frank and the university it would kill him. The unsteady hand of his father jabbled coffee on his saucer and all the time as he sipped at it he tried to speak to Brendan of the coming Christmas and of Uncle Bob's illness –

an illness that may be more serious than one imagined. He padded with his fingers on the tablecloth and then he said as if he were speaking to himself: 'I'm too forgiving! But tonight I'll give him his walking papers.'

CHAPTER FIVE

THAT night the supper had been delayed for over an hour. Mrs. Caffrey asked them to wait until Uncle D. J. arrived as it would save her the trouble of having to make two meals. They were all seated in the kitchen, the father unusually silent as he read a letter from his half-sister Nelly telling him that Bob had neuritis in his right hand, that he was as wretched as a picture of misery's full brother, that she and Dr. O'Neill were unable to persuade him to go up to the city for his X-ray, and that she, herself, was drudged and dragged with over-work. He put away the letter and looked across at Eileen. 'I've just had a letter from your Aunt Nelly,' he said. 'Your Uncle Bob's not too well and I think you could go down and stay for a while. I'll take a day off and go down with you.'

'I'd love to go,' Eileen said brightly.

'You'll be in time for all the dances around Christmas,' Anne said.

'She's going to help in the shop if your Uncle Bob's not fit. She's not going down to jogtrot about the countryside. She can go to a dance only when, and where, her Aunt Nelly permits.'

'That'll be pretty frequently if you heed me,' Anne went on. 'Aunt Nelly's as fond of a dance as Eileen or myself in spite of her age.'

'If she does like a bit of a dance nobody would begrudge her that. And one would think to hear you that she was as old as myself. She's my half-sister remember, and she was running about Monabeg with a skipping rope when I married your mother.'

'Sit over to the table, children,' said Mrs. Caffrey. 'We needn't wait any longer for your uncle.'

The father began to question Frank about his studies, and Anne, weary of that subject, tried to divert his mind to Uncle D. J. but the affectionate kindness by which she referred to him made her father rattle down his cup on the saucer and say with solemn gravity: 'There are a few things I wish to say to all of you. They must be said no matter how much they will hurt you or me. Your Uncle D. J. is a wastrel. He's a gambler and, at times, a dishonest and drunken man. He paid a visit to Brendan's library today and it's almost certain that he took books away with him – stole them and I'd almost swear, sold them in the second-hand bookshops in Smithfield. When he wants money to gamble on a horse there's nothing low enough or mean enough for him to stoop to. I hope in God that none of you will have the misfortune to take after him. Look at him and you'll see what happens to a man who will not stick to his books or be content in a job that he holds. He was given a good education and he made no use of it except in a cunning and underworld way. There he is without a home, without a penny piece, without a job, and almost without a friend.'

'But, Father,' said Anne, 'surely Uncle D. J. wouldn't steal books from the library. He may have pocketed them for a joke just to see if Brendan's as vigilant as that long pencil of a boss he's got.'

Brendan began to explain about his uncle's visit to the library, when suddenly he was interrupted by a rumble at the hall door. They stared at one another in silence. Mr. Caffrey buttoned his coat and rose to his feet but his wife pressed him back to his chair, pleading with him not to say anything to his brother. She opened the door and they could hear the unmistakable voice of their uncle in the hallway. He piloted himself into the kitchen, a new hat pushed to the back of his head, and a burst bag of fruit under one arm. He swayed slightly from side to side, and from all his pockets he took out oranges that had been soiled where they had rolled about on the road. He took apples from the top of the bag and as he handed one to Anne and Eileen he fitted their names into an alphabetical rhyme that made them laugh. For a moment he contemplated Frank, and Frank shuddered from his gaze.

'What will I compose for you?' he said. 'Wait till my muse penetrates the fumes of my spirits. Ah, I've got it,' and he held up his hand to command respectful silence.

> 'F for a fig and F for Frank
> The finest doctor in Killycrank.'

He threw him an orange. 'An orange as you're aware, dear students, is a revitalizer of the haemoglobular – that starry constellation in the blood.'

'Take the weight of your legs, D. J., and have sense. The children are ashamed of you,' said Mary, and she straightened his tie and put her arm under his to lead him to the sofa.

'Now, Mary, none of that if you please . . . linking my arm at your time of day.'

She pushed him gently down on the sofa and tried to take from him a parcel tied with cord.

'No, Mary, that parcel belongs to Brendan. I borrowed some books from his library and I'm now returning them with my full-fed thanks.'

The father rose from the table, and lifting D. J.'s hat from his head he stood erect beside him. 'Now, my fine playboy,' he said, 'when you get your breakfast in the morning clear you out of this house and never cross the doorstep in your life again.'

'Father!' Anne and Eileen said together.

'I mean it. Let him go wherever he likes. He has the house ruined and desolated. Another of Frank's precious evenings is destroyed on the poor boy.'

'I backed two winners. Old Orkney and Double Gift – the Irish and Scotch combination every time. I'll not forget you,' and he pulled from his inside pocket a roll of pound notes.

'No one in this house wants your money,' Mr. Caffrey said. 'It's peace we want.'

'Don't lecture him now,' said Mrs. Caffrey. 'He doesn't understand a word you're saying. Wait till he gets something to eat – the unfortunate man.'

'I'll pay you for your suit. I will indeed. It's a bit tight under the oxters but it'll loosen. Never you fear, it will stretch with wear and tear. Health and strength to wear it out, and may it wear out soon: words taken, my dear friends, from your Uncle Bob's epistle to his customers of Monabeg,' and he laughed till the tears ran out of his eyes. 'Brendan,' and he raised his head, 'I give you the honour of unloosening my boots.'

Brendan didn't hear him for he had already cut the string of his parcel and was noting with a feeling of self-praise that the books he had missed were those in the parcel, but when he scrutinized each book he perceived that all the library – markings had been erased and on the fly-leaf of each was a price scribbled in pencil: what father had said was true – he had sold the books, and then re-bought them because his horse had won.

'Brendan, sergeant-major is speaking,' his uncle called again. 'I bestow on you the rare and coveted honour of unloosing my boots.' Brendan wrapped up the parcel and tied it tightly, and as he knelt to untie the laces in his uncle's boots his Uncle D. J. patted him fondly on the head. 'My fair-haired, bright-eyed Brendan boy,' he kept repeating in a sing-song voice.

Mrs. Caffrey gave him old slippers to put on his feet and bade him sit in to the table. The family retired to the seclusion of the parlour and Mr. Caffrey stretched himself out on the sofa, endeavouring to smother his anger by pondering on the trivial details of his shop but always when he tried to fix his mind clearly on a simple action like the folding of a suit the pleasant voice of his wife and the coarse laugh of his brother drew his eyes to the table. He sat listening to them with stolid patience but on hearing Mary say that Bob was ill and might have to go into the hospital for a while he closed his eyes to hide his annoyance.

'Ill?' said D. J. and he turned round in his chair for corroboration from his brother. 'Anything could happen in this mortal world if Bob gives in his gun.'

'Nelly said he wasn't feeling up to the mark – that's all,' John explained, and he closed his eyes and pretended to doze, and as Mary cleared away the dishes from the table she urged him to go to bed. He said nothing, furtively watching his brother, the slippered feet on the fender and a cigarette in his mouth. She asked him again to go to bed and he turned crossly to her and told her to send the rest of the family to bed and let Frank get an hour's peace to himself. She went quietly into the parlour. The two brothers were left alone, and he suddenly startled D. J. by sitting bolt upright on the sofa and ordering him sharply to clear out of the house in the morning: 'I don't know what kind of a twisted cross-grained man you are! Stealing books out of a library where your own nephew has just been appointed.'

'Now, John, let me explain,' he said with an effort. 'The old brain is ticking slowly. I can explain: they were taken on loan.'

'Liar! You sold them to back a horse. What would have happened if the horse had lost?'

D. J. waved his cigarette in the air, fumbling for words to answer him. He shook his head. 'No, no . . . you're a hard man!'

'Hard, is it? When people are kind to you they're hard.'

'You're as hard and as petrified as a Lough Neagh stick. There's no life where there's no excitement. One must take risks. You're hard and settled.'

'When people rig you out from head to heels they're hard.'

'I'll pay you for the clothes,' and he thrust his hand into his pocket.

'I don't want payment. I want you to clear to hell out of this. In the morning take your walking papers.'

'I'll go now,' and he stooped to take his boots from below the sofa.

Mrs. Caffrey came in again. 'What are you two arguing about? Why are you putting on your boots D. J.?'

John left the kitchen and went up to his room: he knew she would settle him; he wouldn't have it said that he turned his brother out into a wintry night; it was better to leave him to her – women have a managing way.

In bed he lay awake, and at last heard his brother's heavy step on the stairs and Mary's solicitous voice: 'Be careful now, D. J. Watch the turn on those stairs.'

'I'll not sleep tonight, Mary. I'm an abused and insulted man.'

'He didn't mean it, I tell you. He'll forget all about it in the morning. The bad news about Bob has upset him.'

'I'll not close an eye tonight, Mary. I'm insulted.'

'Hm!' said John to himself, 'it would take some insult to keep that boy from sleeping! Tomorrow I'll go out with Eileen to the country but before I go I'll give him another lash with my tongue.'

In the morning he rose early, and after he had taken his breakfast and asked Brendan to send a telegram to Uncle Bob he told Eileen to hurry up and pack her case for her country visit. He went up to the attic, knocked at the door, and entered. D. J. had the bed-clothes rolled round him like an Egyptian mummy, his socks and clothes strewn on the floor.

'Are you awake, D. J.?'

'I am,' he answered, in a wakeful voice. 'I am lying here thinking.'

'I'm going down to the country to see Bob and when I come back this evening I don't want to see sight or trace of you about this house. Do you hear?'

D. J. ran his hand audibly over his stubbled chin and sat up in the bed. He had no pyjamas and he fastened the stud in the open neck-band of his shirt and buttoned the loose sleeves with studied deliberation. He reached out for his trousers that lay in a heap on the floor. 'Turn your back till I jump into these, for the shirt you gave me is disgracefully short.' He pulled on his socks. 'In about five minutes I'll be gone from your hospitable board.'

'You'll take your breakfast first.'

'I'll take no breakfast. You begrudge me every bite I eat!'

'I begrudge you nothing. I have to think of my family. But you have no responsibility. You have no respect for yourself or for anybody belonging to you.'

'Respect! You've a wholesome respect for your poor sick brother in the country,' he said with sarcasm. 'Poor Bob! And you're taking your daughter down to help the invalid. Mary told me all. But let me say here and now that I can see your plan as clearly as the lines in your forehead. You can't deceive a man of the world ... a man that has knocked around the racecourses of England is no Johnny-look-up-at-the-moon.'

'I don't understand you.'

'You don't understand me! Don't anger me for God's sake. I have been lying here since the boys got up thinking of your manoeuvres: you want me to quit the country; you want me to leave Bob and all he possesses to you. Now do you understand me, brother John?'

John shook his head. 'Any mud that is in your mind is of your own making. I don't understand you for I have always mixed with honest people.'

D. J. tightened his braces. 'Don't stand there nodding your

head like a toy in a Christmas window. I could shake you as I'd shake a dice! You're after Bob's money—every cent of it, and you're using Eileen to tighten your grip on it. You're out to deprive me of my just share. But I'll thwart you, my fine pillar of the Church. I'll thwart you. My father cut me out of his will and that's why I have nothing now.'

'That's an old story. It's easy for a man of your kind to reproach the dead. But I'm still alive to choke the lie. You got your chance like us all, and now that you have made a botch of it you hunt outside yourself for someone to blame it on. You only believe what you wish to believe, and I'll not have you in this house to bring ruination on my children.'

'Your children! Frank is a lovely edition. A lovely fellow! I wish you had seen him in a pub yesterday lowering his pint of porter like a man.'

'Get out! You want to turn me against my children,' and he slammed the door and hurried downstairs.

Eileen was standing in the kitchen, a coat over her arm, her suitcase strapped and labelled. 'I think, John, she should take the plaid rug with her,' her mother said. 'Those trains are cold in the mornings and with the snow on the ground it'd be better to be sure than sorry.'

'Eileen's not going,' he said solemnly. 'And don't ask me any questions. She's not going today—that's all!'

'But, John, what's come over you at all? Her heart's set on going and Brendan has already sent the telegram.'

'I'll make the journey myself and I'll explain to Bob and Nelly. Don't ask me any questions . . . And when that man comes down, give him his breakfast if he'll take it and don't palaver him. And, Eileen, if he says anything to you—anything strange about your past visits to your Uncle Bob you need not laugh at him. Your Uncle D. J. has had a hard and strange life and when he meets with decency he believes it is covered with deceit.'

He lifted his hat and coat. Eileen had tears in her eyes and her mother asked that she be allowed to go with him as far as the station itself.

He heard D. J.'s step on the stairs and he took Eileen's hand. 'Come then as far as the station. I'll explain all to your Uncle Bob and Aunt Nelly,' and they left the house.

CHAPTER SIX

BOB was brushing the snow from the shutters on his shop-window when the postman handed him the telegram, and believing it to be from some manufacturer's traveller he put it unconcernedly into his pocket. He carried the shutters one by one into the shop and stood them behind the door. On one shutter there was a chalk inscription scribbled by a child: 'Bob Caffrey is a miser.' He scanned the capital B and C before rubbing them off, and resolved that, if it occurred again, he would carry the shutter as far as the school and report it to the teacher; the long tails on the B and the two eyes on the C would be sure to give her a clue. It was too much of a good thing, he thought, that a decent man's shutters couldn't be left alone of a night without the children using them for a blackboard; and you'd think that the three policemen in the barrack across the way would take a glance out of the window now and again – they'd little else to do and were earning good money for doing it.

He pulled up the blind and in the clear snowy light lifted down his mouse-traps from the shelves, snapped the springs of the empty traps, and emptied the dead mice into the kitchen fire. He had twelve or more traps and he now placed them in a sheltered spot in the yard where the cold air would dissolve the human smell that clung to them. In the evening he would rebait the traps and fix them in their positions, some on the floor and some on the shelves between the bales of flannel. It was surprising the havoc wrought by mice. But traps were pleasanter to deal with than cats: once you got the smell of cats on new clothes it was the very devil to get rid of it. Daly across the road didn't care how many cats he kept or how the clothes smelt. There they were in his window, three of them, stretching themselves and playing like performing animals. 'It's a great wonder,' Bob said aloud to himself, 'Daly's customers don't complain of the cat's hairs on the clothes or the strange smell on them . . . Pooh!' and he blew out his breath as if he had caught the smell from across the road.

He stooped to clear away the snow from the door; he had mittens on his hands, and as he shovelled away at the snow he did so with his left hand, for he still felt a numbing stiffness in his right. Now and again as he heaped the snow at the kerb he would stand for a minute in the silence of the street, looking at the closed doors and at the solid row of houses, aware that they shut out the view of the snow-covered fields that lay hushed and remote, spreading their way across dark hedges, right up to the graveyard whose white headstones were indistinguishable from the mounds on which they stood, and where there would be nothing to catch the eye except the windows of the church, the cold black bell sheltering in its turret, and its rope frozen with snow. There was no sound in the street except that of his shovel, and far down the line the shunting of a train, and at the back of the house the unnoticed sound of the falls continually unrolling their polished web of cold falling water. No one was astir in the village except himself. There was no mark on the snowy road, not a hoof-mark, nothing only the track of the postman's bicycle in the pure snow.

'Oh, that reminds me,' and he took out the telegram, and prized open the envelope with a pencil. He read that his brother John and his niece Eileen would arrive by the early train. He put the envelope back in his pocket and glanced involuntarily at the level-crossing at the end of the village. Within an hour he would hear the whistle of her as sharp as a needle in that transparent stillness. He bent to his work again, and when a cold drop or two dripped on his neck from the slates he glanced up at the roof fearing a fall of snow. But there was little or no snow lying on his roof. Why should there be? Wasn't it well seen that his house was warm? Nelly saw to that, for she kept a good fire blazing in the kitchen in the winter months. The only other house that one could say the same for was the police barracks: they could toast themselves at the public expense. And would you look at Daly's roof? – white as a garden except for a dark 'patch round the base of the chimney!

Soon he had the snow cleared from around the front window where there was a pebbled design of a peacock in the path below it. He sniffed contemptuously at the clear-cut cleanliness of the peacock, and he thought of the foolishness of his father, squandering money on a piece of decoration that the people walked over and spat upon. He shook his head at the grey and red cobble stones that formed the back of the bird and at the blue and green coloured ones that represented the tail and he only wished that they were worn thin and obliterated from his sight. But there was no hope of that, for there was no mistaking the year it had been completed – it was plain to be seen in the corner in white and black stones: 1870; and there it was after all those years as clean and as fresh as if it had been set yesterday. There was one thing certain when he'd enlarged the window in the spring he'd root it out of that – head, tail, legs and all. Wasn't he tired explaining to inquisitive travellers its origin, its age, and who had wrought the design and all the rest of the tomfoolery? You'd think they couldn't read the date: 1870; maybe they thought it was the number of a house – the stupidity of some people is atrocious – atrocious, that's the very word!

He went into the kitchen for a bucket of hot water and

swirled some of it over the window and some of it over the peacock which he swept vigorously with his brush. He put out his iron mat at the door, and he often wished he had the courage to tell his customers to use it. It was painful to see them stepping over it as if it were an ornament. However, some day they'd discover what it was for, and when that day came he'd have an easy enough job sweeping the dry boards of his shop. He breathed in the cold air with satisfaction and withdrew, closing the outside door after him.

'Have you the breakfast ready, Nelly?' he shouted from the shop.

''Tis ready now. Come on inside or you'll get your death of cold on your empty stomach. There'll not be a sinner seen in the village till the snow melts. Why didn't you take a lie in your bed a morning like that?'

'You'll have John and Eileen here on the first train,' and he handed her the telegram.

'Did that come with the postman? And why didn't you tell me and give me time to dress myself?'

'Aren't you dressed enough as it is? Isn't it your own brother that's coming? and as for little Eileen she'll not pay much heed how her aunt is dressed.'

'Aunt, aunt,' she said mockingly. 'A half-sister that's the last of a family is made out to be as old as the oldest in the first family.'

'Pour out the tea till I get to my business. You never know who might be rapping the door -- cold and all as it is.'

'Well, let them rap,' she said. 'It's not much of a business that won't give a man time to enjoy his breakfast.'

'And let my customers go over in a bad temper to Daly's? That's not the way I built my business.'

'If you keep on the way you're doing you won't have much business left to attend on this earth,' she said, and hurried upstairs.

He sat at the table, and as he drank his tea he glanced out

of the window at the white sleeves on the trees and at the sky above them, grey and burdened with snow. It wasn't much of a day for visiting the country, he thought, but, one never knew, it might clear up. He heard the whistle of the train from down the line, and he got up slowly and straightened his tie at the mirror. There was no doubt about it – he had failed since John had seen him last: his collar was slack and loose, and he was sure John would notice the change in him. He rubbed his hand over his sparse grey head, fingering the little cavities here and there. He was getting thinner – there was no doubt about it, but if he was he was also getting older and that surely was the cause of it. He heard the bolts at the level-crossing gates sluck into their long sockets. She'd be here any minute now. He lifted his hat, and Nelly shouted down to him to delay them for a few minutes and give her time to get ready.

He stood within the door of his shop, the leaf of his hat jutting beyond the jamb. The train was there, swirled in steam, the driver looking back from the engine. Presently she chuffed out, and he saw the snow on top of the carriages, the closed windows like pages of ice, and the shadow of her smoke spreading over the sunny road. Silence pressed back into the village again and no one had yet come out of the station. Maybe they changed their minds, he thought. He certainly wouldn't walk from his door till he'd see his visitors, for you never could tell who'd be peering out from an upstair window and laugh at your disappointment. A porter came out of the gate with a bundle of newspapers and left them on the sweet-shop window-sill. The barrack door opened and a policeman in his trousers and vest ran to the bundle, took a newspaper from it and ran back again. 'B-r-r, cold morning, Bob,' he shouted across the road as he put out the recruiting board for the Irish Guards. Then he banged the door, shaking the snow off the knocker. 'They've a grand easy life of it,' Bob said to himself. 'A life like that would have suited D. J.

down to the ground. Pity he didn't go on for the police and he the right height and with a good lining of laziness.' He gave another peep round the jamb of the door but saw no one in the empty street. And then as he turned to go inside to re-read the telegram John emerged from the station accompanied by the porter.

Bob strode from the doorway, his hands under his coat-tails, and walked leisurely through the snow to meet his brother. The white walls of the houses and the bright reflection from the snow dazzled his eyes and he took out his handkerchief to dab the water that trickled from them. He stood in the shade of one of the houses waiting till his brother had finished his chat and then as John came forward with his umbrella in one hand and a rolled-up newspaper in the other he went across to welcome him.

'I'm right and glad you came,' he said, stretching out his hand. 'And you didn't bring Eileen after all. Too cold for her.'

'I didn't; the weather wasn't promising and I thought she could come later on in the spring of the year. And yourself, Bob – how's the health?' and he stole a glance at the pallid face and the bulging shadows below the eyes.

'I'm all right except for the touch of neuritis in the right hand,' and he tried to flex the fingers to show the scant control he had over them. 'It's the raw air that's starving them – they need nourishing heat.'

They had already reached the shop and Bob scraped his feet on the door-scraper and went ahead, John following him. The warm smell of new clothes and the counter polished by the rubbings of the fabric brought back to John's mind the years of his boyhood when he used to sweep the floor for his father, sprinkling water on the dust from a leaking teapot, and how he used to scribble numerals on the floor with the drops before sweeping up the balls of dust on to the roadway. And there on the floor below the hanging-lamp was the dark patch of oil that had expanded with the passing years – it used to remind him of Lough Neagh but now it was so vast it looked more like a map of Ireland.

'You can see I'm fairly well stocked,' Bob was saying. 'But lest I forget I want you to make a list of a few items I'd require immediately. I could do with a few children's waterproofs, men's caps, and a bale of navy serge. "There's nothing like navy blue for smartness," they say around here. And I'm tired telling them that there's nothing like navy blue for showing up stains and creases. But they don't listen to me – they're as stubborn as that,' and he knocked the counter with his knuckles. He turned round. 'What do you think of this new stove I got at an auction? It's very economical on oil and it gives the shop a comfortable appearance. I only light it in the evenings,' he explained when he saw John putting his hand on top of it. 'And do you know what one man said to me the other night about that stove? "Mr. Caffrey," says he, "you might well sit in front of an anvil for all the heat you get from it." He was an ignorant glipe of a fellow that never saw the like before but I soon told him that that stove was only there to preserve the fabrics from damp. I wasn't going to have him mouth around the countryside that I had the stove for my own personal comfort. Do you know, John, I could have laughed when I saw the stupid bewildered look that came on his face.'

'It's not a bad investment,' said John, standing out from the stove the better to admire it. 'But if it were mine I'd certainly put it through its paces these winter months. There's a draught comes under that door that would clean corn.'

'If it does it comes in unknownst to me,' Bob said, and ushered his brother outside the shop to show him where he proposed to make the new alteration. And when John heard that the new window would project two or three feet over the path he expressed his dismay about the peacock.

'The peacock!' said Bob. 'I'll be glad to have it plucked out of that – every stone of it! I really believe the people laugh at it.'

'Could you not get it replaced again at the side of the house?'

'Do you think, man, I'd stand the expense of that foolishness? I haven't money to burn. My father before me was a daft man to waste his money on that useless gargoyle. It's like something you'd see outside a public house or a drawing you'd see in a child's copybook. For goodness' sake have a look at it – isn't it for all the world like a dunghill rooster?'

John remained silent: for him it represented an aspect of his father's nature that he often recalled with an involuntary yearning. He remembered the pride and delight of his father if a passing traveller or a stranger would show any interest in the peacock; he would bring them outside the shop and stooping over the peacock with his pencil he would explain that a real artist drew the design for him for the price of a few bottles of stout, that a local craftsman fitted the pieces together, that the green stones were genuine marble ones that were brought from the island of Iona, that the red ones came from Salruck in Galway, the blue ones from Ballycastle, and the grey ones from Lough Neagh, and that you could travel the length and breadth of Ireland and never come upon its like again.

'Do you know, Bob,' John commented, 'it's my belief you're altering the shop in the wrong quarter. If I were you I would widen the side window. Your front window sits square and decent-looking with the neighbouring houses.'

'The side window! Sure it faces nothing only the pump and the trees. I have given thought to everything and young Doran has approved of my plan. I'll have an awning over the window to keep things fresh and cool from the sun, and in the long run it'll save me money and paint on decoration – the sun blisters the paint and the children pick off the blisters. Look at it! It's a measly and atrocious sight!'

They passed through the shop into the kitchen where Nelly had a vase of fresh chrysanthemums on the table and an extra shine on the plated dish-covers that hung on the wall.

'Where's Eileen?' she asked, taking John's coat and umbrella, and while he was explaining to her the shop bell pinged and Bob lurched out of the kitchen to attend it.

When he was gone Nelly sat beside John on the sofa and pressing her hand on his knee she spoke quickly, her eye cast now and again on the little window which was cut out in the door that led to the shop: 'You'll have to make Bob go to hospital. He's done – there's no mistake about it. He eats nothing. You'll have to see Dr. O'Neill before you go and have a heart-to-heart talk with him. Look at the clothes on Bob. They used to fit him as tight as a rug and only last year I had to put an extra piece in the waist-band of his trousers he was so fat and full-blooded, and now they hang on him, God preserve us, like you'd see on one of his coat-hangers. He's going down the hill fast and the poor man doesn't know it. You can see a change on him yourself?'

'I can. But he's so headstrong it'd be hard for me or anyone else to advise him.'

'But you'll have to do it and you'll have to send Eileen down to help. There's not much life for me here, attending a man that's old enough to be my father.' She sighed and glanced at the snow outside on the trees. 'There's no comfort or joy in the place. I bought that gramophone in the corner and he has raved about the price of it ever since. If I put on a record he goes into the shop and would sit there alone in the dark. If I go to a dance he'll not go to bed like a Christian but sits up here waiting for me. And he sits with no light except that from the holy lamp before the Sacred Heart or the glimmer from the fire which he lets go out.' She took a handkerchief from her sleeve and blew her nose 'That's the way we are living. If he'd even smoke a pipe like another man

77

there'd be some welcome and comfort in the puffs and smell of it. I can't stick it any longer, John. It's wearing me down and if he doesn't go to see a specialist in Belfast soon I'll leave him. I could go to London or Dublin or even Belfast – some place where there's life and movement.'

Hearing Bob's step on the boards of the shop she rose to her feet. 'He's coming, John. Advise him, advise him, it'll be for his own good.'

Bob entered the kitchen in his slow way, tilted his hat to the back of his head, and stood near the window. He rubbed his finger on a drop of water that had fallen from the vase of chrysanthemums on to the polished table and gave a laugh low down in his throat. Nelly signalled to John with her eyes but before he had time to speak Bob was laughing again. 'The things people expect from you nowadays,' he was saying. 'Do you know who that customer was? Mrs. Kerr from the Bog. More clothes on tick as usual. She has a son studying for the teaching and when he's finished she says she'll pay me back every silver shilling she owes me and with interest, too, if I'd like. What was she wanting? – a new suit of woollens for her son. She says he's foundered and famished in the training college and that there's no heat and not enough blankets on his bed. "You don't think that's my fault?" I told her, "I'm not responsible for the heating arrangements of a training college" . . . I may tell you I wasn't one bit soft with her.'

'She's an honest woman,' Nelly said. 'She has reared a decent family and she has a daughter a nun out in the Foreign Missions. I hope you didn't affront her.'

'I did not. She's four feet in debt already for me not to know my business. I gave her the woollens, a cheap cottony set, not the kind she had her eye on. She took them and right and glad she was to get anything. But she didn't even bid me good-day as she went out the door. There's no nature in her at all. The people in this locality are as hard-set as the stones in the old peacock.' He shrugged his shoulders. 'There's the snow falling again. You did right not to bring Eileen, a day like that.'

Big heavy flakes swung down through the trees, falling and drifting silently, alighting on the pane and melting in slow shining drops. A few boys, one in his bare feet carrying a bucket, approached the water pump, and as one of them turned the handle with unnecessary vigour the water gushed out and swept a black patch in the snow.

'Come here, John.' Bob called his brother to the window. 'Wouldn't you think to look at that fellow in his bare feet that there wasn't a rubber boot in the whole village and here I am with a surplus stock covered with brown paper to keep the light from perishing them? It's not worth a body's while trying to fend for the people of this place.'

'He's happy as he is,' John said, watching the boys pelt one another with snowballs. A snowball struck the window, broke in fragments, and slithered down to the sill.

'I'll make them skip,' said Bob, and as he rattled for his stick Nelly told him to have sense in his head and leave them to their bit of play. But Bob went out, and as a few snowballs came hurling at his head John heard with a feeling of indignation the shouts of 'yellow neck' and 'split-the-halfpenny' that accompanied them.

'That's the kind of unmannerly brats we have about here,' Bob said out of breath as he put his stick in the hallway. 'That's the kind of them and there's not one of their mothers that isn't in acres of debt to me. But I'll change my methods once the shop is renovated. Cash Stores, I'll call it.' He sat down, his big hands on his knees, his head erect like one posing for a photographer.

Nelly prepared the dinner, and time and again as she moved to and fro about the range she motioned to John with her eyes.

'About that visit to the city, Bob,' he said with polite

reluctance. 'What about coming back with me and have the job done right off the reel?'

'The job – what job?' Bob started, jolted out of the customary run of his thoughts.

'You remember – the X-ray you mentioned in your letter.'

'Oh, that! Dr. O'Neill hasn't referred to it since. He must have good grounds for thinking I've improved.'

'But you eat nothing,' Nelly put in. 'I make a good dinner for him every day and he picks round it like a sick hen. That's the truth I'm telling you, John. Let the two of you take a walk out the road to the doctor's and talk it over with him. The snow's falling so thick you can't see the sky above the trees. Nobody with any sense will be out shopping today. Go on the pair of you and I'll have a hot dinner ready by the time you come back.'

'I'll decide after the slow train comes in. There might be a traveller or two calling to see me,' Bob said, and he got up and stood looking out of the window.

Nelly made a cup of tea for John to take the edge off his hunger and while he was taking it they heard the slow train hissing at the station, whistle out again and rumble over the bridge across the river. The silence crept slowly back again. John got to his feet, stretched himself, and clapped his hands with feigned good-humour. He began to explain to Bob that his ailment might be only a minor affair, might be an ulcerated stomach that would require only a slight operation to make a new man of him. 'Man alive, Bob,' he went on, 'you can't enjoy a full life when you can't enjoy a good tightener of a meal. Come on. When there's two of us to talk it over with the doctor the job's half done.'

Bob tried to ward him off but with Nelly handing him his overcoat, his stick, and his woollen scarf he found himself weakening and incapable of talk. John put up his umbrella, and passing the pump whose waist was tied with sacking and straw he noticed a large ball of snow stuck on its spiked head and two stones to serve as eyes. He laughed loudly saying that he never saw anything so human-looking since the good God made him.

'The children are half savage – no respect for anything. No trouble to them if the pump freezes,' Bob said solemnly; and John, unable to raise him from his heavy sullen mood, tried to stifle the look of pleasurable reminiscence that his brother might detect from his smile. The snowflakes streaked past his umbrella and he was aware that their glittering whiteness made his face glow with an unsuitable satisfaction. Suddenly Bob gripped his arm and asked him to turn back, that there was nothing the doctor could tell him that he did not know already.

John laughed. 'You'd think we were going to a perfect stranger, and Dr. O'Neill a man that we played football with at school.'

'The smell of his surgery makes me sick. It's as small as a goat's shed and the air in it would suffocate you.'

The noise of wheels crunching the snow made them turn round, and they stood at the edge of the road their hats slightly raised when they saw it was a funeral; the motor-hearse passed in front and they caught a blurred glimpse of an oak coffin with heavy brass fittings. Behind came a long line of cars, the windows streaked with snow except for the dark sector swept out on the windscreens. The air was filled with an oily smell of petrol.

'Who'd that be?' Bob said in a whisper.

'Some big fellow, I'd say,' and John gazed after the cars, cutting black lines in the snow.

'The coffin was the last word in elegance,' Bob said.

'If his soul is half as elegant he'll have all his worries over him by this time.'

'A man like that would leave plenty of money for Masses to be offered up for his soul. He'll be all right.'

'Men can be selfish even in death,' John said, 'and unknown

to him the grace from that man's Masses would spread to us all. It's the good you do while you're alive that will stand to you. Do you know, Bob, the nearer I draw to the grave the more I wish I could destroy the years in which I had injured people. I would try to undo it all.'

'A thought like that would never strike me. When I'm finished with a person I'm finished with them for good! That's my belief. You can't let people walk over you as if you were a door-mat.'

They had reached the drive that led to the doctor's and Bob stood irresolute, looking at the car-tracks in the snow. 'We'll turn back. It's no comfort listening to the old story and he charging a guinea for taking my pulse.'

John lowered his umbrella and the air seemed to him to be filled with sound; lumps of snow fell from the burdened trees and a phistling, like sand, came from the bushes. They heard the doctor's voice bidding someone goodbye and then there was the dull sound of a door closing.

'He's in,' John said, and he touched Bob's arm and moved to the gateway, and there coming down the drive and humming to himself was D. J. He had his head bent from the snow and he didn't see them until he had reached the open gate.

'Well, well,' he said. 'Is this where the pair of you are? You never know what you will meet in the snow.'

'What are you doing here?' John said.

'And what are you doing?' D. J. said back to him. 'It's a free country,' and he glanced at Bob to see if there was any sign of a welcome in that pallid, inscrutable face. Bob was staring at him with stupid consternation, his lower lip hanging loose and trembling. His heart pounded in his breast. 'What takes you here?' he said at last. 'I thought you were in England.'

'So John didn't tell you,' he said. 'Do you think that Bob has no concern for me and I have no concern for him?'

'I hadn't a chance to tell him and I hadn't the time. We

were just taking a walk up to see Dr. O'Neill,' and he turned to Bob for agreement.

'I'll not go now. I'm not in a fit condition to see anyone,' and he turned towards the village, John and D. J. following at each side of him.

'Come on and we'll have a bumper at my expense,' D. J. said.

'I'll have no drink,' Bob said. 'You know I don't touch spirits. Go back to wherever you came from and leave me in peace. It's the police I should send on your tracks for all the money you borrowed from me.'

They reached the village and Bob eyed the footprints in the road leading to his shop and then followed the same tracks across to Daly's. He turned suddenly on D. J. 'Didn't I tell you to go away and not be obstructing me? And what right had you to give my name and address to the landladies you left in the lurch? Go off before I get the police.'

D. J. halted beside the pump. 'John has warped your mind against me. I'm not the down-and-out you think I am,' and he opened his coat and displayed some of his money.

'How do I know it was honestly come by?'

John whispered to him to take him in for a bite of dinner, but Bob ignored the suggestion, and John followed him into the house leaving D. J. confusedly crumbling the ball of snow on the pump's head.

They took off their coats in heavy silence and awaited the dinner that Nelly was bringing to the table. Bob stood at the window, and sat down only when he was satisfied that D. J. was gone. And while they were at the table John related all of D. J.'s movements since his arrival in the city, omitting, however, his singing in the snow, the incident of the stolen library books, and his ordering him out of the house.

'I thought he was still in Belfast,' he went on, 'but he must have followed in the slow train. I told him you weren't feeling up to the mark of late – that news must have worried him.'

'That's none of his business, and if he's visiting Dr. O'Neill on my account I'll soon change my doctor. I don't want a man like that foraging into my affairs. He's depraved – I know by the letters he sent to me from England from time to time.'

'It's hard to know and it's harder to judge,' John said. 'And there's none of us so degraded that we won't be a bit better for a kindness shown to us. You shouldn't have turned him away.'

'You should not,' Nelly agreed. 'It's scandalous to turn your own brother away from the doorstep where he was reared. You'll rue this day. And what's more you'll give friend Daly the laugh of his life.'

Bob put down his knife and fork and asked her to put on her coat and go out and look for him.

She came back without him. He was nowhere to be found: neither in the pub, the newsagent's, nor the waiting-room at the railway station; and as she took off her coat she lamented that it was a disgraceful action for one brother to clash his door on another's face, and that, too, in the dead of winter. 'It was enough to make father turn in his grave,' she said, 'a father that never turned a beggar from the door without handing him a copper or two or the makings of a supper.'

'I better open the shop,' Bob said, 'I haven't the health to stand this. If he's in the village at all he'll be the ruin of me. And you, John, know more about his manoeuvres than you pretend to. It's strange you both came on different trains. No, there's nothing straight – not even among your own flesh and blood. No honest dealing,' and he got up from the table and lumbered into the seclusion of his shop.

John rubbed his hand over his forehead and shook his head in despair. He looked at his watch and decided to take the first train home. His visit was a failure. Nothing was done, and as Nelly took the tablecloth from under his hands she, too, regretted that nothing was done, that her life was becoming more burdensome, that it would grow more miserable now that D. J. was rambling about the country and she having to stand the strain, the talk, the spying, and the intolerable restlessness it would cause Bob.

'Oh!' she continued, 'it is no comfort for me to watch a man dying on his feet and renovating a shop that he'll not live to enjoy. And I dread the long nights with no one to talk to. None of you know what it is to have a tortured mind!'

'A tortured mind, how are you!' John said to himself. Weren't his brothers a continual worry to him! And then there was Frank: he would have to look into that remark of D. J.'s about Frank drinking. He was sure there was no truth in it. How could Frank start to drink — a lad that you may say is still at school. It was nonsense.

A train whistled in the distance, and as Nelly helped him into his coat he noticed tears in her eyes. She pleaded with him to wait for a later train but he told her he must catch this one as he wished to put in an hour or two's work in his own shop.

'You'll promise to send Eileen soon,' she said, holding tight his hand that she was shaking in farewell. 'Promise me that! I can't stick here any longer.'

'I will,' he said, and he passed into the shop.

Bob held out his hand over the counter to bid him goodbye. 'It was good of you to send my money so promptly. And when young Doran has the new window put in you'll take a run down to see it ... And you'll dispatch that little order of mine as soon as you get back. I'd like to have it for Christmas.'

Through the window they saw the cars returning from the funeral and pass rapidly through the village. They looked on in silence, and in their own minds they saw the fresh dark mound of clay in the graveyard, the snow falling on it and merging it with the common whiteness of the neighbouring graves.

85

CHAPTER SEVEN

THE next day John dispatched Bob's order, and in the succeeding days he watched Frank closely. He noted his eyes, the colour of his cheeks, the sound of his voice, trying to find a convincing sign that his son was drinking. He would pretend to show him some important item in the newspaper and when Frank would bend over his shoulder he would inaudibly sniff the air around him. But he was glad to say there was never a sign, nothing in the boy's manner or behaviour that could make him believe in D. J.'s announcement. Frank, no doubt, was unusually late coming home of an evening but one couldn't blame him for that. He was always discussing his work and his problems with his class companions, he told them. Anne always supported him and tried to persuade her father that Frank's method of study was the best possible for strengthening his grip on his lectures. The father always shook his head doubtfully and would refer to the Mallon nephews – boys who got their examinations by pitching into their books morning, noon, and night.

From these gentle wranglings in the evening Brendan kept aloof though once or twice he felt impelled to get to his feet and tell his father that Frank wasn't at the university at all, and that he had squandered his second-year enrolment fees that had been given to him. He always restrained himself in time by going off to the parlour and singing a few songs to Eileen's accompaniment. He yearned for the months to pass quickly and give Frank an opportunity of saying that he had failed in his second medical examination. After all more than half the students failed in that examination and his father would understand and attribute the blame to Frank's new-fangled methods of studying. And Frank, he was sure, was keeping in touch with other students, for one evening in the attic he saw a notebook of Frank's and on perusing it he discovered that he had been making a copy of all the second-year lectures. But whether or not he was studying them was another matter, and the few times he had questioned Frank he was told to mind his own damned business and not to be meddling in problems that didn't concern him. Brendan confessed that he had glanced at his notebook and Frank accused him of searching for passages in obstetrics and that he was no better than the fellows who prowled around the salacious bookshops in Smithfield.

'I have my own plans,' Frank told him. 'And if you don't stop interfering in my affairs and stalking after me through the town I'll not be responsible for what I'll do to you. Now that's my last and final warning!'

'Do you ever think of anybody except yourself?' Brendan lectured him. 'Do you not realize that if father or mother or Anne or Eileen get to hear about you you'll break their very hearts? They'll be ashamed to speak of you just as I'm ashamed to speak of Uncle D. J. when the janitor in the library worries me about tips for horse-racing.'

'You're a fellow took the wrong turn. 'Tis a wonder you didn't go into a monastery and become a missioner. And if you want to know I envy Uncle D. J. I envy him his rambling roundabout life. Up and down the length and breadth of England – a man so interesting you'd gladly forfeit a night's sleep listening to his adventures.'

'It'll be a long time, Frank, till he'll have an adventure at your expense. You'll be going in and out of the university, day after day, and year after year, till the people will think you're one of the staff. You'll be one of the hardy annuals.'

'There's no damned fear of that, my tuppence-halfpenny librarian! If I chucked it tomorrow I've a decent enough education that would get me a respectable job. I could go anywhere – Canada, Australia, New Zealand.'

'If that's your intention why don't you tell father? He'll have to know some time and it'd be better for you to speak it out than for him to hear it from an outsider – someone that would put a twist on it that would madden and sour the very soul out of him.'

To all this Frank never gave him any satisfaction or any inkling of what he intended to do. The days sped towards Christmas, and the university vacation began. Frank was free to lie in bed in the mornings and his mother brought his breakfast to him, advising him to take a good rest for she was sure his poor nerves needed it.

Anne, too, got her vacation from school, but on the last day, after the Christmas tests had been corrected, Miss Mallon had reprimanded her for faulty teaching in tones loud enough to be heard by the whole class; and Anne, instead of arriving home thankful to be free for a while from the fetid air of school, was heavily dispirited. Eileen and her mother tried to drag from her what was wrong but she answered them sharply and told them that she hated the school and she was not going back to it.

That evening at the tea-table her mother asked if she had had a tiff with Miss Mallon, for Miss Mallon had passed her very curtly in the street – a sharpness that she couldn't fathom, especially at Christmas time when even the stiffest had a smile for you.

'I had a row with her,' Anne said without enthusiasm.

'A row!' her father said with mock surprise. 'You didn't pull one another's hair, I hope.'

'We had a quarrel over the teaching of English,' Anne went on. 'Miss Mallon won't allow me to teach in the way I feel is right.'

'But, maybe, Miss Mallon is right and you are wrong. She has the experience; she has a weight of years you should respect,' her father counselled.

'Oh, Father, I know all that. You are always ready to take her part. But can you not see how boring it is for me to teach a subject in a way that revolts me?'

'What really happened?' Brendan asked. 'For goodness' sake tell us what happened till we have a laugh.'

'It's no laughing matter let me tell you,' Anne said, almost in tears. 'My class was reciting poetry in chorus. Joseph Campbell's poem "The Old Woman", it was; and Miss Mallon bounded into the room in the middle of it and told me to cease immediately. "If it's a poem about a mother you intend to teach then let it be 'Somebody's Mother' – the new inspector likes that," she told me. "Well, I don't," I told her back to her face. "But you've other things I object to," she said; and she sent a girl to my press for the composition exercise books. She opened a few of them greedily. "Now," she said, "look here! There's what I call a deluge of indiscretion," and she pointed her finger at sentences that I had marked *very good* with red pencil: *A boy speeled up a lamp-post to tie my rope* – a little girl had written that, and I loved it. But Miss Mallon said it was bad English and that *speeled* was a common, vulgar street-word. I told her it was a lovely word – a word that conveyed the sound and feel and movement of the boy's hand on the lamp-post. Then she perused a few compositions on "Rain" and tut-tutted as she read aloud a few extracts: . . . *a row of raindrops hanging on a bare clothes-line . . . the rain pitted against the paper . . . the rainbow-colours on drops of oil lying on the wet street . . . from the window I watched the rain looping little bracelets on a puddle of water* – all that she said was not about rain at all and that a girl would get no marks for such in examinations. I smiled at her and she told me I was insolent and intractable. "But I'm teaching a child to live," I said, "I'm not teaching for dessicated examinations." "But what about me, Miss Caffrey?" she said. "I being principal have to think of the success of my school." '

'She has, indeed, poor woman,' the mother put in.

'Oh, Mother,' said Eileen, 'let Anne finish till we hear the climax.'

Anne sighed and continued: 'Miss Mallon then asked me

how I had approached the subject of "Rain" and I explained how I had read out aloud to my class Seamus O'Sullivan's poem on "Rain" and also a very beautiful extract of Austin Clarke's:

> There by dim wells the women tied
> A wish on thorn, while rainfall
> Was quiet as the turning of books
> In the holy schools at dawn.

She told me it was no wonder that I got the results I did get after an approach of that kind. "First of all, Miss Caffrey, you should always have a preliminary talk with your class before they put pen to paper: for instance how rain is useful to man, how rain feeds the crops and makes the grass grow, and how it provides the cows with nourishment and hence provides us with rich milk; and then how rain is formed, and how some countries have a low rainfall and some a heavy rainfall and the effects of this on vegetation. It's information we want from compositions, Miss Caffrey, and not this rainbow-chasing nonsense," and she slapped the books with her hand. "But that's all wrong," I told her. "There's no feeling for life in that method, no respect for human distinctions, nothing in it only a stifling of originality. A child, more than we, can feel everything as life, as movement, as lived experience, as imagination, as loveliness. They possess fresh vision, Miss Mallon, for I have seen examples of it, but we crush it and destroy it by imposing our own dry ideas upon them. Instead of nourishing that vision we starve it, and so we get stale impressions instead of self-expression; and for me who has to correct that stuff – instead of refreshment from my school work I get stagnation. Compositions by recipe is your method," I told her. Don't allow them to write what the heart dictates or what they feel and hear in their own vital environment! When I had said that she flung down the books on the desk and turned on me. "So, Miss Caffrey, you are finding fault with my teaching. A girl just out of the training college to advise *me*! Before you leave today I demand an apology!'' and she left the room and banged the door. And that's the whole story.'

'Well, well,' said Mr. Caffrey. 'I'd teach the way she wants and have peace.'

'That's what Pilate would do. But I'll not – even if I have to throw it up altogether.'

'I hope you apologized,' her mother said.

'I tried to see her before I left and when I went into her room she raised her head from her desk and waved her hand: ''I'm busy at the moment, Miss Caffrey,'' was all she said and I went out of her room with my face on fire. That's the reception I got for going to apologize!'

Mr. Caffrey finished his tea and raised his eyes to the holly leaves that decorated the pictures. 'It's an unfortunate occurrence and she so decent in getting you that appointment, and her brother ready to make a wireless set for me any time we desire one. It's too bad altogether and you'll have to try and alter your attitude to it and don't let it mar your Christmas. Like a good girl send her a tasteful calendar at Christmas and invite her down as usual on Christmas evening. When she simmers down she may respect you all the more for clinging to your own opinions.'

Anne said nothing, but two days before Christmas when she and Eileen were down among the shops selecting Christmas cards she relented somewhat of her outburst and fingered a few calendars in the hope of finding a suitable one for Miss Mallon. Eileen lifted one depicting a mountainy cottage in Donegal and Anne pondered a moment and said: 'I'd be afraid to send it. She might read a meaning into the picture that that was the place where I yearned to go.'

'But surely she doesn't think you're crazy enough to go up into the mountains?'

'I have enough sense to know that one must be bred and

reared there to settle contentedly in it. I'd like a place nearer home.'

Anne put the calendar in its tray and looked at one that had a Celtic tracery design: 'Peace on Earth to Men of Goodwill'. 'Oh, Eileen,' she said, 'I never realized how difficult it is to select a calendar. Everyone of them has something she might construe as being insolent.'

'You're far too complex,' Eileen said. 'That's what too much reading has done for you – you see motives where none exist. People at Christmas are so delighted at receiving cards they haven't time to think somebody is sending one to insult them. Here!' and she lifted a coloured calendar showing Ardglass herring-boats. 'She can hang that up in her class-room to remind them that Ardglass is noted for fish.'

'I'll take that one,' Anne agreed, and having settled on that they moved from shop to shop buying presents; ties and handkerchiefs for Frank and Brendan, tobacco and socks for their father, and envelopes and notepaper for mother.

'And I'll have to send Aunt Nelly something, this Christmas,' Eileen said. 'She's always very kind to me.'

'And what about your friend Doran, the young builder? You'll send a card to him, I hope. He was more kind to you than Aunt Nelly from what you've told me from time to time. And look at the lovely bangle he bought you when you were down last. If I were admired like that I wouldn't treat it lightly.'

'But his job isn't a good one.'

'He's steady and he'll go ahead. And that house down by the river with only himself and his sister in it – I loved it when I saw it last summer: the flowers in the garden, the piano in that lovely cool drawing-room, and the wooden steps down to his boat. It was all so peaceful, anyone could be content there if one were in love.'

'I like him, but I'm not sure if I could like him in that way. I love Monabeg but I wonder if I could spend all my days in it. There's Aunt Nelly and she loathes it. Every time I go down on a visit it's her whole complaint: the deadness of the place, the sound of the falls, and the trains leaving the station and dragging her heart away with them. There was a young policeman used to bring her to a few dances but since he was transferred to Armagh she has no interest left.'

'It'd be different for you. You'd have your husband, and if you had children you'd wonder how easily you could adapt yourself. Poor Aunt Nelly has nothing to look at except Uncle Bob and she'll not get much fun out of that museum piece.'

They stood at a tram-stop. A Salvation Army band played Christmas carols in the grounds of the City Hall, and an old man, bent with age, carried a placard: 'Flee from the Wrath to come'. They bought mistletoe and chrysanthemums from the street flower-sellers, and boarding a tram they sat inside with their parcels on their laps. The faces of the passengers were strained and dispirited. They all sat quite still except for two ragged boys who kept wiping their noses on their coat-sleeves and admiring a blue-grey pigeon that the bigger boy held in his right hand. He stroked the pigeon gently and it shook its head and blinked its white eyelids. The conductor came along for the fares and the big boy asked in a husky voice for two halves. The conductor eyed him critically, punched one ticket with studied deliberation and handed it with a smile to the smaller boy. Once more the conductor scanned the big lad from head to heels and asked him was he sure it was a 'half' he wanted.

'Aye,' said the lad, 'a half.'

The conductor punched another ticket, and handing it to him with pretended reluctance he said: 'There's your first Christmas box. Give my respects to your wife.'

The strained faces relaxed, and a smile broke from Anne and Eileen. The boy reddened, put the pigeon in the breast of his coat and wiped his nose on his snot-polished sleeve. Anne handed him a sixpence to ease his embarrassment and he smiled and nudged his brother: 'Tommy, show her what you have got.'

Tommy took a black and white mouse from his pocket and placed it on the palms of his hands. The mouse, dazed with the light, ran round the little platform of the boy's hands, sniffed the air, ran out to the tips of his fingers, doubled back again, and running up the outside of his sleeve, it circled his neck and fell on to the lap of the lady beside him. She screamed and jumped to her feet, and the boy picked up the mouse from the floor and put it back in his pocket. The conductor came forward and ordered them to get off to hell out of the road. 'That's the thanks I get for giving you a half, my oul' bucko,' he said to the big lad, who was moving off with stubborn slowness; and the lad once out on the safety of the road shouted at the conductor: 'Come out here till I get a clout at your clock!'

The tram started once more on its journey, the conductor saying to anyone who cared to listen to him: 'That's an example of the coming generation. They're taught everything in school except manners.'

The remark sent Anne's mind back to school and to Miss Mallon informing her that the children of this town do not appreciate kindness. To ward off the thought of school she asked Eileen if the mouse had frightened her and did she consider the conductor justified in ordering them off the tram, seeing they had already paid their fares? Eileen was considering the lawfulness of it when suddenly her mind was distracted by an onrush of fresh passengers, one of them a drunken man carrying a wrapped-up turkey by the legs. There was no seat for him and he swayed unsteadily on his feet, lurching forward and back again, shouting out that it was a stormy passage, a rough crossing, and that the captain was blind drunk. Anne rose and gave him her seat and he slumped down heavily beside Eileen wishing her a happy Christmas. The shoulders of the man jogged against her own

94

and he kept begging her pardon and nodding his head to the rhythm of his own words. Then he held up the legs of the turkey and asked if the bird by any chance could be a goose, for the shopkeepers could palm anything off on you when you're tight.

'The legs are the legs of a turkey,' Eileen told him.

He fingered the feet of the turkey and ran its claws over the back of his hand. 'You're sure it's not a goose, daughter?' he asked again.

'It couldn't be a goose. A goose has webbed feet,' and she turned away from him and laughed into her handkerchief.

The man shut his eyes, his head bobbing with the movement of the tram. Then suddenly he jerked his head erect and held aloft his forefinger to command attention: 'I have it now, daughter,' he said, cutting the air with his finger. 'I have it now. Sure, how the hell could a goose swim if it hadn't webbed feet? That's the best ever I heard,' he went on, arguing with himself and telling himself that he was a stupid bloody man not to know that a goose had webbed feet. Eileen and Anne came to their stop and he raised his hat and wished them once more a very happy Christmas. The tram sped on to the terminus and as they looked after it they hoped he hadn't missed his stop.

Walking up the street they noticed lights in the parlour windows: blinds were undrawn and young children were helping their fathers to erect the Christmas trees, swinging coloured balls among the branches and clipping red candles to the outside tips. They stood gazing over the hedge at one house, fascinated by a little boy who was up on his knees on the table, switching and unswitching the coloured electric bulbs that adorned his Christmas tree.

'Wouldn't it be lovely, Eileen, if that were your little boy and the lights shining out on the river?'

Eileen hugged her sister's arm and told her not to be so foolish, and going into their own house they placed their baskets on the table, and before taking off their coats they sifted the Christmas letters, Eileen seizing a small packet addressed to her in heavy Gothic penscript. She knew it was rom Philip Doran, and because of her parents' presence she curbed her immediate inclination to open it. There was no card as yet from Miss Mallon and Anne decided to withhold her own calendar from the post until tomorrow.

The father sat in his armchair, unaware of the excited chatter around him and staring into the fire absent-mindedly. He smoked his pipe, his hand now and again passing slowly over his head. A letter had come to him from D. J. and he burnt it at once endeavouring to destroy all thought of the enraged bitterness it contained. But the sentences, one by one, grew all the more strongly in his mind, thwarting all his efforts to uproot them. He was an outcast, D. J. had written: everyone was ranged against him, planning to dispossess him from his rightful share in Bob's money. John he blamed most, for without him the others were lost. He blamed him for stiffening Bob's mind against him. He had called recently at the shop and was received like an income-tax collector and all that in spite of Nelly's support – a good girl that had no thought of anything except what was just. But you John (and he had underlined his name three times) are the hypocrite, pushing your family forward to gain a share in something that doesn't belong to them. But mark these words he wouldn't be foiled this time – he would fight, even to proving that Bob was insane. Bob would make no will if left alone – he was too cowardly to sign the countryman's death warrant. He was sure of that! and he had concluded the letter by printing the words: LEAVE HIM ALONE.

What could you do with a man like that except pray for him – pray that God would simplify his mind? All that he did for him was misread, was turned and twisted and flung back at him in loathesome abasement. It's a strange world when kindness nourishes ill-nature. There was no doubt about it

96

Bob was finished with D. J. and he meant as little to him as the old peacock that lay in stolid indifference underneath the shop window. If Bob makes a will – and God grant that he wouldn't – D. J.'s name would never occur to him as he penned it. And now with D. J. hanging around Monabeg he would irritate him at a time when even the hardest are inclined to weaken. For himself he could honestly say that he'd strive for their reconcilement: the distress and conflict of two minds gradually ceasing, merging together, so that the one who was left behind in the world would remember the other with a prayer and not with a malediction. He smiled then at D. J.'s sudden folly – the gambler's belief in chance: ordaining who was to die first. There they were the two of them each convinced of the other's worthlessness, each desiring the other's death and not desiring his repentance. D. J. coveting what Bob has and not desiring a change in what he is. And Bob so absorbed in his possessions, wrenching every penny from the poor, and forgetting that some day he would have to leave it all behind him. Maybe they were all in a way to blame for D. J.'s irresponsibility: the father that reared them, the blood he gave them, and the will that he had made, leaving the shop to Bob and nothing to D. J. But his father did what anybody would have done – leave his business to the eldest son, a son who would build on it and not destroy it. He never condemned his father for the will or ever thought of it with remorse. If D. J. had married it would have made a different man of him: in the rearing of a family he would have been able, perhaps, to forget himself; he would have known sorrow and joy, and in experiencing both, the meaning of his life would have been revealed to him as clearly as the wintry winds reveal the branches and limbs of a tree. Winter and spring, sorrow and joy – that was life: one could not experience the fullness of each without having experienced the other. Suffering, as his father was never tired of saying, was the tether of God; it was sorrow that nourished and held men fast.

He knocked out his pipe on the range, yawned and stretched himself. The family had gone to the hall door and he could hear the St. Vincent de Paul carol singers outside singing 'Noel'. He went to the door, shuddering from the sudden grasp of cold air that met him. The carol singers, youths and girls, were arranged in a group on the roadway, and from the upstair lighted windows in the adjacent houses children awakened from their sleep had pulled the curtains to the side and were gazing down at them, seeing the swaying lamps above the heads of the singers, the open song books and their red hands reflecting the soft light. The singers laughed and joked together after each song, the collector rattling his box and going from house to house asking the listeners to help the poor. Mr. Caffrey put a few shillings in the box and Mrs. Caffrey asked them to sing 'Holy Night', and after the collector had gone Brendan said it was little odds what they sang for they were all singing out of tune. His father reproved him for the remark, telling him that it was a shame for a boy of his age with such a lovely voice not to be out with the carol singers and helping the poor.

'And if he were out,' Mrs. Caffrey said, 'you'd be worrying about him, fearing that he get his death of cold.'

'There'd be no fear of my saying that,' he said without conviction, and trembling once more from the cold he went up to his room, hearing as from a distance the lovely melody of 'Holy Night'.

CHAPTER EIGHT

ON Christmas morning Mr. Caffrey arose early to go to six o'clock Mass and on coming downstairs he found the fire already lighted and his shoes and spats warming on the rack above the range. On the table were his presents from the family and though he did not wish to look at them until he returned from the church he noticed with pride that there was a large handkerchief from Frank – a poor fellow that had barely enough money to keep himself in cigarettes! He lifted the handkerchief, smelt its perfumed newness, and placed it on the table again. His family had gone to midnight Mass and were now in bed, and so he set off alone, enjoying the quiet darkness of the morning, the star-pointed frost on the road, and the echoing sounds of his own footfall. Near the chapel people passed him black as shadows, and in the warm light from the door he noticed that they were mostly poor people, grateful for the darkness that hid the shabbiness of their clothes.

He waited for the three Masses, collected for the St. Vincent de Paul for a while, and then set off, a piece of fresh straw from the crib sticking out from the pages of his missal. A few thin stars lingered in the sky but darkness had already shrunk from the trees along the road and from the windows and doors of the houses. Near home he overtook Mr. Mallon and after wishing him a happy Christmas he expressed a hope that he and his sister would be free to come down for a while in the evening. Mr. Mallon excused himself as two of his nephews had arrived for the holidays. Mr. Caffrey included them in his invitation but Mr. Mallon replied that he thought his sister had booked seats for them all at the pantomime. He walked slowly then, detaining his friend as best he could, and resisting an inclination to refer to Anne's little differences with Miss Mallon. It was wiser to say nothing, he decided, for it would only give heavy emphasis to a matter of slight importance.

'And the doctor,' he found himself saying. 'I suppose he will come back from England some day for good?'

'I don't think my nephew will ever countenance that,' Mr. Mallon said dryly. 'He's attached to a hospital that possesses every modern equipment. He's specializing in radiology and he's preparing a thesis for his M.D.'

'More power to him,' Mr. Caffrey said, 'more power to him. There's no mistake but you Mallons have more than your share of brains. I wish you could give Frank a grain or two. When he's finished he'll have to cross the Irish Sea to gather the wherewith to set-up in his own town. Maybe if the doctor has a minute or two to spare he'd have a heart-to-heart talk with Frank. It'd do my boy good, you know.' At the garden gate as Mr. Mallon was leaving him he again announced his invitation, saying that the door would be always open for them at any time of the evening they'd find time to call.

'Don't expect us,' Mr. Mallon said. 'The nephews will be on the tired side after the pantomime.'

Mr. Caffrey hung up his coat in the hall and went into the parlour. The Christmas cards were four deep on the mantelpiece and Eileen was polishing the piano and placing a sheet of music on the stand. Her father looked at the rich attractiveness of the well-laid table, the white cloth showing its stiff creases, the firelight streaking the tumblers which held serviettes crimped and fanned like sea-shells. There was a smell of burnt leather and he felt the back of one of the chairs and drew it away from the heat of the fire.

'We got two cards less than last year, Father,' Eileen said, rubbing her duster along the sideboard. 'None from the Mallons and, strange to say, none from Aunt Nelly. Maybe Uncle Bob's not well and she couldn't get her post off.'

'She'll write – there's no fear of that,' and he stood warming himself with his back to the fire.

'Could I go down to see her after Christmas, Father?'

'We'll see. We'll see. The weather's a bit on the cold side. There's an icy breath from the old river that'd give you your death.'

He went into the kitchen for his breakfast and before sitting down to the table he took envelopes from his pocket and handed one to each of his children. 'Your Christmas presents,' he said. 'You'll see I have made a slight difference from last year,' he added with a slow smile. 'One pound to each of the employed, Anne and Brendan. And three pounds each to the unemployed.'

Brendan and Anne protested with childish affectation and Eileen shouted them down, laughing and saying they had no cause for grumbling. Frank put his envelope unopened in his pocket, yawning and giving a forced smile.

'And by the way,' the father continued, tucking his napkin under his chin, 'the Mallons will not be able to come down this evening.'

'On account of me, I suppose,' Anne said.

'No, it's on account of their nephews. Two of them are here for a short holiday.'

'A fine excuse,' Anne said. 'When they didn't see fit to send us a card I know too well what has riled them. She'll have no cause for worrying when the holidays are at an end – I'm not going back to that school!'

'What nonsense,' said the mother, 'don't let us have all that talk again. Let you and Brendan and Frank go for a walk as far as the mountain's foot and get an appetite for your Christmas dinner. There's Frank and he's dying for a breath of fresh air.'

'I've a few things to tidy, yet,' Anne said, and she told Frank to go on by himself and they would meet him on the way back.

Frank was glad to get out alone. He walked quickly past the tram terminus and out on to the country road that led to the mountain. He tore open the envelope, counted the three pounds, and flung the empty envelope over the hedge. He breathed in the cold air, feeling it penetrate his throat like a hot flame. He tightened his scarf and turned up the collar of his coat. His breath hung like smoke in the air and tiny grains of frost settled on the hairs of his scarf. Thrushes, ragged and hunched with the cold, foraged under the hedges, turning over the starved and withered leaves, and stared at Frank with a boldness that surprised him. Twice he looked back along the road but there was no one in sight, and time and again he took off his gloves and with his warm hands tried to rub life into his stinging ears. He came to a wayside pub and glanced to his right and left before entering. Inside it was chilly and the noise of his feet on the boards echoed hollowly from the empty snugs. He tapped on the counter, and between the snowy letters of a Christmas greeting on a large pierglass he saw his pale reflection and the panting fog of his breath. He pushed his hat back, but feeling the cold air on his warm forehead he drew it forward again, and once more hammered the counter. He ordered a small whisky and was glad that the barman went off again while he was taking it. He sipped it slowly, glancing now and again at the misted window. He heard footsteps outside, and he pulled his hat well down over his eyes and hunched his shoulders. Two men came in and stood beside him, and without turning his head he eyed them in the pierglass opposite. They had two greyhounds on leads, and with shrinking apprehension he felt one of the greyhounds sniffing at his leg. He moved his leg away with a jerk and the greyhound sprang away from him and entangled itself in its lead.

'He'll not touch you, lad,' one of the men said and stooped to pat the greyhound. The word 'lad' annoyed Frank and he spread his elbows on the counter to convey an impression of age and experience. The dogs stretched out at full length and rested their heads on their muddy paws. One of the men ordered two large whiskies, spat out on the floor, and placed a canvas bag on the counter. There was a movement inside the canvas and the tip of a ferret's nose appeared at a net-covered hole; it sniffed audibly and spattered a moist speck on to the counter. Frank turned his head from the revolting slimy movements of the ferret and fixed his eyes on the pierglass where he studied the reflections of the men who had so suddenly invaded his peace. They were unshaven, the loops of the dog-leads over their blood-scratched wrists, their clothes covered with drying mud. He took another sip of whisky — he would take his time. He sensed that the men were wanting rid of him but he would show them he was in no hurry. The two whiskies were placed before them. They rested their arms on the counter and he had to give way to make room for them. He slowly took out a cigarette, struck a match and flung it on the floor; the match alighted on one of the grey-hounds and it leapt to its feet with a whine, wrenching the lead out of the man's hand and upsetting the whisky.

'I'm sorry,' Frank said, feeling his face burn.

'Why the hell don't you look what you're doing? . . . Come here, dog,' and he bent down to examine the dog's eyes. 'What about the whisky?'

''Twasn't my fault!'

'Maybe you'll bloody well tell me it was mine!' and he stared at Frank with a hard look. 'What age are you? You're not the age to be served — a young fella that's hardly started to shave.'

'Take his name and address, Bill, in case the dog's eye gives you trouble.'

'I'll pay for the whisky I've spilt,' Frank said. 'It was an accident.'

He ordered a whisky for the man, and going out from the pub he heard them laughing behind him. He put a clove in his mouth to camouflage the smell of the whisky and hurried back along the road. Ahead of him he saw Anne and Brendan coming along, playfully swinging each other's hand, the laugh of their voices bright and rising in the frosted air. They were still laughing when he neared them, and for some reason their happiness disturbed him, and filled him with a mood of pulsing anger. Before they could speak he reproached Anne for taking her school troubles so lightly.

'Oh, well,' she said with a shake of her head. 'I'm sure

Miss Mallon isn't worrying herself about me.' She smiled and looked at the mountain that was cleft with snow. 'Come on and we'll go as far as its foot. Are you game, Frank?'

'I've done all the walking I'm going to do,' and he stepped towards home, and Brendan and Anne walked at each side of him. She began to hum and swing Frank's arm to the rhythm but he wrenched away from her and plunged his hand into his pocket.

'What's wrong with you at all?' she said. 'Why can't you relax in your holidays?'

'Hm, holidays! I've been on holidays since October, if you want to know. I'm not at the university at all. Isn't that a lovely bit of Christmas news?'

'Frank!'

'Yes,' he said. 'And Brendan knows all about it.' Brendan intervened, trying to halt the rush of his words. But Frank shunned him and continued with evident relish, maligning himself and blaming his father and mother for pushing him on for medicine.

'That's untrue,' Brendan said. 'You wanted to be a doctor.'

'They shouldn't have allowed me. They shouldn't have listened to me. They should have known that I'm not the kind of fellow that can sit in, evening after evening, and pore over books. I didn't know what I was undertaking but I know now. And what's more I'm not going to let this day pass without telling them. I can't continue like this any longer – I'm finished with it!'

'Allow the year to pass and enrol next October,' Brendan said. 'You got your first medical with ease and it wouldn't cost you much sweat to get your next.'

'It's the length of the course that frightens me. I'm through with it.'

'Then you're through with everything that will cost some effort,' Brendan said. 'You'll be another Uncle D. J. – a failure, and a damned nuisance to everyone belonging to you.'

'I'm asking nothing from you. You keep out of it!'

'It's terrible, Frank,' Anne said, almost in tears. 'Why didn't you tell me before this and maybe I could have helped? You're everything to father. He thinks of nothing all day but you and your success. For the love of God say nothing until I get time to think out some plan, some means of breaking it to them. Oh, Frank, you'll ruin your life if you don't go on.'

'I'll break it to him myself. I've no need of an aide-de-camp.'

'You can't do it on this day of all days,' Brendan said.

'Can't I!'

Anne caught Frank's arm and halted him on the road. She pressed it tightly as he struggled to free it. 'Frank,' she said. 'Look at me.' Her eyes sought his but he averted them. 'Look at me, Frank, and promise you'll let Christmas Day pass without destroying the share of joy it brings to them.'

'I'll promise nothing,' and he shrugged his shoulders and tightened his scarf.

In her mind she prayed that he would relent. They reached their own street and she walked slowly, aware of a harried weariness, a limpness in body and mind that plucked all joy from her. Children on new tricycles or dressed as Indians called to her to admire their toys and she smiled wanly at them and walked on. Going through the garden gate of the house she appealed to Frank for the love of God to take the murderous look off his face. They hung up their coats in heavy silence and went into the parlour, awaiting the serving of the Christmas dinner. From the kitchen there came the warm smell of roast turkey, the sizzle of gravy, and Eileen singing to herself as she cleaned their best dinner-service.

Frank leafed through a Christmas magazine and Anne sat at the piano, playing Herbert Hughes's arrangement of 'Down by the Salley Gardens'. Eileen came in, her fair hair combed back and tied in a loose knot with black velvet. She stood at the window, listening to the music, and watching the children playing in the street. 'It's the loveliest of all the arrangements of that song,' she said as Anne slowly lifted her fingers from the keyboard and sat back. 'Dinner will be ready in a tick,' she whispered to Anne and tiptoed over to Frank who was lying in an armchair, the magazine on his lap and his eyes closed. She kissed him on the forehead and he opened his eyes with a start and she ran laughing from the room.

The mother carried in the turkey while Eileen and Anne helped with the vegetable dishes. They arranged themselves around the table and the sun shone through the curtains, reflecting on Eileen's hair and on the bangle on her wrist. She pulled her blue blouse tight against her firm bosom, joined and unjoined her hands, and smiled at her father's solemn determination as he sharpened the knife on the steel. 'Thank God we're all spared to enjoy this Christmas and may we live to enjoy the next,' he said, transfixing the turkey with the fork. He dislodged a leg from the turkey and placed it on one of the plates. 'That'll do Frank; he likes a drum-stick.' And when they were all served he blessed himself and sat down. Anne stole a glance, now and then, at Frank. His head was bowed, and once when she stared yearningly at him he deliberately dropped his knife on the floor, avoiding his inclination to look at her. The father and mother talked of former Christmases: Christmases spent in the country or Christmases spent among them when they were all very small.

'Oh,' said Anne, 'there's the Mallons gone past the window with their nephews.'

'Well, let them pass, there's plenty of room for them to expand,' the father said. 'I'll swear if I walked down the street this very minute nobody would turn their heads to say "There's Mister Caffrey away past." Aye, but some day, some day soon, they'll turn their heads and say, "There's Doctor Caffrey away past." Am I right?' and he shook his head with firm pleasure.

'I wonder where Uncle D. J. will be spending his Christmas,' Anne said quickly.

But her father went on: 'The Mallons won't have it all their own way with their theses for their M.D.s and their F.R.C.S.s and their God-knows-what. Wait till a Caffrey shoots his head forward and we'll show them how to take the jumps. Aye, we'll show them.'

'He'll fly past us in his motor car when that day comes,' Eileen said and laughed towards Frank.

'We'll all go to the pantomime or the pictures tonight. What do you say, Brendan?' Anne said, and stretched out her hand for the cider. 'Some of this old Burgundy for you, Brendan,' and she filled up his glass and Frank's. Eileen passed hers and Anne turned to her mother with affected gravity: 'I don't know if we should let Eileen have a jorum of this heady liqueur.'

'Fill it up for the girl,' the father said, and he lifted the decanter of whisky and poured some out for himself and his wife. 'When Frank's finished we'll celebrate that day in fine style – never you fear,' and he raised his glass to Frank. 'Here's luck to you, my boy, and to all of you. And Anne, my girl, you'll show the Mallons that a Caffrey can live and let live. You'll go back to your school again. Am I right?'

'Yes, father, you're right,' Anne said. 'I wouldn't let a silly squabble like that defeat me!'

'That's the way to talk to them,' the father said, rattling his spoon against the tumbler in roguish applause.

In the happy silence that followed Anne turned to Frank. His knife and fork lay on his plate and he was stroking the tablecloth with the tip of his dessert spoon, line upon line converging to a point. God in Heaven, let him keep his silence, she said to herself. Her own troubles were trifling ones when confronted with the baleful unrest of his own mind. And she knew, too, that her own sharp resolutions would flinch before his, and that she would adapt herself to whatever he would say to her or ask of her. Never again, she decided, would she involve her father and mother in the feeble worries that filled her days at school. She would have plenty of them but henceforward she would not unburden them. She was old enough to know that they had all passed out of childhood and that they should strive to conceal that which would cause sorrow and share that which would give joy. She glanced, then, at Eileen and at the vivid brightness in her eyes. Oh, if they could hide Frank's affairs from her until all was righted – that would be something. Eileen had her love – let her keep it and fill her days with it. Frank raised his head as his plum pudding was passed to him. Anne sought his eyes and cast upon them a look of earnest unselfishness. He smiled back with his lips closed.

'Who's game for the pictures tonight?' he said at last.

'Me!' said Eileen.

'And me!' said Anne. She sighed, and a depressed feeling spread away from her and left her limp with a sweet relief. She knew that, for that day at least, she had won.

CHAPTER NINE

THE Christmas holidays came to an end; Anne went back to her school, Brendan to the library, and Frank, once more, was rising at his usual time in the mornings and striding out after his breakfast with a notebook under his arm. And Eileen, bright and cheerful, would prepare the table and the fire, persuading her mother to take a rest in bed in the dark January mornings while she would bring her breakfast up to her; and the mother lying in bed with a light shawl around her shoulders would reprimand her daughter for the way she was spoiling her. 'Eileen,' she would say, 'you will send me to an early grave with your kindness. It's activity that keeps a woman of my years alive, and here you are coddling me as if I were a convalescent, forcing me to stay in bed and allowing my limbs to stiffen. I should be out at Mass these mornings thanking God for sparing me to see you all reared. Upon my word, girl, I feel you want rid of me.'

'There's not enough stretch in the mornings, Mother, they're too dark,' Eileen would answer, standing at the window and gazing down at their frozen patch of garden. 'Indeed it's no comfort to any of us to think of you picking your steps along the frosty ground and maybe slip and fall on the roadway. And then that chapel is as cold as a grave. Have sense in your head till the mornings are bright and fresh again. It won't be long now for I see a tiny growth on the snowdrops.'

'Do you know, Eileen,' her mother would sometimes add in a mood of warm confidence, ' 'tis a great pity you haven't a profession like Anne or Brendan. All you have is your music, girl, and I wouldn't like to think of a daughter of mine dragged and drudged all her life in giving music lessons.' She would pause then, pat the eiderdown, expecting Eileen to return her mood of quiet confidence. But Eileen, sitting on the bed with her hands clasped about her knees, would toss her head in contemptuous good humour and say: 'You never know the success I could make with music lessons – especially when one likes it the way I do.'

'But surely, Eileen, you'd marry if the right person came along. It'd be unnatural if you gave no thought in that direction.'

'I do and I don't.' She would smile evasively and rise from the bed.

'Marry young and marry a man that's young. If you wait too long and are fortunate in having a child or two you'd be continually worried, wondering if you'd see them reared and coming of age. Marry young, Eileen.'

'I'll have to wait until someone asks me,' she would laugh

and hurry from the room. She would stand at the parlour window, watching for the postman and yearning for a letter that would invite her to the country. There was nothing she would like better than to be in the country for the spring of the year. But no letter came to her from Aunt Nelly; once or twice she wrote to her father but to Eileen's annoyance he would only read out to her a few sentences: sentences pertaining to Bob's illness, to the weather, or to the local gossip.

And then one day as she was digging in the garden and loosening the soil around the daffodils Aunt Nelly arrived.

'So there you are, Eileen,' she said, 'and not a scrape from you since your card at Christmas and not one "yes" or "no" to all my invitations and pleas.'

'But you didn't ask me, Aunty.'

'Well that's a good one. And me underlining it in every letter I wrote to your father. Did he not tell you I needed your help with the spring-cleaning, with Uncle Bob, and with the renovation to the shop that Philip Doran is to make? Do you remember Mr. Doran?'

'I do,' Eileen said. 'The young fellow that rowed us down the river to the island.'

'Yes, that's the man. He's not as young as he looks though. It's he that's going to do the alteration to the shop window and I'll need some help.'

They went into the house and Mrs. Caffrey welcomed her warmly and told her that she was getting younger and fresher every year.

'Ah, Mary, if you could see my heart – there must be as many wrinkles on it as there is in the dried mud of the old river. It's a wonder I'm not grey or in my grave long ago. Oh, the martyrdom that I've put in with Bob!' She was ready to enlarge on her woes but restrained herself, intending to reserve her wrath till she was face to face with her brother John.

Eileen was sent down on the tram for her father and when

he arrived Aunt Nelly immediately flared out at him in front of the family, spilling out with many a cry all that she had suffered since D. J. arrived in Monabeg, and how she had striven by prayer, by flattery, and by coercion to bring about a reconciliation between the two brothers, and how Bob's stolidity had smothered all her efforts. John hushed her and told her to calm herself. He brought her into the parlour out of earshot of the family, and when she was seated in an armchair and a glass of wine and a piece of cake beside her he asked her once again to lower her voice and control herself.

'I can't help it, John,' she defended, and coiled a piece of string around her finger. 'My nerves are as chafed and frayed as an old rope. I've no energy. Bob would break the patience of a canonized saint – and I'm no saint, I may tell you. But D. J.'s a changed man. He is thoughtful and kind and on New Year's Night he brought me to a ceilidhe in the hall and I wish you had seen the way the crowd cheered him and stamped their feet after he had sung for them. And there he is, the poor man, living with a doting old pensioner, baking his own bread in a cubby-hole of a place that is not fit for a relation of ours. On Christmas Day I invited D. J. for dinner with us but Bob wouldn't hear of it. I told him I would walk out and never return and he agreed then to have D. J. But what do you think he did when D. J. arrived! He went off and locked himself in his bedroom. But myself and D. J. enjoyed ourselves and we played all the records on the gramophone twice over. I brought Bob's dinner up to him on a tray but he wouldn't open the door for me and he didn't come down the stairs that day until D. J. had gone. He took a glass of milk then and a bit of turkey and not one word did he speak to me until the following day and then it was to reprimand me for inviting D. J. to the house and to accuse me of handing out by the back door a pair of new trousers and new shirts to D. J.' She sighed, took a sip of the wine, and shook her head in despair. 'He'd let his brother run naked before he'd raise a hand to clothe him. He grows harder and odder every day; and yesterday, although I tried to prevent him, he carried one of the shutters to the school and commanded the schoolmistress to find the brat that scribbles the chalk-marks on his shutters. He got nothing for his pains, I may tell you, except the sweat of carrying that awkward board under his arm. That, John, is what I have to face, day in and day out. So you'll let Eileen come and give me a rest or it's me that'll be going into the hospital and not Bob. Bob's fond of Eileen and she can turn him round her finger as easily as I turn that bit of string.'

'What about Bob's illness?' he asked, avoiding all mention of Eileen.

'He has changed his doctor and goes on the train on Sundays to Magheraglass. He feels the new doctor understands his case better than Doctor O'Neill but I'm afraid it's the old story: new brooms sweep clean. But he's still on a diet and a slave to his shop, giving himself no time to take his bit of dinner.' She finished the wine and arranged her hair before the mantel-piece. 'Well, I suppose you'll have no objections to letting Eileen come with me now? It'll not take her long to pack her few things.'

He made an excuse about Eileen having to help with their own spring-cleaning and that she would not be ready for at least three weeks.

'Three weeks! I'll be in my grave by that time for my heart is sore afflicted with him already. I can't endure it any longer. He's your brother as well as mine and I have done my share of nursing and humouring him. I've worn out my youth with him and look at me now with a few grey hairs stealing into my head. If I don't get help I'm leaving and he can get in a housekeeper to attend him.' She went into the kitchen to bid goodbye to the others and he, himself, put on his hat and coat and accompanied her to the station. He was oppressed by a guilty feeling of indecision, and all he could say to her by way of comfort was: 'Don't worry any more, Nelly, you'll have help soon.'

As she leaned out of the carriage window with her two hands clasping his the tears in her eyes hurt him and he looked guiltily away from her. Why, he thought, should he bruise the heart of this sister of his for the sake of stifling D. J.'s suspicions; why should he tangle his own life by pampering to a wastrel's? Eileen's place was in the country, he was sure of that! And he would send her no matter what D. J. should say to her when she arrived. Money, money, money – he wished to God that Bob had none of it and then there'd be an end to this indecision, to this criss-cross of life that was twisting and torturing their very souls.

The whistle blew and she looked intently into his face and held on to his hand. 'Promise me, promise me, that you'll send Eileen before the month is out!'

'I will, Nelly, I will – have no fear!'

She watched his retreating figure on the concrete platform, appearing and disappearing under the overhead lamps, and then as the thick darkness swept behind the train she leant back in the empty carriage and wept herself to sleep. Now and again she wakened as the train halted and she would rub the mist off the window and read the name of the station that was printed on the face of the lamps.

It was dark and wet when the train reached her lamplit station and as she descended from the warm carriage she stood to the side as the train moved off again, dragging into the dark country its reflected squares of light. The platform was wet and a sleety rain beat against the one lamp and hummed in the unseen telegraph wires. She pushed open the wet railway gate with her foot, stepped into a puddle in the darkness and emerged on to the street where the open wind drew the breath from her. Blinds were drawn in all the houses except that of the police barracks and as she passed it she saw in the glow of the fire a young policeman playing a melodeon.

The sight of him recalled a smarting memory. She reached the shop. A rod of light shone through a knot-hole in the shutters and she knew Bob was within, patiently waiting for a stray customer. She shook the rain off her coat before turning in. Bob was seated behind the counter with an old catalogue in his hands, its edges curled and swollen with damp. He looked at her over his spectacles. 'So you got back all right,' he said, and licked his thumb to turn a page in the catalogue.

'I did,' she said, and stared at his bowed head and at the lead half-crown that was nailed to the counter as a challenge to all counterfeiters. Something in her rebelled, and she quelled the impulse to shout something insulting at him. She put her hand on top of the stove and tch-tched with disgust. 'Why don't you turn it up and put some heat through the place? It would founder you.'

He took off his spectacles and rubbed his eyes with his forefinger. 'I don't feel the cold, Nelly. I'm as snug here as a moth in a bale of cloth,' and he affixed his spectacles on his nose again.

'You didn't ask me how John and his family are keeping,' she said.

'Aye, how are they?' he said and blew at pages in the catalogue that were stuck together.

'I don't know how they are!' she answered and lifted up the flap in the counter and let it fall with a bang behind her. He went on thumbing the pages as if nothing had happened and in a few minutes he heard her raking at the range and filling up the kettle. He rose slowly, hung up the catalogue by its loop of cord, brought in his iron door-mat and closed the outside door. He got his mouse-traps from the yard, and after baiting them with bacon-rinds he stood on a step-ladder and placed them carefully on the shelves. He turned out the stove and the lamp, and in the dark groped his way back to the kitchen. Nelly was spreading the cloth on the table with subdued anger and he stood out of her way near the window. On the small mahogany table was a rolled-up sheet of paper with a coloured drawing of the proposed alteration to the shop. He slipped the elastic band from it and unrolled it on the table, placing ash-trays at the corners of the sheet to keep it flat.

'Philip Doran left that in with me today,' he said, standing out to let the full lamplight shine on it.

Nelly showed no interest in it and he sat down in the arm-chair and awaited his supper. She called him to the table and gave him his milk and a raw egg.

'It's a nice job he's going to make of it and by the same token it'll cost a nice penny,' he said slowly, glancing round at the drawing.

'It'd have cost a much stiffer penny if you'd employed a builder from Ballymena or Belfast. Quit worrying about it – as long as you have money enough and to spare all you need think about is the finished product.' She wondered what possessed her to mention money to him for whenever she did so she had to listen to a litany of the unrecoverable debts he was owed, the slackness of trade, and the rise in wholesale prices. Now he only gave a slow nod of his head. 'I'm owed more money than I possess. I'm afraid to look at my books because of the dishonesty that would assail me. For myself I pay my bills – my doctor's, my grocer's, and my whole-saler's – in a manner that is prompt and pleasing. And the day that Doran finishes the job I'll pay him right on the nail.' He glanced over his shoulder at the drawing. She said nothing.

He lit his candle, and from the foot of the stairs he called to her to look at the design and let him know in the morning what she thought of it. With the teacup to her lips she nodded, and on hearing the pad of his footsteps in the room above her she turned to the drawing. For a long time she studied the careful printing, the wash of blue on the new window, and the in-clusion of the waterpump and trees at the side of the house. 'If he had made a sketch of Bob at the door it would have been complete,' she smiled. The tip-tap of a coin on the window-pane drew her to the door to admit D. J.

'He's in bed,' he said in a whisper. 'I saw the light go out in his room.'

'You needn't whisper, D. J.' she said aloud. 'I have a right to ask my brother to the house and extend any kindness I wish.'

'That's all right,' he whispered, 'but we must think of poor Bob's ailments and the way my princely presence enrages him.' He looked at the drawing. 'I say that's an attractive bit of work. He's a fine fellow that Doran, and do you know, Nelly, the way he danced with you on New Year's Night makes me think he's a bit struck on you.'

'Philip Doran! It's somebody a year or two younger he'd be angling after.'

'He might think that a time might come when his name would be printed above the shop window. I'm sure he feels, like myself, that Bob will leave the shop to you.'

Nelly rolled up the sheet and slipped the elastic band around it. 'That thought never occurred to me, D. J.,' she said shortly and remained silent. Sensing that he had annoyed her he hastened to inquire of her day in the town and of John and his family. She told him Eileen was coming down to the country soon.

'Eileen! What's taking her down here at this time of the year? John must think her piano solos interrupt Frank's studies,' and he laughed loudly and then put his hand to his mouth and cast his eyes to the ceiling.

'It was me that asked her and it's much against John's wishes, I may tell you.'

He stood with his back to the range. 'Ah, Nelly,' he said with an air of discovery, 'I see all their moves very clearly. Eileen's mother has her eye on that Doran fellow. He's a sober, steady, go-ahead chap and he'd make a good match for Eileen. Leave it to D. J. to see far down the course!'

'Sit over and take this cup of tea and maybe it'll clear the fog out of your head,' and she beckoned him to a chair at the table. He was about to sit down when there was a sound of heavy steps on the stairs, and Bob came into the kitchen in his trousers and shirt, his hair disarranged, and a candle-holder in his hand.

D. J. stood with his hand clasping the back of the chair, and as Bob confronted him with silent hostility D. J. shrunk with puny resolution. Bob was like an effigy cut out on a rock-face and as his eye slowly ranged round the table D. J. recalled him when he was a boy at school, sitting always at the end of a desk, no words for anyone, doing his work with dumb passivity, and rushing home at the end of the school day to help in the shop.

'Get out of my house!' Bob said.

'He came on my invitation,' Nelly intervened. 'Haven't I the right to ask my own brother to the house of an evening? Am I to sit here in loneliness, night after night, and grow as odd as yourself? I have ceased asking the schoolmistress or the dressmaker because your manner showed them they weren't wanted.'

'Get out,' Bob said again without raising his voice. 'Get out before I cross the road to the police barracks.'

'Sure I am doing no harm to anyone, Bob,' D. J. said. 'What wrong is there in speaking to my own sister? And, as for myself, I'm always ready to help you in any way I can. I would row you down the river if you ever wanted to catch a pike or two.'

'I don't want your help. You disgraced the name of your father and you disgraced us all the day you pilfered the railway company's money.'

'That was thirty years ago, I believe,' Nelly said. 'Can a man not reform himself or are you to be the last to forget that? – and you his brother.'

'There's many a one remembers it and casts it up to me. A dishonest act among a rising family is never forgotten in a country place. And there's another whisper or two about him that I haven't come to the bottom of. I hear he has advertised in a newspaper as a tipster – I'm sure there is some trickery or dishonesty behind that. Now you understand me. Go on now wherever you have to go and maybe when you're shown no kindness you'll leave this village in peace. I see you are wearing one of my shirts – Nelly has you well decked out in what doesn't belong to her.'

'The little I gave him was dearly owed to me and doesn't trouble my conscience. Have you ever thought of what a housekeeper would cost you?'

D. J. moved towards the door and Nelly asked him to stay until he had heard a record or two. She went to the gramophone and as she lifted a record Bob pulled it from her hands and smashed it on the floor. D. J. closed the door behind him, and Nelly looking at Bob suddenly burst into tears. 'May God forgive you, Bob Caffrey. May God forgive you! You are damning your soul and you drawing near the grave!'

'I know my business.'

'You're damning your soul, I tell you. Show some charity to your own flesh and blood; give to the old beggars that call at your door. For the love of God change your ways before it's too late.'

'You'd think I was going to die to hear you. Couldn't D. J. be away before any of us? – there's no flesh on him. What has he done for anyone? When he was at school he mitched; he did no school exercises; he was put off the altar for misconduct; and when he stole the money from the railway he lost his job as clerk and disgraced the name.'

'Maybe we're all to blame – our father and your mother; and because of D. J. and his weaknesses it may all have been to make us better than we are. You may try to hide all this; you may try to choke it but you know in your heart and soul you can't get rid of it. You needn't tell me you're a happy man. Look at Major Allen's house out the road – an empty shell, a cupboard for the winds, a place where no tramp would lay his head for they'll all tell you it's haunted. He lived for himself, for his money, and when he died he hadn't enough friends at his funeral to carry his coffin.'

'What would you want me to do? To feed and fend for a man that never did an honest day's work in his life. Encourage him in laziness and sloth. Man alive, I wouldn't give him the bad half-crown that's nailed to the counter. And as for the tramps and beggars that flock to the door – what are they but the misfits, the cast-offs, the shiftless and the thriftless who'd rather beg than work?'

'You'd see your own brother in rags and you wouldn't give him a shirt-button!'

'He'll batten on you like a maggot.'

'From people you usually get what you search for. If you look and search for love and kindness you'll get them. If you mistrust people you'll make enemies where there were none before.'

'It's easy to be kind to people at my expense. Shirts and trousers handed out to him and not paid for.'

'It's a lie,' she said, the tears rising to her eyes again. 'I have slaved for you and wasted the best years of my life. I'm to have nothing. You deny me the simple company of that gramophone,' and seeing the bits of the record on the floor her anger blazed up in her and seizing the handbrush and a shovel she swept them up and hurled them into the range. The flames roared and bellowed up the chimney and they stared at the range in silence. The roaring increased and burnt soot toppled somewhere at the back of the fire.

'The chimney's on fire,' he said.

'It'll not do it a bit of harm,' she answered firmly and halted him as he made to go out to the street in his trousers and shirt.

'I'll go out,' she said, and pulling her coat over her head she went outside and looked up at the roof. Flaring bushes of sparks grew up from the chimney pot and were grasped by the wind and fell hissing on the wet street, and then a red tail of flame streeled out spreading its glow on the wet slates and on the trunks of the trees. The air was filled with a smell of soot and burnt smoke, but the coldness of the night had kept the people indoors and she was grateful for that and hoped that the blazing chimney would pass unnoticed. But as she watched, the chimney pot turned red and a piece of it flew off, rattled over the slates, and fell in pieces at her feet. She ran towards the barracks in fright but before knocking she once more looked up at the roof, and on seeing the flame shrink and disappear, and huge cauliflowers of smoke emerging she knew that the fire had spent itself. She returned and met Bob at the door. The wild look in his eyes dismayed her. 'It's well cleaned now,' she tried to say calmly. 'That's the best cleaning it ever got since it was built,' and she stood staring at the range and listening to an odd rumble in the chimney. 'Let that be a warning to you,' she went on, feeling her courage return. 'Let that be a warning to you. Where there's anger and ill-will there's no grace or luck about a house.'

'There's never luck with that D. J.,' he said, and halted on hearing the chimney rumble again and a shower of soot falling into the fire. 'I don't believe he has gone on his knees this many a long year.'

'Some of those who are often on their knees are not much of an example to him. Go on now to your bed after you've destroyed my evening. Go on,' she pleaded, seeing the terror in his eyes. 'You need have no fear – I'll stay in the kitchen until the range cools.' He took his candle and at the foot of the stairs he turned and looked at her. 'Good night, Nelly, good night.' He paused and then mumbled: 'Forgive me.'

She shook her head, knowing how hard it was for him to add the last words, and when he had gone from the kitchen she rested her arms on the table and wept for him.

CHAPTER TEN

THE days that followed were bright and white with sun, cool and fresh with the urgency of a hurrying spring; but with Bob and Nelly there was an undergrowth of strain, and the few words that they exchanged with one another invariably included D. J.'s name and in trying to justify their different attitudes towards him they would find themselves bitterly quarrelling and cleft once more by a hostile silence. Nelly would take her knitting to the window that overlooked the tree-lined road that led to the river, and when barefooted boys with wooden boats under their arms would noisily pass the window or later repass with a glass jam-jar of swimming spricks she would call to them in a momentary feeling of joy and offer them sixpence if they would bring her a bunch of pussy-willows from down the river. The next day they would bring her an armful of a black and silver variety, and arranging these in vases in her sitting-room she would survey the room from different angles, filling her soul with an unshared and secret pride.

On Thursdays the shop was closed for a half-day and Bob, now that the days were lengthening, would put on his heavy overcoat, take his stick, and saunter along the river bank. She would open the window after he was gone, put a record on the gramophone, smoke a cigarette, and enjoy for a while the sweet freedom that came from his absence. And one Thursday as she was resting like that and re-reading a letter from Eileen a knock came to the door. It was Philip Doran who had come to see Bob about the proposed alteration, and she brought him in and arranged a cushion in an armchair for him.

'He shouldn't be long, Philip. It's a wonder you didn't see him along by the river. He usually takes a walk as far as the falls. But one never knows what crooked notion would come into his old head and he might change his beat and take some other route. He'll not be long for he's not too fond of the walking.' She sat down, crossed her legs, and clasped her hands about her knee. She laughed. 'Philip, you should get a medal for patience. Oh, the way you have tholed and humoured that old man has astounded me. Really, Philip, I don't know how you have put up with him for so long.'

'We'll all have to grow old sometime,' he said, 'and we mightn't be one bit pleasanter than Bob.'

'That's true – but somehow Bob has grown ten years older in the last six months: he's so cantankerous he can't bear to listen to the gramophone or know I'm at a dance. I suppose you were at the dance the other night yourself, Philip?'

'I wasn't, Nelly. I was working late that night making furniture. It's pleasanter work than boat-building.'

'You didn't miss much from what I hear, Philip,' and she laughed, disguising the annoyance his gravity was causing her.

He continued to talk about his own work, and in order to detain him for a while she pleaded with him to make a cabinet for her gramophone records. 'Many a one Bob has sat on and broken on me,' she said, and getting a sheet of note-paper she drew a rough design of the cabinet she desired. He noticed her clean hands and the long slender fingers curving over the page.

'Oh, I can't draw,' and she threw back her head, aware of his eyes upon her. 'When I was at the boarding-school my drawings were a standing joke with the nuns. Here – you take the pencil.'

She leaned her hand on his shoulder and bent over him, praising each firm stroke that he made. He was conscious of her warm scented presence and acutely aware of the roughness of his own hands and the ragged edges of his finger-nails. 'It'll be something like that I'll make but not as dirty,' and he laughed and said he must be on his way. She insisted on his staying to meet Bob and she pushed him down into the arm-chair and went off to prepare a tray for a cup of tea. When she had come back again she had freshly rouged her lips. He was standing at the mantelpiece looking at a snapshot that was stuck loosely in the corner of a framed portrait of herself. 'Who's that?' he said, pointing to the loose card.

'That's Eileen in her Confirmation rig-out,' she said.

'I wouldn't recognize her. She has grown such a big girl since that was taken.'

'She's only a child, yet – twenty her next birthday, I think,' and she went on to say that she was coming down to the country soon and that then they would be able to get to a dance or two and maybe go on a picnic down the river. He turned to Eileen's photograph again and Nelly laughed and told him he had a great interest in schoolgirls. She lifted her own portrait and taking it to the window she wiped the frame with her handkerchief, held it at arm's length and asked him what he thought of it.

'It's a good likeness,' he said.

'D. J. thinks it makes me look years older than I am.'

'Aye, I suppose he's right. But it's a good likeness all the same.'

'You wouldn't think I was the slightest bit solemn in it, Philip?'

He studied it for a minute and then looked at her and back again at the portrait. 'I would not. It's a good picture. You'd think now it was your reflection I was looking at.'

Bob's shadow passed the window, and Nelly snatching the portrait put it back on the mantelpiece and went to the tray to pour out the tea.

'I came to see you about the new window,' Philip began as soon as Bob was seated in the armchair. 'I can start tomorrow afternoon if the weather holds.' He showed no further interest in the tea as he enlarged on each detail of the new alteration, bending forward and rubbing his hands with enthusiasm, and allaying Bob's fears that business could not be carried on as usual, and that at night the ripped-out window space would be covered by a large green tarpaulin that was free of mildew, oil-stains, and vents. He would have two men to help him and a lad to mix the cement and carry sand. Bob listened quietly, unperturbed and unaffected by Philip's energetic movements and hand-demonstrations. He closed his eyes, calculating the amount of money it would take for Doran to pay his workmen and the cost of material. He concluded that a hundred and fifty pounds was a big figure for what seemed a small job. He told him what he thought.

'I couldn't do it for less,' Philip said. 'I made the lowest estimate I could for old friends' sake. My father before me left his mark on that shop-front—look how fresh the old peacock is after nearly sixty years of rain and frost and hob-nailed boots.'

'You can have every feather of it back again and I'll not ask a solitary halfpenny for them,' Bob said. 'But I'll ask this—you'll have to reduce your big figure.'

'I can't,' Philip said.

'Material is a big price,' Nelly put in.

Bob ignored her and continued to wrangle about prices, telling Doran that his wage-bill would amount to no more than thirty or forty pounds. Philip reddened and he only wished that Nelly was away from the room until he could tell him to go to hell and employ somebody else, and that he had plenty of work in hand without undertaking a piece of work that would underpay him. He turned to the table, finished the tea that remained in his cup, thanked Nelly and got to his feet. 'I'll make a start tomorrow or next day if I don't hear from you,' he said and went out.

From the hall the grandfather clock ticked loudly and outside a motor car back-fired and the crows in the trees rose up screeching and circled over the houses and the river.

'You shouldn't have badgered him like that about his estimate,' Nelly said. 'After all you agreed to it months ago.'

'That fellow is making money hand over fist. I was passing his house today and the fences and the garden gate and the new steps down to his boat are the last word in extravagance. He has only himself and his sister to fend for – and there he is ready to fleece his neighbour if you'd let him. He has sand and gravel at his own backside and all he has to buy for the bit of a job are a few bricks, a few bags of cement, two or three boards, and a pane of glass. He's a daylight robber and though he's making plenty of money he didn't raise his stipend at the last collection in the chapel. I have my eye on him, let me tell you.'

She was tired of rows and she held her peace, letting him ramble freely in his thoughts until he was weary of the sound of his own voice. She saw him take out his notebook, make calculations in it with pencil, snort with disgust, and mumble to himself: 'A robber – a double-dyed robber!'

The following morning Bob rose earlier than usual and Nelly lay in bed listening to the rattle of the shutters as he unfastened them from the window and dumped them behind the door of the shop. There must be a good-sized dent in the floor-boards after all the years of thumping, she thought, and decided that she'd have no regrets after the new window was installed and she'd hear the familiar thump of the shutters no more.

From down the line came the whistle of the train and she threw aside the bedclothes and dressed hurriedly, afraid that Eileen might step in on her by the early train. As she went downstairs the train hissed into the station. She put a match to the range that she had prepared the previous night, and as the flames roared up the chimney she peeped slyly through the window space that led into the shop. The door of the shop was open to the sunlit street and Bob, himself, stood inside near the window spying out between two jerseys that hung over a brass rail. He had his hands on his hinches and she saw him draw back from the window and Eileen appear in the doorway.

'I'm glad and happy to see you, Eileen,' and he stretched

his hand across the counter. 'Come on, come on,' he said, lifting up the flap in the counter. 'I don't know if your aunt is up out of her bed yet but we'll see.'

'Oh, Eileen, it's lovely to see you,' Nelly said, hurrying forward and throwing her arms around her. 'I had nearly given up hope – seeing how I've been disappointed so often . . . And you look beautiful in green,' and she drew back to admire her. 'Upon my word you're growing very tall.' Eileen smiled and her aunt made her turn her back and then her front till she had satisfied her eyes with the perfect tailoring of the coat. 'And it's lovely stuff, too,' she said, as she fingered the material of the coat and looked at the lining. 'Your father's the man won't affront you with anything shoddy,' and she preceded Eileen upstairs, carrying her suitcase, and talking away to her over her shoulder. 'The room you always loved, Eileen,' and she drew back the blue curtains to let the spring sunshine fill up the little room.

'And the river,' said Eileen, looking out, 'there's not a bit of change in it. And your little garden, and the summer-house, and the blossom on the fruit trees – it's all so perfect I could cry with joy. I often thought of it when I was seated in our own cheerless parlour at home.'

'The whole house will look much better when the new window's put in. Philip Doran and his men may start at it today.'

'So I heard,' Eileen said, pushing down the window to release an autumn-coloured butterfly that was purring against the warm pane. 'Philip told me about it in a letter he sent to me.'

'He doesn't write to you, does he?'

'He wrote to me a few times.'

'And you didn't answer him, I hope?'

Eileen smiled. 'I wrote to him once or twice but I hate writing letters and I didn't answer his last.'

'You did perfectly right, Eileen. He's far too settled in his ways for the likes of you. And to think he never as much as mentioned to me that he wrote to you. He's a sly one,' and she paused, believing now that Philip had danced often with her because of his interest in Eileen. 'Wait till I see him.'

'Oh, Aunt, say nothing to him, please. He'd die of embarrassment and he might think I showed his letters to you. You'll say nothing to him, please!'

'And what if you did show his letters to me? – there'd be no harm in that. You'll meet better and nicer boys in the city, Eileen. It's because you don't see him often that you think of him at all. And supposing you were married to him you'd be stuck for ever in this hole-in-a-corner of a village and your life would be starved.'

'But I love this place, Aunt Nelly. At home it brings sleep quickly to me when I think of the river slipping by.'

'So you've even thought about marrying him, Eileen?'

'Oh, no, no! It's just that I think of the river and then I see Philip's house beside it and the boat swaying beside the wooden steps at the water's edge. And there's the smell of new paint and there's the reflection of the clouds in the water. I really don't know what I feel. I just think of the river – that's all.'

'Maybe if you saw it in the winter you'd think less of it. You've always seen it in spring or in summer and you have never lived in it in winter. To see only one side of life is to see it wrong. You must be careful, Eileen, and not let summery feelings like this run off with you . . . We'll have another chat later. Take your things off while I'm making the breakfast.'

Later when Eileen came downstairs in a green frock, a handkerchief tucked in a bangle on her arm, Aunt Nelly realized that her niece was no longer the young girl whom she had sponsored at Confirmation but had now the height and firm-breasted attractiveness of a young lady.

'What age are you now, Eileen?' she asked as they finished their breakfast.

Eileen threw up her head and smiled. 'I'm growing old. You'd never guess that I was twenty-one my last birthday.'

Nelly eyed every movement of her – admiring the careless arrangement of her fair hair, hanging a little down her back and tied with black velvet. And in the freshness of her face and eyes she read the defeat of her own years. There was no doubt that she had wasted the best part of her life – wasted them on a man who had never expressed a thanks for what she had done for him; if she had gone away, even ten years ago, her life might have been different, and God knows she might have met someone whom she could have loved and who could, in return, have loved and appreciated her. Now, perhaps, she was too old to have children. In her youth she had had one lover – the young policeman: he had written once or twice to her after he had been posted to Armagh but that was all she had ever heard from him and he was nothing to her now except a thinning memory. Day by day she was being ground deeper into the life around her, and to flee from it all would be as difficult as remaining on and seeing it out to whatever end God had ordained. She sighed audibly and Eileen smiled across the table at her.

'You're tired, Aunt Nelly. Let me do the dishes for you.'

'On your first day! You'll do no such thing.'

'But mother told me that I wasn't to let you wet your finger where the dishes were concerned.'

'Rest yourself,' Nelly said, and put the dishes on a tray. Eileen took her arm. 'We'll do them together and chat at the same time.'

In the bright sunlit kitchen that looked out upon the patch of garden Eileen dried the dishes and as she did so she suddenly burst into song, and her voice echoing pure and sweet filled Aunt Nelly with a sharp and tearful joy. They spread the cloth on a bush to dry and sat in their little summer house that overlooked the river. A smell of tar came from the railway line, and from the river the sound of its drish and driggle and the rattle of a boat's chain as it swung round on its moorings.

'I see two new boats since last year,' Eileen said.

'The white one belongs to the doctor and the other one is the curate's. Philip made them both.'

'They're beautiful. It's a pity Uncle Bob doesn't get him to make one.'

'Your Uncle Bob has no interest outside his shop. His shop is his whole life – his work and his recreation. Even in the good weather you'd think the warm stuffy smell from the clothes and the heat of the shop would drive him out to the fresh air – it doesn't and that's what is killing him. God preserve us all from such an existence.' She lit a cigarette and lay back with a sigh of deep contentment. There was silence, and a gentle wind stirred in the bushes, and from Eileen's presence there spread a deep and urging happiness. Eileen, too, shared in it as she sat in the full blaze of the sun and idly stripped the leaves off a twig.

'This will never do, Eileen girl. I must rise and get my work done in case Doran and his men would step in on us unannounced.' She threw the end of her cigarette on to the grass and watched it burn to ash in the wind. 'Wash your hands, Eileen, after fingering those leaves – they could leave a stain on your white collar that the devil himself couldn't take off . . . Would you like to take my bike and go out to Gormans for a few dozen fresh eggs? And you could call to see your Uncle D. J. on the way out – he lives in the thatched house this side of the school. I'm sure he'd be glad to see you, for the old pensioner he lives with is a bit off the rails.'

Eileen wheeled out the bicycle from the shed at the side of the house and as she cycled along the tree-lined road that stretched out flatly from the village she heard the larks in the naked sky madly unreeling their breathless song. Near the thatched house she encountered Uncle D. J. sauntering out of his lonin, a coat on him that was very short in the sleeves, his cap pushed to the back of his head, and his face unshaven. The haggard sight of him roused her affection and she dismounted and held out her hand to him. 'How are you, Uncle D. J.?' she said.

'How am I? Well, well, that's a good one. Sure nobody cares how I am. Nobody cares whether I am under the sod or on top of the world.'

'That's untrue, Uncle. We all care and we are always wondering where you are and what you are doing.'

'Leave your bicycle against the hedge till I show you the smoky precincts of my sequestered nookery,' and he walked ahead of her, leaving her to pick her steps in the soft mud. He lifted the latch, and the wind rushed in with them and whirled the white ash that smouldered on the hearth.

'Make yourself at home,' he said with dry sarcasm, and knelt to pile turf on the fire. She glanced at the pictures of racehorses pasted on the walls and at the table that was strewn with breadcrusts. 'Make yourself at home,' he repeated, and taking a cup from the dresser he plunged it into a bucket of spring water and asked her to take a drink as it was all he had to offer her. Shy of offending him she took the cup but the sight of a few tea leaves floating in it revolted her and she looked up at her uncle and said she wasn't thirsty. 'Drink it to please me,' he said. She took a few sips and it was so cold it made her teeth ache and she left it on the window ledge beside her.

'How would you like to share this house?' he asked. 'There's only the two of us: Johnny P.M., a bit lopsided in his mind, and myself – he's drawing the pension and I help him to spend it. And do you know the reason? – I'm a tipster and there's no honesty left in the world and I make little or no money. I advertise in the newspapers and I ask no money from my clients: all I ask them to do is to put a few shillings for me on the horse I send them. I have sent out many winners and only a few honest clients have sent me a share of their winnings. There's nothing but roguery in this mortal world.'

Eileen laughed. 'I'm afraid, Uncle, I know nothing about racehorses.'

'But I'll tell you what you do know,' he said suddenly. 'You know what has brought you to the country.'

'I'm here to help Aunt Nelly.'

'You were sent here to get round your Uncle Bob.'

'I'm afraid I don't know what you mean,' and she turned the bangle on her wrist.

'It was your father that sent you – wasn't it?'

'He was against my coming and only for mother I wouldn't be here at all.'

'It's a lie, Eileen,' and he caught her wrist. 'Tell me the truth! You were sent out to be nice to Uncle Bob so that he'd not forget you in his will. It was your father that sent you – wasn't it?'

She struggled to escape from him. 'Let me go, Uncle D. J. I have told you the truth.' He let go her wrist, and as she saw the white marks of his fingers on her flesh she flared out at him: 'I'm no longer a little girl that you can tease and make fun of. I used to have respect for you – I've none now. And while you were tending the fire I was thinking of coming up some day soon and cleaning your house from top to bottom. I'll do nothing for you now and I'll tell Uncle Bob and Aunt Nelly what you said to me.'

She went to the door but he stood with his back to it. 'You're not leaving till you hear what I have to say! Remember this – you nor your father nor anybody else will get Bob's shop after his day. I'd burn it down before I'd be tricked out of my share in it. My father cut me out of his will and it was that injustice that has left me the way I am. And now my own brother and his family are conspiring against me.'

'It's not true, Uncle; it's not true.'

He withdrew from the door and sat on a chair by the fire.

'Don't go yet, Eileen. Come here to me – don't be frightened.' He clutched his head in his two hands and stared into the fire. The pale look on his face drew her towards him.

'For the love of God, Eileen, tell me the truth.'

'I've told you the truth, Uncle; I've told you the truth,' and she shook her head with fervour. 'I cannot and I wouldn't tell you a lie.'

'My head aches with it all. I would go away only I'm afraid you're all ranged against me and would defraud me after I'm gone.'

'Uncle D.J.,' she said gently, putting her hand on his shoulder. 'Don't be twisting and souring yourself. Nobody is against you – my father least of all. And the day he ordered you away from the house he wasn't to blame.'

'I suppose I could blame myself. I never had much in my life and anything I had I couldn't keep it. I would go away from here only I'm afraid – afraid that Bob would die and your father pounce on what he possesses.'

'It's wrong to say that. Why can't you live for each day that comes. God knows you might be dead before Uncle Bob – and look what you're doing now to yourself.'

He turned to her and noticing the red mark on her wrist he said he was sorry for hurting her. 'It's nothing, Uncle. It's nothing at all. Goodbye,' she called from the door, 'and don't be torturing yourself and piling up this hateful suspicion against my father – you'll find he's always ready to help you.'

As she picked her steps down the muddy lonin she reflected on what he had told her, and she was alarmed that a man of his years should have his mind worn and wasted by worrying over something that he might never live to see. At the foot of the lonin she saw an old man with a stick peering at the name on her bicycle. He was mumbling away to himself and didn't see her till her shadow fell across him. She coughed and he looked up with a start.

'That's a fine bicycle you have, daughter,' and he pointed

at the shining handle-bars with his stick. 'Ah, you'll be one of D. J.'s nieces, I suppose. You're the dead spit of a Caffrey anyway. You wouldn't be the girl that's teaching school. It's nice to meet a body that'll talk to you for a minute or two on the road.' Eileen hadn't exchanged a word with him and she smiled at the companionable inference of his greeting and watched him sit down beside her bicycle. She might learn something about D. J. if she'd the patience to listen without interruption; and to encourage him she said she was one of the Caffreys.

'Ah, ah, I knowed it all right. D. J. told me all about you. You've a brother going on to be a doctor and you've a brother in charge of all the reading books in the city. I know all — tell your father he has done well for his family. Tell him I said it — Johnny P.M. Do you know how I got that name? One day in school the Master asked me what A.M. meant and I said "At morning", and then he asked what P.M. meant and I said "Past morning". I was the only scholar in the school could answer him and he laughed that day with joy and he gave me a fine orange for myself and said: "God bless you for you're the intelligent child — P.M. is 'past morning': that's the best answer I ever heard since I put foot in the school." Since that day to this they call me Johnny P.M.' He stretched out his fist and pressed the tyre of the bicycle. 'There's a good tube in that wheel. Your uncle is good company — he's good company for me and I'm good company for him. He can bake bread and he's helping me to put in the spuds. The spuds is a wholesome dish if you have an eel to go with them. We set an odd line after dark for an eel when the peelers is asleep. But it'll not always be like that with us. Whisper now,' and he looked up and down the road. 'Bob Caffrey's dying and he's to leave all to D. J. — shop and clothes and money and all. And D. J.'s going to take me into the shop, and I'll brush it out every morning, chop his sticks every evening, and walk over to the newsagents for the paper every day. And I'll meet all the trains to see if they've a hamper of stuff for Caffrey's store. We'll have a great time with only the two of us under that fine slated roof – there's not many houses with good Bangor blues covering the rafters. I'll be living beside the stir and see the motor cars passing on the road and the trains at night with all their lights rattling over the bridge. Do you know, girl, I love the darksomeness of the railway line; it's always draughty and lonesome with the green lights and red lights on the signals and the thin wires trying to hold up the wind. I'll not need my pension money and I'll give it to the priest and he'll see that I'll have a nice grave near the road and a white cross on it with my name in black letters and if a girl like you is passing you'll not forget to say a prayer for me. D. J. will have many a one to pray for him but I'll have nobody. It's a queer thing I'm going to say to you – I'm over seventy years of age and I never saw my father and I never saw my mother and I don't know if I ever had a brother, a sister, or a cousin.' He got to his feet with difficulty and Eileen lifted his bag of groceries and looped the strap of it over his arm. 'You'll come to see us in our new house,' he went on. 'Bob Caffrey is getting a new face in it today and the men are working at it. Every Caffrey will be welcome. We'll not be like your Uncle Bob – a man that wouldn't give you a safety-pin to fasten your shirt against the cold.' He turned up the lonin and stopped to shake his stick in farewell. 'You're a good wholesome girl for talking to me on the road . . . You'll always be welcome.'

On her way for the eggs and on her return the sunny wind fingered her hair, dispelling the mood of sadness that the old man and D. J. had roused. She reached the village and saw the ripped-out window of the shop, the bare scaffolding framing it, and Philip Doran with his back to her and a trowel in his hand. For a minute she stood at the edge of the group of idle onlookers who were busily making fun of Philip's apprentice, telling him to take his hands out of his pockets, not to be walking on Bob's peacock, and to give back to the old man the packet of pins he stole from him. In his embarrassment the young apprentice tripped over a bag of cement and put his foot through one of the panes of glass that had just been removed. Philip, turning round angrily, told the scoffers to give the young fellow a chance for the love of God, and then seeing Eileen he came across to her, his face red because he had sworn at them.

'I didn't expect you in the country till we'd the job complete,' he said. 'It was your Aunt Nelly told me you came by the early train. . . .'

'I came suddenly,' she smiled up at him, the sun shining on her fair hair, her cheeks flushed by the excitement of the day.

'I'm going to make a fine job of this, Eileen — on your account, of course. I'll make it as pleasing to look at as yourself.' Both turned round simultaneously to the shop and saw Bob stare at them with grim displeasure. 'Oh, Philip, Uncle Bob's watching us,' and as she made off from him he caught the saddle of the bicycle and asked her to come down to the house in the evening for a game of whist. 'I'll have to ask Aunt Nelly first,' and she glanced furtively at her uncle, but he had his back turned to her, examining the pane of glass that had been broken.

'The dinner's ready an hour ago,' her Aunt Nelly said to her. 'I was beginning to think you had run off with Johnny P.M. . . . Hurry now like a good girl and wash your hands.' And when they were seated round the table Eileen told them of her visit to Uncle D. J. and how it hurt her to see him living in such a mean place with nobody for company but an old man who was barely able to tie his shoe-lace because of his rheumatism.

'It's a good sight better than he deserves,' Uncle Bob said. 'And while you're here, Eileen, it would be better to avoid him as much as possible.'

'He's her uncle,' Aunt Nelly defended, 'and you've no right to turn her against her own and your own flesh and blood.'

'There are things about D. J. that are better left unsaid. It would be better for her to keep away from him. And she should keep away from that gossiping Doran fellow and his clumsy workmen and let them get on with the job. The sooner they're finished the sooner I'll be content.'

'It'd be better to put Eileen in a cage if you're going to tabulate any more "don'ts" for her.'

'I don't want any harm to come to her while she's here.'

'I'll do whatever you want me to do,' Eileen said, and gave a forced smile to disguise her awareness of their snapping differences of opinion.

'You're here to enjoy yourself and not to listen to the fitful vagaries of an old man,' Nelly said.

'There you go again. Women never understand me—when I tender some advice, they think I'm finding fault,' and he went on to explain how his women customers misunderstood him every time he tried to persuade them to buy an article of value.

He rose from the table, not waiting for his usual cup of tea, and stood at the window looking at Doran's three workmen who were smoking under the sunny wall, the dregs of their tea-cans flung on the roadway. 'That's the laziest·pack of workmen I ever clapped an eye on. You'd think after they'd eaten their fill they'd go back and get the work finished while the good weather lasts. If the weather breaks and there comes a wind from the north I'll get my death of cold in the shop. I was a stupid man to give that Doran fellow the job. A stranger would give you a better deal.'

'For pity's sake give yourself peace, sometime,' Nelly said. 'If Philip Doran said he would do it in a certain time he'll keep his word.'

'His word depends too much on the weather,' and he pushed open the window and glared at the workmen, and they rose with leisurely contempt, knocked out their pipes, and rolling up their lunch-papers into a ball, kicked it to one another till Bob shouted at them to go back to their jobs or he would employ another contractor. Then Philip arrived from his dinner and the sight of him in a clean collar and tie, his best jacket over his dungarees, drove Bob to such a fit of desperation that he asked him was he going to the chapel to attend a wedding or was he going to finish the job that was given to him out of respect for his dead father?

Presently there was the clink-clink of a trowel against stone, the rattle of sand in the sieve, the sound of the pump-handle outside the window, and now and again the pleasurable ring of the shop-bell as a customer entered and business was carried on as usual. Twice Philip came to the side door but it was Aunt Nelly who answered his knock, and from her seat in the armchair Eileen, hearing their laughter and the blurred edges of their talk, hoped Philip would mention the evening's visit. But to Eileen's distress the afternoon merged into evening and still Aunt Nelly did not refer to it and Eileen awaited an opportunity to announce it to her herself.

The men fastened the tarpaulin to the bare window, pushed the handcart into the side passage, and hurrying off left the silence to the crows and to the sunlight that lit up the fresh green of the chestnut trees.

'The young leaves are like green moths with folded wings,' Eileen said, standing near the window.

'You're very fond of green, Eileen,' and her aunt put an arm round her waist. 'Is that what you'll wear tonight at Philip's?'

'Oh, Aunty, I didn't know how to tell you about it. I didn't think it right to go visiting on my first night and I didn't give Philip a no or yes when he asked me.'

'But I did it for you, Eileen. We'll certainly go – it will be a relief for me to get away for an evening. And since we'll be together your Uncle Bob won't be sitting up in the dark till we return and there'll be nothing nagging at the tail of my mind – I'll feel as free as the wind.'

They hurried with the tea. Aunt Nelly put on a black frock and Eileen a green and the bangle Philip had given her. On buttoning the back of her aunt's frock she told her that black made her slim and young-looking.

'As long as it makes me as young as my years I don't mind. Fastened to an old man as I have been would dull anyone's interest in dress and style. But I mustn't start that litany.'

They set off, leaving Bob at the table poring once more over the design of the shop-front. Stars sparkled in the sky and the rising moon nested for a while in the branches of a tree at the side of the house. There was stillness and peace, a cold air from the river, and a smell of burning quicksets from the flat fields. They crossed the bridge and walked along the bank where the river lapped and lipped against the moored boats and where the moon's reflection spread out like a wing of gold on the water's surface. 'It's so quiet here,' Aunt Nelly said in a hushed voice. 'The calmness of it always lifts my own mind.' They stood still. High above them stretched the curved blue of the sky, pricked with stars, and the rising moon like a polished port-hole of light. 'Thank God, Eileen, to be alive on such a night – it's wonderful and glorious!' Below them reeds stood each in a nest of moon-rings, and a disturbed water hen moving jerkily out from the bank broke the rings into tiny rafts of light that bobbed and floated for a while on the cold water. Then suddenly from the opposite bank the headlights of a motor swerved through the village, glared on the white houses, and swept harshly across the fields. Eileen moved, shuddering from the abrupt intrusion that grasped and tore at the peace of the evening.

Ahead of them dogs barked from the flat fields and their sounds intensified by the river seemed to rise into the air and echo from the vast ceiling of sky. Philip and his sister, Martha, hurried from the house to welcome them – a welcome that was so full of courtesy and kindness, ease and laughter, that Eileen was in the brightly lit kitchen before she could find words to say to them; and then with everyone talking at the same time, the dog barking and Philip shouting at it to keep quiet, Martha brought them into a bedroom to take off their coats, and there Eileen sat for a moment to repress the rush of excitement that overwhelmed her. But through the partly opened door she saw into the sitting-room and the light of the fire reflecting on the piano. 'Oh, Aunty,' she said, 'I hope they don't ask me to play. Last summer their piano needed tuning and some of the keys were stuck together with the damp.'

'If they ask you don't refuse or they'd be offended,' said her aunt, her back to the oval mirror on the dressing-table as she powdered her face and licked the tips of her fingers to smooth her eyebrows. Eileen stood up and looking into the mirror arranged her hair with a few careless sweeps of the comb.

'Does that mirror not give you a queer appearance?' said Aunt Nelly.

Eileen glanced at herself again in the mirror and shook her head. 'No, it seems to me to be all right.'

'It must be my imagination,' said her aunt, and led the way into the sitting-room.

'You take the armchair, Nelly,' Martha said. 'And Eileen you sit here beside me . . . You have grown quite a young lady since you were here last. Hasn't she, Philip?'

Philip hung his head quizzically to the side and affected a studious air. 'She's looking like herself – that's the best I can say. But I think she has grown an inch or two since last summer. Stand up, Eileen, till I make sure.'

'Spare her blushes,' Martha said, and told Eileen not to heed him.

Eileen smiled and asked him if he had still the same boat as he had in the summer.

'I have but I'm making a new one. It's only a skeleton at the moment – would you like to see it?'

'For goodness' sake, Philip, give the girl peace,' Martha intervened. 'What on earth interest would Eileen have in the building of a boat? Now if it was my new incubator you wanted to show her there'd be some sense in it.'

'Come on, Eileen, and I'll show it to you,' Philip coaxed. 'We'll not be a minute.'

Eileen turned the bangle on her wrist, and on raising her head her aunt noticed the irresolute expression on her face and told her to go on with Philip if she wished to.

'Will I need to put on my coat?' she asked.

'Run on, you'll not be a tick. You'll do as you are,' Nelly said.

In the kitchen Philip lifted a hurricane lamp and taking Eileen by the hand he led her to a shed at the back of the house. There was a chill in the air but when he opened the shed, the close warmth of it, the smell of oil, and the cheep-cheep of chickens flowed around her with mysterious attractiveness. He lifted the lid of the incubator, and as they leaned over, shoulder to shoulder, she saw in the haygold light the tiny chickens mischievously darting in and out from the hanging flaps of grey flannel. She laughed at their playfulness especially one little black one that was the most forward of all. 'They're sweet and lovely, Philip,' she said. He lifted one and placed it in her cupped hands, and as she felt the tremorings in its throat like a heart-beat she smoothed and fondled its head with her lips.

'It's well for some chickens,' he said with a laugh; and as she stooped to release the chicken he saw her bangle circled with gold light. She stood up and he toyed with the bangle asking her in a low voice if it fitted her well.

'It's perfect,' she said, turning it on her wrist. 'It was kind of you to give me that.'

'It's more than that I'd give to the girl I love,' and he put his arm around her and she yielded to him with shy reserve.

'I love you, Eileen. I've said that often in the clumsy letters I wrote to you. You know I love you – don't you?' She gave a low, nervous laugh. He looked down at her and holding her head firmly in his hands he gazed at her with such tense penetration that she had to close her eyes to shut out the terrible sincerity that flowed out from him. Whether she loved him or not she could not say; never before had she felt drawn to anyone, and it was only last summer after he had taken her for rows on the river that she found herself often recalling the fresh bronzed vigour of his face and the strong sweep and creak of the oars. Whether that was love or not she could not say, and now the same honest strength was drawing her to him and she felt herself swaying under its warm, forceful appeal.

'Oh, Philip, we must go in!' and she broke away from him with a tremulous smile. 'Aunt Nelly will wonder what on earth's keeping us.'

'Och! Let her wonder!' he said, and taking her hand he led her from the warm seclusion of the shed.

Nelly met them at the door. 'I was just going out to look for the pair of you. The tea is ready,' and as she spoke she noticed the flush on Eileen's cheeks and the dishevelled comb-tracks in her hair.

'There was no call to worry,' Philip joked, 'I couldn't drag her away from the chickens and there's one wee black fellow you should take home with you in a paper bag – she fell in love with him.'

Later they seated themselves round the table to play whist; Philip took Eileen for his partner, and Aunt Nelly, perceiving their fumbling playing and the laughs of Philip every time Eileen beat his own card, knew that Philip was in love; and with her cards studiously fanned out in front of her eyes she covertly glanced at Eileen, seeing, but not sharing, the brightness of her smile.

On their way home along the river bank Aunt Nelly walked with a slow lingering weariness, unaware of the moon-mist that drenched the fields.

'Did you enjoy your evening, Eileen?'

'I did, Aunt,' and she linked her arm and pressed it to her side. 'It was lovely. But I played the piano very badly, I thought.'

'It gave us all great pleasure. And there was Philip and he never took his eyes off your hands as they ran along the keyboard. He's more than fond of you I believe.'

Eileen said nothing and they walked on, linked together in silence.

Aunt Nelly sighed, preparing to unloose the strands that had fastened her to a desire that she now knew was beyond her. She had been afraid to look in the oval mirror in the room they had just left. She had been afraid to admit to herself that her freshness was gone. For a long time past she had pursued a hope – a hope that was already rotted by her years; and in that vain striving she was never at rest. But henceforth she would change all that: she would meet what is and not try to live for what she hoped would be, and in that attitude to what was real she might gain the contentment of mind that had always escaped her.

'Eileen,' she said, pressing her hand. 'You love Philip?'

'I don't know, Aunt. Honestly, I don't know my own mind. I certainly like him well.'

'He's strong, he's kind, and he could give you a comfortable home. If you care for him take my advice and marry him. If you don't,' and she paused for a moment as if she had heard a step behind her, 'if you don't you might one day be like myself – a woman yearning to relive my share of life again. You're happy, Eileen?'

'I am, Aunt Nelly – very happy.'

'Marry him, marry him then! He'll make a fine husband for you.' She had said now what she had thought she could never bring herself to say; she had cleared her mind, and in wishing for Eileen what she had all along wanted for herself she felt her heart race forward in a rush of pained joy. The harmony and completeness of her spirit stretched out from her, and in the tightened clasp of Eileen's hand she knew that what she was doing was being valued, and from that knowledge her own face and eyes shone suddenly with a brightness that submerged, for the moment, the jaded look of her own years. She drew herself erect, and on reaching the bridge she paused, glorying in the loveliness of the falls, its shoulders polished by the moon, and the broken water below it split and shaken with a quicksilver of light.

CHAPTER ELEVEN

AT the end of the following week the alteration to the shop window had been completed, and a new awning having arrived from Belfast Philip was now busily fitting it in its position while a group of idlers, among them D. J., had gathered to watch him. With his hands in his pockets D. J. stared with insolent silence as the white canvas was given its first unfurling and he saw, printed diagonally across it in black letters, R. CAFFREY. The sun striking through the canvas shed a cool glow on the window and it suddenly reminded him of a wake.

'I'm thinking that Bob won't have many months left to him to drag that gadget back and forward,' an old man said, echoing the gist of D. J.'s mind.

'It's a sad thing to say but that's what I feel about it myself,' D. J. agreed, trying to stem the casual tone of his voice. 'And it wasn't that I didn't advise him against it – spending money on a new shop-face and he with one foot and a half in the grave.'

'You advised him right. But he didn't listen to a man of the world.'

'He did not. He's beginning to dote and he acts like a man going soft in the head,' D. J. went on.

'Damn the dote and damn the soft in the head! Try any of you to palm off a bad coin on him or try to get him to throw off a few coppers from the price of a shirt – you'd be wasting your good warm breath.'

With a long pole Philip pushed back the awning into its wooden slot and pulled it forward again a few times to ease the stiff newness of the rollers.

'The rain will wriggle into that bit of a shelter and the snow will rot the canvas,' the old man went on. 'But it'll last out Bob's day and he'll not be here to see the rusty rags and tatters the years will make of it. Man, D. J., when you're planted safe and snug behind the counter you'll not waste your strength pulling out that mainsail. And what, under God, possessed him to root out your father's peacock. It was the only attraction in the village. Sure nobody would stop to look at an eyelid on a shop window and them as common as curtains in the big towns. But the peacock was a strange and uncommon sight.'

'Didn't I tell you he acts strange of late? It was daft of him to dig up the old peacock,' D. J. said.

The old man spat out on the grey patch on the road where the cement had been mixed. ''Tis a queer country – the old rooting out the valuable and hankering after the new.'

From the room above the shop Bob was looking down with pride at the awning lifting in the wind and his name rising in bold black letters – the downstrokes thick and heavy, and the upstrokes thin and delicate as a thread. 'That'll give them something to talk about,' he said to himself and glanced at Daly's shop whose painted front had lost its gloss in the snows of the recent winter. The group of idlers now attracted him and he knew they were discussing the awning – praising it, or more than likely finding fault; it was easy to find fault with a thing that somebody else has paid for. And there was D. J. among them and his head bobbing like a frightened coot. He was a maddening and upsetting sight to look at, day after day, scrounging about the village. Only for Nelly's misdirected kindness he would, he was sure, have quitted the village long ago and left him in peace. And it wasn't that he hadn't prayed for him night and day – prayed that he'd be delivered from his baleful and lazy presence. But there he was – tall and stiff and dishevelled as a May scarecrow.

He came from the room and joined Philip in the street, and Philip handed him the pole to test the smoothness of the awning's rollers. Bob manoeuvred the steel point of the pole into its socket and gave a mighty heave. The awning creaked but did not move. The idlers laughed and one shouted: 'Keep at it, Bob. Four tries free and a penny change!'

'You're standing too much to the side,' Philip said, ignoring the scoffers, and directing Bob to stand mid-way. 'Now! Lift and push at the same time! Steady and easy does the trick.'

Bob did as he was ordered. He heaved and pushed, the canvas wavered, and then as he was about to desist it moved back with miraculous smoothness and Bob pushed it home to the cheers of the group on the roadway. Once more he pulled it forward and shot it home with fierce concentration, heedless of the derisive shouts about him, his mind bent on mastering and subduing the stubbornness of the awning.

'To be so new it runs freely,' he said to Philip in a loud, self-assured voice.

'There'll be a gallon of froth on your braces after work like that,' the old man laughed. 'You better employ a shop-boy right off the reel!'

Bob pushed back the hat from his brow, feeling the cold sweat on it, and aware also of his heavy nasal breathing. He rested against the varnished pole upright in his hands, its S-shaped metal point flashing in the sun like an ancient insignia.

'Spit on your hands, Bob, and give her another spin,' someone shouted, and a volley of laughter rang through the village.

D. J. fidgeted uneasily; some dormant family pride roused

within him, and he suddenly felt a wretched abasement as he stood among that group, encouraging them by his silence to poke fun at his own brother. Near him a youth was doubled up with laughing, and D. J. lunging forward, pulled off the youth's cap, and struck him on the head with the peak of it. The youth raised startled eyes to him and D. J. struck him again. 'Whose brother do you think you're laughing at – you miserable son of a get!' He would have scattered the rest of them but at that moment Bob had gathered his breath and clenching the pole he made another attack on the awning. With a mighty effort he sent it flying but the impetus of his rush carried him too far forward and he stumbled and fell, the steel point of the pole crashing through the window. Uncontrollable laughter swept the group, and even Daly, who had been eyeing it all from the dark seclusion of his shop, came to the doorway grinning away to himself as D. J. ran to help Bob to his feet.

'I'm all right,' Bob said, taking his hat from D. J. and dusting it with a handkerchief. 'Go on off to your clownish scum and have another laugh.' He turned his back and examined the damaged window. 'It's unfortunate, Philip. And everything looking so trim. If the rollers had been a little on the stiff side this wouldn't have happened.' He shook his head. 'However, I must settle the little bill of fare and you can put in a new pane at your very earliest.'

Philip went with him into the shop, and in about fifteen minutes Philip came out again, and turned down the road at the side of the house. D. J. hurried after him calling out: 'Philip, just a minute like a decent man!' Philip rested against the hedge that bordered the garden and which hid from view the little summer-house where Eileen, at that moment, was writing a letter to her mother. She sat up on hearing the familiar voices.

'Philip,' D. J. was saying, 'I was wondering if you'd do me a little favour and help me to leave this village where I was

146

born. It's only a little favour and I'll return it. And as a token of my warm affection for you I'll say a good word about you to the girl you love. She's my favourite niece and I know every mood and move and nerve of her. Now her sister Anne is a charming girl too but she hasn't got that sleek and graceful action that Eileen has. Wait till I meet her father and mother! I'm the man to stake your claim. They'd do any mortal thing for me. And now for the favour lest I forget: Would it be too much to ask you, Philip, my lad, to advance me a loan of thirty pounds?'

'It would be thirty times too much,' Philip said coldly. 'I gave you a pound a few weeks ago.'

'A pound! Well, well, I'm surprised at a man like you remembering such trifles. Man, alive, I'd give a fellow a pound as quickly as I'd give him a cigarette and forget all about it the next day. That's the kind of me. I've a touch of class about me. I'm not one of your common beggars coming with hat in hand and asking for a few shillings. The loan I ask is large because I've too much respect for myself and for you.'

'I'm afraid, D. J., you can try your respect on somebody else. I'm ashamed of you.'

'Even for what I'd do for you?'

'You can keep Eileen's name out of this. She'd be ashamed of you borrowing like this.'

'For the last time: will you advance the loan or not?'

'I will not!'

'To hell with you – and you with a well-lined pocket. To hell with you for a stingy, hungry hound! You and Bob should be tied together and flung over the falls. But let me tell you you'll never have a share in Eileen if I know anything,' and he went off mumbling and cursing. Philip asked him to stay for a minute but he shook his head and said he was finished with the Dorans for ever!

Five minutes later Aunt Nelly came down the garden to the summer-house and found Eileen in tears, her hands folded on her lap, and the writing-pad fallen at her feet. She said she wanted to go home as no one had written to her for the past two weeks and that there must be something seriously wrong – her mother sick or, maybe, Frank.

'But this morning, Eileen, you had no notion of going home. You were looking forward to Philip taking you to Abbey Island tomorrow. What has come over you at all? Has he said anything to you? No. Has your Uncle Bob done anything to you? No. Then, Mother of God, what is wrong with you?' And she cast her arms about her, shook her playfully, and coaxed her to confess her troubles. She put a finger under Eileen's chin and asked her to smile. At last she gave a tearful laugh and revealed the conversation she had overheard. Aunt Nelly advised her not to think anything more about it. Everyone knew D. J. for what he was. People enjoyed him and pitied him but few despised him. It was her own opinion that there was some good in him if he'd only give up the gambling and the rambling and the borrowing. Some day she might be in a position to help him. If only he had the responsibility of minding the shop, of buying and selling, he might pull himself together. Until that day comes no one can be blamed for the mean things that his mind feeds on.

'Oh, Aunt Nelly, you don't know what he has done to me. I feel I can never be the same with Philip again. The thought of Uncle D. J. will start coming between us, rending and twisting the easy way we've always had with one another.' She put a handkerchief to her eyes. 'I detest lies and dishonesty in anyone! Father and mother always taught us to hate lies and to follow honest ways. And to think Uncle D. J. gets money from Philip and I not to know!'

'Eileen, girl,' and she pressed her head against her breast. 'You mustn't let little things like that burden and cripple you. Your life is just beginning and you must have faith in what you are yourself and put your trust in the goodness of God.' She stroked her head.

The sweet cool air coming across the river drew the anxiety from her eyes and she looked away under the blossoming apple tree in the garden and saw a boat on the bank of the river almost hidden by tall green rushes and above it swallows lacing the air and dipping for an instant on top of their own shadows in the water.

'I wish I'd never see Uncle D. J. again,' Eileen said.

'Sh-s-sh,' Nelly said. 'Never wish like that – desiring ease and flying from the first contact of unpleasantness. You must learn to make these things strengthen your character. You must strike this gloom from your heart. Remember the young apple's sourness grows to sweetness under the joy of the sun. It's a sin for you to be lamenting and crying on such a lovely day. Promise me you'll put him from your mind and not worry any more.'

Eileen nodded, and picking up her writing-pad Aunt Nelly led her out by the side gate to see the new awning and the unfortunate mishap to the window. A long iron-toothed strap was screwed along the sill of the window to prevent the youths of the village from using it as an evening resting-place, and as Aunt Nelly was dislodging the pieces of glass from between its teeth Bob came to the door and held a ten-shilling note up to the light of the sky. He gave a snort of contempt, and without a bow of recognition to Nelly or Eileen he withdrew again to the shop and they could hear his voice, loud and dry with indignation: 'Tell your mother I couldn't accept money like that. It's dirty and torn and you'd think the baby had chewed it. It's defaced money into the bargain.'

A ragged little girl came out of the shop, crying bitterly as she ran home, heedless of the sympathetic voice of Nelly asking her what's wrong.

'There's what's wrong,' and Bob showed her a pencilled note on which was written: 'Give my little girl a pair of stockings for herself and be sure to wrap the change in paper and put it in her pocket. I am sending you a ten-shilling note. Mrs. Bruce.'

'I couldn't accept the money,' he explained. 'The number on it was barely decipherable.'

'You shouldn't have sent her home in tears and without the stockings.'

He hammered the counter with his knuckles and went on to explain that from now on he was a changed man and that his attitude to the people of Monabeg would be one of hard strict business. He would be polite but aloof, and never again would he give them anything on tick. They had laughed at him today; they were responsible for breaking his window and they took as much delight in that as they would on seeing a circus clown break a cracked plate. Today he learnt a lesson or two about the Monabeg people which he wouldn't forget in a hurry. And never to his dying day would he forget the laughs and sniggers of D. J. That man, he was sure, would come to a bad end for scoffing at his own brother!

Nelly listened to him in silence, and tried to assemble in her own mind the fragments of his talk and the irksome source of it all. She was contriving an excuse for D. J. when she was suddenly startled by the appearance of Mrs. Bruce who rushed into the shop, an apron around her, and a tablefork in her hand.

'What do you mean by sending my wee girl home in tears? Whose money is disgraced?' and she drew near the counter, waving the fork in his face. He backed away from her, staring with stupefied astonishment, and not bothering to wipe away from his face the spits that accompanied her enraged language. 'Whose money is disgraced? If your brother D. J. had it in his fist he wouldn't feel it was disgraced. He wasn't particular what kind of money the railway had when he made off with it. Dirty, chewed, or disgraced didn't matter to him. And remember the Bruces never robbed anyone – their money was honestly wrought for and honestly come by. Do you hear what I say?' and she shouted louder, trying to rouse him from that stupor of contempt by which he silently assailed her. 'Do you hear me?' and she jabbed the fork into the counter. 'Only you're at death's door I'd pock-mark that yellow face of yours. Disgraced money! What way is your brother D. J. making his money! A tipster – if you please! A man in the know! The real stuff for the Handicap on Friday! He that sends out every horse in the race – isn't he sure to tip the winner! That's a clean and lovely way to make money! I suppose he gives you a share of his dirty earnings.'

'I know nothing of D. J.,' he said quietly, turned his back, and took down a box of shirts, and opened them on the counter.

'You'll listen to me!' she said, exasperated by his cold contempt. 'You can go on with your work when I've finished with you,' and with one swipe she flung the box on the floor and proceeded to kick the contents into the street.

'Nelly,' Bob said calmly, 'go across to the barracks and tell the sergeant I want him.'

Nelly stood where she was—too frightened to pass the angry woman. Mrs. Bruce kicked the box into the shop again and standing at the door she called out: 'Bob Caffrey, I never put a curse on anyone, but I am going to put one on you.'

'Mrs. Bruce,' Bob pleaded in a changed anxious voice. 'Your little girl made a mistake. It was defaced money I said – not disgraced.'

Her threatened curse had, at last, roused him and she gave a laugh of malevolent triumph. She looked at the fork in her hand as if seeing it for the first time. 'Sweet God, the dinner will be destroyed on me,' and banging the door they heard, in the rush of silence, bits of glass falling from the pane and tinkling on to the street.

'That's how I'm misunderstood! That's how I'm misunderstood!' Bob said over and over again as they helped him to pick up the shirts from the floor. 'D. J. is killing me. Cheating over horses is the next of it! He'll drag us all down in his ruin. Write to your father, Eileen, and maybe he'll get D. J. a job in the city. Your father should turn a hand to help me.'

Eileen went off and added a long postscript to her letter, mentioning Uncle Bob's suggestion about D. J., and reproaching her mother and Anne for not answering her last three letters. When she had finished the writing of the letter a load of sorrow lay about her heart. Mrs. Bruce had terrified her and her remark about D. J. and the railway filled her mind with dreaded anticipation. Maybe Aunt Nelly would tell her what had happened without her asking! Whatever it was it was something dishonourable. Poor D. J. – God in Heaven help him!

Aunt Nelly pretended not to notice the unhappy mood that had chilled Eileen's customary brightness and that evening as they walked along the river as far as the falls she would gaze at the reddish glow in the sky and look at the mist covering the far-away hedges and say: 'Philip and yourself are going to have a lovely day for your trip to the Island tomorrow. It'll be very warm. Look how close the midges dance above the water and listen to the screech of the swallows. It'll be a beautiful God-given day!' and she pressed Eileen's arm.

About them was the rainy sound of the falls and from a boat on the river the singing of boys and girls, their voices made clear and sweet by the cold stretches of water. Trees overhung the path and under their thick leaves there lingered the heat of the day; and as they walked past they felt the heat eddy around them and caught the heavy perfume from the flowering hawthorn hedges while petals lay like scattered confetti on the path.

'A reminder of your wedding,' Aunt Nelly said, halting on the path and touching the petals with her toe. 'Oh, Eileen, that will be the happiest day of my life. And then you will be living near me and I'll have something to live for.

It will be a new life for me, for you, and for us all. Pray, Eileen, that nothing will happen to destroy it.'

Eileen linked her arm and they walked on, keeping in step, their shreds of sorrow being rended and consumed by their anticipated joy, by the dew-quiet of the evening, and by the untroubled reflections in the water that were fascinatingly deep and clear. But on their return to the village they saw D. J. standing in front of a group of laughing youths. He was swaying unsteadily on his feet, pulling back his cuffs, and waving a leafy twig in front of the group like a conductor of a choir. Someone had pinned a rag of a towel to the tail of his coat and as D. J. waved the twig and urged the boys to sing up and sing out for the love of God the towel would swing in unison, leaving whorls in the dust of the road. He hummed a bar or two of a song and raising his hands he said: 'Now, my boys, let us render that.' But the lads ceased laughing. Nelly rushed forward and abused them with her tongue for making fun of a man in his foolishness. She unpinned the towel and kicked it out of the dust where it had fallen, and taking D. J. by the arm she led him out along the road to his home, telling him she was ashamed of him for making himself so low, so cheap – a laughing-stock for those playboys. He agreed and protested at the same time; it was longer than a month since he had taken a drink and it'd be a long time before she'd see him like that again. He drew up on the road and looked back at the village. 'A crowd of frog-spawn – that's what they are! Tying a tail on me and me trying to elevate them. Sing? They wouldn't know a bloody note from a sheet of notepaper.' She left him at the lonin of his house and hurried back.

''Tis a long time since I've seen him in such a state,' she said to Eileen as she hung up her coat. 'He has promised me he'll take better care of himself. For all his swagger he doesn't like anyone to make a fool of him. Now there's Philip Doran and you'd never see him making game of a defenceless beggar or a drunken man.'

Tears came into Eileen's eyes and she told her aunt not to heed her. 'Something has come over me,' she said. 'I can't go with Philip tomorrow. I feel unworthy of anyone's love.'

'May God forgive you, Eileen, for speaking like that. Oh, you mustn't – must never think like that again. And to speak like that is utterly shameful. Remember always that it is you yourself that matters to Philip – your own goodness and grace and sweetness. Think of that when you lie down tonight.'

She went with her to her room, drew her curtains, and lighted her lamp. And on returning later to bid her good-night she saw her kneeling in a blue nightdress, her fair hair fluffed around her shoulders, the soles of her bare feet stained brown by her shoes. Her eyes were closed, and in the fervour of her concentration she was unaware of her aunt's presence in the room, and her aunt watching the quiet purity of her hands, the mouldings of her breasts, was suddenly filled with an anguish of strong protectiveness towards her. Stemming back an onrush of tears she withdrew unheard, and purged by what she had just seen she went on her knees and prayed for Eileen and Philip, for D. J. and Bob, for John and his family, and prayed, too, that the peace in her own soul would not desert her.

For a while she did not sleep as she went over the events of the day, and then when sleep did come she was awakened out of it by the cry of cattle passing on the road. Ever since she was a child these herds of cattle moving through the night to the waiting wagons at the station had always wakened her, and their crying and their breathing and their shuffling huddled through her mind in a terrifying mystery to which she could give no name. They always come in the semi-darkness, in the cold no-light of the predawn; they are driven from wide flat fields where mists make light of night; their dew-wet hoofs lift the dust on the road and swirl it into their gaping eyes and on to the low-hanging leaves on the trees. They brush and lurch against the hedges, and the thorns grasp hair to stream in the daylight's wind. They cry, and their calls are echoed by distant cattle lying in the warm nests of their own sweat. A crack from the drover's stick sends them leaping forward; they steam and sweat and make the road a river of mist. They cry again, and strings and clots of froth fall from their mouths on to the thirsty road. They reach the village, and windows rattle in the pad-pad of their hoofs. Their gasping breaths and their crushed and driven roughness are narrowed into an intense shadow of sound. At the station there is the shunt of wagons, then the thump of harried feet on bare boards, and, at last, the rick-rack of wheels as the train rattles with its terrified load into the cold light of dawn. Outside on the road and over the fields the silence falls, and falling into Nelly's mind come fear and mystery and sorrow – life approaching death.

CHAPTER TWELVE

NEXT morning the rising sun quickly scattered the mists from the river, the trees, and the fields. The cow-dung dried on the road, and the slates on the roofs were warm under the feet of the resting pigeons. The postman complained to himself of the heat on the handlebars of his bicycle as he wheeled it from the post-office window. He opened the neck of his tunic, and as he passed Bob Caffrey stretching out the awning he told him with a touch of envy that he'd be as cool as a leaf under that shade. From an upstair window Eileen was watching the postman and seeing him wheel off without opening his bag she wondered, with a stab of disappointment, what on earth had come over them at home that they didn't think it worth their notice to send her even a card. She didn't blame her mother – her mother, God knows, had plenty to do; she blamed Anne — surely Anne wasn't so frightened of Miss Mallon that she'd be afraid to sit down for a few minutes in school and scribble off a letter. Well, there was one thing certain, they wouldn't get another letter from her till they thought fit of answering her last one. Today she'd enjoy herself on the river with Philip; she'd put every worry from her mind and she'd not allow this disappointment of the postman to overshadow and spoil the brightness of the day.

She had an early dinner and set off wearing a straw hat, a blue frock with a black belt, and white canvas shoes. She had a coat over her arm to guard against the evening chill from the river. Philip was in the boat when she arrived and he had two cushions in the stern and a basket covered with large green leaves to protect the milk and sandwiches from the sun. Martha came to the bottom of the steps to see them off, and the two dogs ran along the bank, keeping pace with the boat, until Philip shouted at them to go home. They sat eyeing him eagerly, their tongues panting, and then with many a backward glance they trotted homewards as the boat turned a bend and lost them from view. The river narrowed between tall trees that almost roofed out the sky, and here the air was cold like that above a well and their voices echoed in the dark aisles between the trees. From the cloistered coolness of the arching branches pigeons flew out with a wooden clapping of wings and the sleek black water reflected the candelabra of the blossoming chestnut. Eileen put the coat around her shoulders and Philip leaning on the oars sent the boat forward with quick, urgent strokes, only slackening his pace when they had emerged from the cold tunnel of trees into the bright sunlight. The sun shone through Eileen's straw hat and freckled her face with diamond-specks of light; the specks shimmered like a veil and Philip told her she looked like an Eastern lady. She took off her hat, then, with a careless sweep of her arm and exposed her face to the sun and to Philip's steady gaze.

The river widened into a large lake where wild duck lay like long lines of stepping-stones on its smooth surface. They arose at the boat's approach, mounting into the great width of sky, and circling over three small islands that lay near the lake's edge. Smoke arose from one of these islands, and in the air Philip caught the smell of poteen. He eyed the duck as they wheeled high around the islands, too frightened to land, and he watched them wheel back again and settle down in the wake of the boat. There was no wind and the smell of poteen lay thick over the lake. He noticed that Eileen was aware of it but he said nothing as he had heard that her Uncle D. J. was drunk from poteen last night. A crazy, silly man, he said to himself, and sent the boat flying forward to escape from all thought of him. Ahead was the thickly wooded island with its ruined church and its old graveyard where Philip's father and mother lay buried.

He piloted the boat to a causeway of stones and carried Eileen ashore to a huge boulder that lay under the shade of a thorn tree. St. Patrick's Stone it was called, and he showed her holes in it the size of a man's knee and an imprint of fingers which he told her were those of St. Patrick, worn out on the stone when he retreated there to pray. On the branches of the hawthorn tree were decayed rags, and on a neighbouring stone lay a collection of mildewed religious medals, rusty pins, and pieces of rosary beads. He had to explain everything to her and he told her of his first memory of the island. He was six or seven at the time, and from a sickness his eyes had become red and inflamed. His father and mother put a heavy overcoat on him, though it was a warm day, and rowed him down the river to the island. He remembered sitting on a stone and swinging a blue pair of rosary beads round his finger and smiling at his father and mother as they took off their shoes and walked round the old church in their bare feet saying their beads. Time and time again his father cried out that the crabbed young nettles were stinging the legs off him but his mother came behind. 'Thole it, man,' she said. 'It'll cure your rheumatism. You're doing penance for your son's eyes.' They put on their shoes then and came over to me and pouring water from the lake into the holes of the stone they bathed my eyes and called out to St. Patrick to cure my eyes if it was the Will of God. They made me put my blue beads on the stone, and tying the wet rag to the branch of the tree they carried me to the boat. I roared and yelled for my beads and my father told me he lent them to St. Patrick and that the postman would bring them back to me. "I want them now," I shouted, and I kicked at the boat so much that I put a hole in the timber and the water rushed in. We weren't far out at the time and my father put ashore again. They were simple people and they regarded it as a bad omen but after my father had found an old tin on the shore and a few rusty nails on St. Patrick's Stone he was able to flatten out the tin and mend the hole. "The Saint wants you to have your beads," he said. "Maybe you'll be a man of prayer a priest of God." He took out a small bottle of poteen from his pocket and he gave it to my mother to take a drink and took the rest himself and hurled the empty bottle into the lake. I kept a steady eye on that bottle as it floated with its neck up, and my poor father and mother stared at me as if there was a halo on top of my head. "He'll be a priest," they said, and they kept repeating it like a litany. "He sees things that we don't see." It was years later that I understood their commotion but it was too late to tell them for they were dead then. But they talked about that journey to everyone, and every old woman that came to the house used to put a hand on top of my head as if I were something holy – something that dropped from the sky. But there was one old woman with a withered face that frightened me. One day I told her to go to hell and on that day my sainthood ended. My father was going to slap me but she shouted and laughed: "Leave him be, leave him be! He's just like one of ourselves with as much white in his eye as there is in a duck egg! There's more devil in him than saint. There's more black on his head than there is in a crow's wing. He can pick up bad words as quick as a hen can pick up good grain. And now I'll make good out of bad and I'll give him an old woman's blessing: May the Lord breathe upon him and send him a good wife." '

'And you didn't become a priest after all?' Eileen smiled naively at him.

'I did not. I hadn't a vocation. But maybe some day I'll get someone to marry me and let Martha go where her heart is bent – a nun on the Foreign Missions. What would you think of that?' and before she had time to reply he shot away from her, bounded across the causeway to the boat, and back again with the basket, two cushions, and a rug. They spread the rug on the soft grass below a sycamore tree, and there they lay in one another's arms, and above them the leaves swayed, folding and unfolding the sunlight that moved through the branches. Below them the lake spread wide, sparkling where a thin wind now and then scuffed the water; there was no ebb and flow on its sandy shore, only a few sticks with dried froth, a white feather smooth and unbroken, the marks of birds' feet, and the movement of the fins of perch that sunned themselves in the shallow edges. Unaware of the presence of the lovers the wild duck approached, calling unnervously to one another, the ripples from their feet lipping against the stones of the causeway and making a reflected honeycomb of light on the side of the boat.

It was there that Philip asked her to marry him, telling her how much money he had saved, telling her of the improvements he had made in the house and the improvements he would make on it if she would be his wife. She sat up then, his arm about her waist.

'I couldn't give you an answer, yet,' she said. He was hurt and she felt his arm slip away from her. He lifted a bunch of young sycamore blossom that lay on the grass beside him, and

as he plucked the sticky flowers from their stem he told her
he would do anything for her: he would go and live in the city,
if she wished, and set up as a building contractor. She
wouldn't want him to do that, she said, for she loved the
country, the village, and the river; it was her real home, she
felt, and she could be content in it all her life.

'Then why in God's name can you not give me an answer
now?' he said. 'I suppose I'm not good enough for you!'

'Oh, Philip, how can you say a thing like that?' she said,
hurt. 'Do you think I'd have come down here with you if I'd
thought that? Do you think I would have written to you and
accepted that bangle? Do you think I would face the confes-
sional and deceive myself with such deceit? Philip, you
don't know me yet or you wouldn't come out with a thing
like that. Not good enough for you! What have I? – I have
no sacrifice to make – no profession to give up. I have
nothing to give you.'

'You have yourself to give and that's everything. But it
was your family I was thinking of: Frank will be a doctor,
Anne's a teacher, Brendan's a librarian, and your Uncle
Bob's the richest man in the whole parish. *They* might think
I'm not good enough.'

'And don't forget Uncle D. J.,' she said with slight scorn
and lifted the scraps of sycamore blossom. 'A man that none
of you respects! A man whose pockets are empty. And didn't
he do some theft at the railway years ago, for I heard a woman
in the shop casting it up to Uncle Bob? Isn't that so?'

'There may be some truth in it. But it has nothing to do
with us. Nothing to do with the love that exists between us.'

'It has a lot to do with us. He could cause us many a
heartbreak. He has done so already to Uncle Bob, to my
father, and, if the truth were known, to Aunt Nelly.' There
came to her mind, then, his theft of books from Brendan's
library, his attempt at borrowing money from Philip yesterday, and the encounter she, herself, had had with him in the

thatched cottage and how he had bruised her wrist and would only believe what he wanted to believe – that her father was trying to deprive him from a just share in the shop if Bob should die. She gave a long, loud sigh but said nothing, and dusting the sycamore flowers from her lap she smiled wanly at Philip.

'Eileen, you cannot live another's life like that. What D. J. does or doesn't is his own concern.'

'One would think so! But where a close relationship exists, where there is loyalty and love then a dishonourable act affects the rest.'

Philip couldn't understand why she should feel so deeply for a man that, to his mind, wasn't worth a spent match. He told her what he thought, and since he offered no explanation that could satisfy or solace her, all her anticipated dread lay in a confused and weary heap, terrifying her future, frightening her out of making a decision. And why, after all, should she be afraid, she tried to console herself? She had done no harm. Why then should she be so irresolute, so fearful of tomorrow? God in Heaven, it was wrong of her to be like that – to be so anxious, crowded in by cares, harrying herself with what might never be. She had laughed at Anne the time she was distraught over her row with Miss Mallon and she had laughed and misunderstood Anne's finical anxiety over her selection of a simple Christmas card. Now it had come her own time to be shaken by scruples, to be beset with doubts, and to be fretted with what at times seemed meaningless worry. Two years or a year ago these would have lain lightly upon her and she would have cast them aside without a thought. Now life had changed for her – what you did and said and what others did to you were part of an experience that did not die with each day. That, she told herself, was what growing up meant.

Far across the lake and over the flat fields there came the whistle of the train as it left the station, and presently it rumbled over the bridge and into the country where its white smoke rose above the trees, hung for an instant and then disappeared in thin shreds. Today was Thursday: it was the half-day and Uncle Bob was in that train going off to Magheraglass to see his doctor.

'Philip,' she said, 'I will go home on Saturday and will tell my father and mother all that there is between us. Next week I will come back again and will tell you what I know is true: I love you.'

He kissed her for saying that, and over and over again he told her how happy they could be together. A few strings of rain fell from a sky that was bare of cloud, they fell silver and scant, making large rings in the water that you could count, and Eileen looking at them thought of Anne's compositions and the child who had written: 'The rain made little bracelets on the water.'

'That's just what it is like,' she said aloud, looking at the rings in the water.

'What's like what?' Philip laughed.

'Oh, nothing – I was just thinking,' Eileen said and laughed to hide her discomfort at being caught talking to herself. At that moment, high in the tree above them, the chiff-chaff gave out his two-noted song: chiff-chaff, chiff-chaff, like water dripping from a tap. They stood out from the tree to find the bird and Philip, peering slowly from branch to branch at last discovered it on a topmost twig that swayed under its tiny weight. Try as he could to point it out to Eileen she failed to see it, and the bird continued in a tantalizing way to give out its drip-drop, drip-drop of song. He stood close to her, his cheek against hers, and asked her to look where he was looking; then he stood behind her and resting his outstretched arm on her shoulder he told her to follow the direction of his forefinger but she squirmed under the weight of his arm and he stumbled, the bird flying off and losing itself in the spraying foliage of a silver birch. They laughed at one another and their laughs echoed across the still lake, and echoed also from the walls of the old church that lay browned and warmed by the sun behind them.

They ate the cool tomato sandwiches and drank the thick cream that Martha had prepared for them, and afterwards Philip stole away and visited his parents' grave and did a station for their souls round the ruins of the church. Eileen kicked off her canvas shoes and washed the vessels in the edges of the lake but the blue milky scum spreading out from the cups destroyed the transparency of the lovely leaf-brown water and she looked at it with an injured sense of guilt and repulsion. She moved away from it along the shore, past stones that were grey with dried flaky mud, over the firm hot sand, and sitting on a projecting rock she dabbled her feet in the silky ebbless stillness of the water. She sang aloud to herself and rejoiced in the resonant clarity of her voice as it carried across the lake and echoed from the arching trees that rose behind her.

Cattle were calling to one another from the fields and a mist was rising from the far margins of the lake when they set off for home again. No smoke came from any of the smaller islands, and in the air there was no longer the smell of poteen but as they entered the narrow river the air was smothered with the perfume of hawthorn, and the heat that had matured all day under the warm hedges escaped in drifts across the cold evening water. Every sound was alert and sharp and one could hear the whorl and spin of the water in the clefts scooped out by the oars. They passed small boats fishing for pike, and then a white motor boat passed them bridging the river with large waves.

'That's a boat I built,' Philip said proudly. 'It belongs to Doctor O'Neill. He might lend it to us some day if he could forget that your Uncle Bob is no longer one of his customers.'

'I wouldn't sit in it if that's the conditions under which it would be lent.'

'I won't ask him then,' he said, 'and I'll have no call to – in a year or two we'll have one of our own.'

She smiled pleasantly back at him and trailed her hand in the water. Her bare arms were red from the sun, and time and again she shook water on them to soothe their raw and burning tenderness.

She was tired and listless as she walked home along the river bank carrying her straw hat in her hand. On trunks of trees and old gate posts were coloured posters, glossy with wet paste, announcing a Monster Carnival and Circus. Youths were standing at the gable ends of the village and small boys were trundling rusty hoops out along the road to meet the caravans, the piebald ponies, and the swing-boats. Aunt Nelly was in her garden and she greeted Eileen through the hedge before going to the door to let her in.

The curtains were drawn and the sitting-room was cool and refreshing after the heat of the day. Eileen sat down on the settee with a grateful sigh, closed her eyes for a moment and let her hands fall listlessly by her side. She told of the lovely day that she had had and of Philip's intention of marrying her.

'It's great news, Eileen. It's great. It's great,' said her Aunt, congratulating her and putting her arms around her.

'I'll go home on Saturday and tell father and mother and I'll come back again next week. No letter came this evening?'

'Not a letter, not a scrap!' she said, parting the curtains to let in the evening light. 'Oh, Eileen, they'll be delighted! It'll be a new life for me with you living beside me,' and her voice rose excitedly and then cut off abruptly for she remembered that Bob had gone early to his bed. 'I forgot,' and she put a finger to her lips. 'Your Uncle Bob got a bad report today. The doctor ordered him to rest plenty and avoid over-anxiety. You'd have pitied him, Eileen, to see him come in that door with hardly a breath in him. He noticed his own pallor in the glass and I tried to persuade him it was due to the heat but he kept on saying it was D. J. that was wearing him out.

Oh, if he had taken Doctor O'Neill's advice and gone to the hospital my own belief is he'd be a different man today.'

There was a great commotion in the street outside: dogs were barking, children were shouting, and someone was blowing a bugle. 'It's the circus people,' said Nelly. 'Come on till we have a look at the procession,' and they hurried through the shop. The blind was down and the shadow of the cracked window was visible upon it. Nelly opened the shop door and they stood together on the step and smiled at a cowboy mounted on his horse and blowing a bugle. Behind him came a long line of yellow and green caravans some with weary greyhounds walking underneath between the wheels, others with roofs of shaking canvas, vans crammed with poles and rolled-up tents, swing-boats with their chains clanging, a circle of hobby horses, stiff and wide-eyed, their pink tongues chipped and spotted, their brass stirrups shaking with the movement of the van. Then came piebald ponies with long sweeping tails; dirty men with battered hats, black-haired women with shawls and creaking baskets, and lastly over the level crossing thundered the black steam engine with high thin chest and powerful wheels. They watched it approach and stood well within the door, afraid of its hissing steam and the crunch of the gravel under its wheels. The noise had brought Bob from his bed and he came into the shop, mumbling and lamenting.

'Blast them and their circus and their halfpenny amusements. Who the devil wants to look at them? The same troupe every year and the same noisy old bucket-music that gives me neuralgia.' The engine was opposite the shop now and he could feel the vibration in the boards under his feet. 'It'll shiver the window to remnants. The very lamp on the ceiling is shaking. Blast you! Hurry past before you bring the window crashing on to the street!' At that moment on one of the shelves a mouse-trap snapped in the vibration and Nelly jumped. 'Mother of God that put the heart out of me!'

'That Doran should have fixed that window today. I was a

foolish man to pay him so soon.' Bob went on, angry now because Nelly and Eileen were still laughing over the mouse-trap. 'A gust of wind would make short work of that broken window. If there was a big enough gap in it those thieves of circus men wouldn't think twice of robbing me. What would your father say, Eileen, if he heard you were away your lone on the Island with Philip Doran?'

'He'd hope it didn't rain on them,' Nelly defended. 'Go on to your bed and stop worrying for goodness' sake.'

'I wonder should I bring in a couple of boards and cross them on the inside of that window. Those gypsies are always prowling about at night.'

'Quit worrying, Bob. Bad and all as that crack is it could stand out for many a long month yet. And the gypsies wouldn't be lurking about here and the barracks across the way. Oh, I forgot to tell you,' she said to divert the worry from his mind. 'I think Eileen and Philip will be getting married soon.'

'He'll not do any marrying till he fixes that window if I know anything,' he said absent-mindedly.

'It's Eileen, your own neice, he's going to marry,' Nelly raised her voice, trying to break through his inertness.

'That's good, that's right,' he said, and patted Eileen's shoulder.

'But there's nothing arranged yet, Uncle Bob,' Eileen said. 'I haven't told Philip yet that I would marry him. You see he asked me today and I want to think it over.'

'That's right — always think things over,' Bob said as if he was talking to himself. 'Always think things over. He has a good solid house on the riverside and he could give you a good holiday with the money he got for doing that new window. He'll have to put in a new pane tomorrow. Don't go on any more trips with him till he does that job for your uncle.' He went over to the shop door that Nelly had closed and satisfied himself that it was securely locked. He peered into the window space, following with his eye the shadow of the crack on the blind and at the top the shadow of the jagged hole – a hole hardly big enough, he comforted himself, to swallow a man's fist.

'Do you think it would stand up to a breeze of wind?' he asked Nelly.

'I think it would stand up to a hurricane if that's any comfort to you,' Nelly assured him.

He stood on the small step-ladder and refixed the mousetrap that had sprung. 'It has turned cold,' he said, shrugging his shoulders and rubbing his hands.

'Is it any wonder you feel cold?' Nelly said. 'And you after leaving your warm bed. Shout down if you want a hot jar for I'll be boiling the kettle to make Eileen and myself a cup of tea.'

'I'll be warm enough. I'll put on the eiderdown tonight. Good night to you,' he said from the stairs, 'and if you're saying the rosary don't forget to say a prayer for me.'

CHAPTER THIRTEEN

BOB closed his eyes, and listening to the newsagent's sign swinging in the night wind a fitful sleep crowded upon him. He dreamt that the wind had grown stronger with the night and had widened the crack in the window till it was as broad as a gap in a hedge, and through the gap there stepped three greasy-looking gypsy men carrying huge wicker baskets. They were smoking and all three simultaneously nicked their cigarettes on the heels of their boots and kicked the ashes on to the street. They yawned, stretched their arms, and lazily began to fill the baskets with the display of shirts and ties and caps that was in the window. They impertinently scrutinized each tie before dropping it into the basket and, more often than not, threw it on the floor and snatched a brighter coloured one that took their fancy. Having denuded the window space they stepped out of it into the shop, scraped their feet on the door-scraper that was on the inside of the door, struck matches on the black-leaded stove and relit their cigarettes. They began to throw down the bales of cloth from the shelves and the bales seemed so light that they swayed through the air and alighted upon the ground as softly as a feather. One of the gypsies slowly beckoned to his companions to come up to the top shelf, and they arose, lifting their feet high and sailed up into the air. With rounded mouths they gazed with hushed reverence at a mouse that was caught in a trap. Its eyes were as black as wet ink and there was no movement in them or in the tail. One of the gypsies tapped the red ash of his cigarette on top of the mouse and at once there arose a smell of singed hair; the gypsies laughed, a laugh that had no sound – just a fantastic gesture of mouth and of hands and of eyes. They sailed down to the floor again but one of them alighted on top of the cold stove and with one foot pirouetted himself at such a speed that his coat-tails swirled in a solid circle and the lamp above his head swung in the draught.

'That will do for one night,' they said, and as they lifted their baskets from the floor one of them spotted the half-crown that was nailed to the counter. He levered it up with the blade of his knife, bit it with his teeth, spun it into the air with an oily thumb and finally stowed it in his pocket. Once more they heaved themselves into the window space and stepping out into the street the gap in the window closed up behind them. Out in the street ties and collars and socks fell out from their laden baskets, and a policeman who was standing at the barrack door whistled to them to draw their attention to the loss. He even strode forward himself to help to pick up the articles from the road, and blowing the dust off them he dropped them into the basket, all the time smiling and humming to himself. He was a tall policeman and his bare wrists protruded from the sleeves of his uniform. He laughed. 'You never heard of me! I am Mr. Robert Caffrey's brother. You call me by the musical name of D. J. I personally attend all racecourses – circular ones, elliptical ones, flat ones, and round ones, those in the torrid zone and those in the north frigid zone, those in the tropic of Capricorn and those in the tropic of Cancer. I am the world's best tipster – always come to me. Come back for more shirts if you haven't enough. You are welcome to them – my dark-eyed lovely man.' He sailed back to the barrack door again and going inside he tried to close the door behind him. There was a pebble wedged at the bottom of it and he pulled savagely at the door, the pebble screeching and leaving white scratches on the doorstep. At last the door was free and he banged it behind him, the knocker rising up and tapping twice before coming to rest.

Bob awoke; his hair was plastered with sweat and he pushed off the eiderdown and sat up, listening. He could hear the thump of his own heart but outside there was no sound except the brushing of the wind in the trees. There was a smell of cigarette smoke in the room and he knew that Nelly must have been smoking in bed, the smoke percolating across the landing and in under his door. He got up and looked out on to the street from the open window. The air was pleasantly cold, and he could see lights through the trees from the circus encampment and could hear the sound of a mandolin. It couldn't be very late, he said to himself, and he struck a match and looked at his watch. It was only half an hour after midnight. He pulled on a coat and went downstairs, and the noise of him moving about the shop drew Nelly from her room, and she hurried down to him and upbraided him for walking about like somebody that was losing his senses. She saw him into his bed again, and standing at his window she had to listen to his dream. 'It bodes no good,' he kept saying. 'I'd rest content if the window were repaired.'

'Sure those circus men have been coming here regularly for the past fifteen years and to my knowledge not even a stud or a spool of thread was stolen from the shop. In God's name close your eyes and forget about that window.'

'Do you think will John do something for D. J.? Get him a job in the city and take him out of this. 'Tisn't right or fair for a brother like John to burden me with the likes of D. J. The sight of him sailing through the street gives me a scunder.'

'You'll do yourself harm with all this worrying. Could I bring you a couple of aspirins to settle your nerves?'

'They don't agree with me. They make my heart shake like a weaver's shuttle.'

In the dusky light from the window his face, hair, and arms were visible, and she fixed the clothes around him and gave a despairing sigh. But accidentally she touched the flesh on his arm – it was soft and unmanly, and she recoiled from it with involuntary fear.

'I'm sure that Doran fellow's sound asleep,' he said, pushing down the weight of clothes from around his chest. 'I may tell you I didn't delay long about paying him. I did my part like an honest man.'

'Didn't the doctor tell you to take things easy and not cause yourself any anxiety?' she said impatiently.

'It's not me that's causing myself anxiety – it's other people: John and Doran and the like! People are thoughtless nowadays. They think of nothing but their own comforts.'

'That's just what's wrong with us all,' she said, and gave him a comprehending look that was lost in the gloom of the room. He made no answer. She could never change him. She shook her head and stood at the window looking down at the deserted street and the lights to her left shaking through the trees. In the quiet she could hear the water going over the falls and could hear the rubbing of Bob's hand across his brow – rubbing, rubbing without pause, and making a sound like cattle moving through the night. She put a hand on his brow, and on withdrawing on tiptoe from the room he called her and asked if she herself slept well.

'Not too well,' she said, knowing that it was fear that made him ask her. 'I waken at the slightest sound ... Good night now. Take your beads in your hand and pray yourself to sleep.'

He dozed on and off through the long night, and rising earlier than usual he went downstairs, and on entering the shop he noticed specks of rain like grease marks on the yellow blind. He should have pasted a piece of paper over the hole, he said to himself. He'd make sure to do that tonight if anything prevents Doran from fixing the window. Fix it! He'd have to fix it! And what's more he'd give him timely warning!

He pulled on his overcoat and walked towards the river bank in the cold light of the early morning. The hedges were soaked with a wet mist. The girders of the bridge were polished with rain, and as his boots rumbled over the metal plates the raindrops fell into the river below, and the water-hens disturbed by the unexpected patter flittered across the surface and hid in a cold tangle of weeds. Boats lay soaked and half-filled with rainwater, their mooring ropes tautened with wet-ness and scarcely moving in the drift of the river. He walked steadily past them along the bank, and snails that were returning to the wet grass were crushed beneath his heavy tread.

He halted at Philip's bedroom window that faced the river. It was propped open at the bottom with a hair-brush and through this open space he kept calling and hammering at the window-sill till Philip awoke. Philip sat up in bed and stared at the window.

'It's all right, Philip; it's only me,' Bob said, putting his mouth to the opening.

'In God's Holy Name what's wrong?' Philip said, coming to the window and rubbing his eyes.

'The window, Philip – the window.'

'Sure there's nothing wrong with the bloody window,' Philip said, and he took the brush from below it and pulled it down at the top, sticking out his head and shoulders. 'There's nothing the matter with that window. There's a cord broken in the sash – that's all.'

Bob stared up at him with pained astonishment. 'Is that it?' he said with an ache in his voice. 'Is that it?'

'Is what it?' Philip said. 'What the hell are you talking about? Speak up and don't keep me shivering here in the cold.'

'It's my window I'm talking about – the one we broke with the pole. I want you to start at it as soon as you get your breakfast.'

'Good God! Is that it? And you waken me out of my sleep to tell me that! Do you know what I'd like to do with you – do you? I'd like to bloody well pitch you and your window into that river! Do you hear that?'

'No bad language! No violence now! My nerves wouldn't stand it,' Bob said, stepping back a pace, and going on to describe about his sleepless night and about the great craftsman Philip's father was – a man that wouldn't have closed an eye till his work was wrought to perfection.

'You didn't think much of his peacock when you made me remove it.'

'Even the best of eyes can squint occasionally,' Bob said. 'But that's taking me away from the gaping window.'

'I've ordered the glass from Belfast and if it comes today I'll fix it. I can't do better than that,' and in his anger Philip violently pulled up the window, snapped the snib into place, a piece of dislodged putty falling on to the floor.

Bob turned on his heel and went off. Oh, the thoughtlessness of some people, he commiserated with himself. Nelly was right – thoughtlessness was the trouble. Oh, the selfishness of them! Anyone could see that the broken window was far away from that man's mind! If he hadn't been paid he'd have given more thought to my affairs. Young people nowadays think of nothing only their own comfort. They'd sleep in bed all day if they could live without eating.

As he picked his way over the puddles on the bank the sky above the lough turned a primrose yellow and the slender spikes of the rising sun fanned out above the clouds, then thinned to sharp needles that pricked the shoulders of the falls and sent the water limping and tumbling in a fret of light that pained the tired eyes of Bob. He pulled his hat down to shield himself from its baleful glare. The sun was crooked like everything else – if you wanted it to shine it would go and hide itself!

On nearing the village he saw a woman closing her door and buttoning her coat as she hurried along the road. She was going to morning Mass. There was still an hour or so before the arrival of the first train and there was no better way of spending the time than to go to Mass himself. He went into the house, got his prayer-book, *The Key of Heaven*, and set off. Half way to the chapel he discovered he had forgotten his spectacles, and in the dim light of the building he couldn't read his prayer-book and he fixed his mind on the movements of the priest but it soon wandered to the bald patches on the carpet, to the dirt on his own finger-nails, and to the wall where there was a Station of the Cross which he, himself, had donated to the memory of his parents. He could see the brass plate below the framed station and he knew every letter that was printed on it: 'Of your Charity pray for the souls of Robert and Kathleen Caffrey – R.I.P.'. He was sure that very few of the faithful ever gave a single thought to that plea – they were too much concerned with their own affairs. They were all like that Doran fellow – sleeping as sound as judges and unaware of other people's worries and anxieties.

He yawned, blessed himself, and offered up a prayer for the souls of his parents. He was sure they were in Heaven – they had lived an honest life, never used violent language, minded their own business quietly, and never did anyone any harm. It was true that D. J. was their son as well as he himself was – but then wasn't there a black sheep in every family? Parents can't be held responsible for the ill-doings of their children.

The sound of the priest giving the final blessing turned Bob's eyes to the altar and he blessed himself and rose stiffly for the last gospel. On his way home he walked slowly, saluting, with an uninviting nod of the head, the people who passed him. He wasn't going to encourage any of them to walk home with him – too well did he know that a familiarity with any of them brought an increasing list of names on credit in his books.

Across the flat fields came the whistle of the train and he saw her to his left with her flying scarf of smoke black against the yellow sky. In the village he saw the postman cycle past the shop without stopping. Once again there was no letter from John. He was a strange kind of a father, he thought, that wouldn't think it worth his while to send a line or two to his little daughter. Ah, well, she'd have to swallow her disappointment!

Johnny P.M. was resting on his stick near the window of the shop, unable to sit down on the ledge because of the iron-toothed strip that was fastened along its whole length. Bob opened the door and let him pass in in front of him. He was wanting a pair of bootlaces.

'Are these for Mr. D. J. Caffrey, your lord and master?' Bob said, leaning over the counter with the bootlaces in his hand. 'A man like him with no business to attend to should be up for Mass every morning. He's no good, Johnny, and it beats me why an intelligent man like yourself doesn't bar the door on him some fine night.'

'I'm lonesome,' Johnny said. 'The dog I had was poisoned on me going after sheep and I was my lone after that till your D. J. kept me company. He's the boy knows how to get a good drop of poteen.'

'He's the boy could bring the police down on top of you some fine morning. Do you ever think of that?'

'We do not. We've great crack together in the night. Ah,

if you heard him singing and laughing you'd forget that some day you'd be screwed down in a box no broader than that counter. It's a great gift to be able to sing.'

'There's your laces – three coppers for the pair.'

'Two to a friend of the family,' and he put two pennies on the counter.

Bob withdrew the laces. 'I'll give you the laces for nothing if you do a message for me. Go down to the railway and ask the stationmaster if a pane of glass came for Philip Doran. Wait now,' and Bob scribbled the message on the back of an envelope in case it would slip from Johnny's memory.

In about ten minutes Johnny came back with Bob's newspaper that the newsagent asked him to deliver. There was no glass for Doran on the first train; there was nothing only a consignment of goods for Bob himself.

'There's the laces, Johnny. The porter will wheel up the goods for me,' he said, and he stood at the window watching Johnny shuffle along the road. He looked across at Daly's – his shop wasn't open yet, his window was barely stocked, and a ginger cat lay asleep on the inside of the window. There was no doubt that Daly was going down the hill badly; he had no business methods and the lay-out of his window was as slovenly as himself. He was a jealous man, too, by all accounts, for he had heard that he had laughed himself sick when the pole crashed through the new window. This morning he'd have another laugh when he'd look out and see the crack staring him in the face. 'But it would be his last laugh at my expense,' Bob said aloud to himself. 'If the glass isn't on the second train I'll make Doran send a telegram for immediate delivery of the pane.' He turned from the window, opened out the newspaper on the counter, and put on his spectacles. Eileen came in and asked him if there were any letters.

'There's no letter for anybody. And by the way, Eileen, don't be going off on any more trips with that Doran till he mends the window.'

'Yes, Uncle. But I'm going to go home tomorrow. Mother or father must be sick or they'd have written.'

'It's my belief your father wants no truck with the country. He doesn't want to be reminded of your Uncle D. J.,' and he turned over the paper and went on reading.

Eileen went in for her breakfast and while she was taking it Bob hurried in from the shop, stumbling against the door in his haste. 'Look at this! Look at this!' he said, and placed the newspaper in front of Eileen, pointing with his thumb at a small paragraph in an obscure corner of the paper. Eileen read what was shown to her, her face reddened, and she burst into tears. 'Oh, Uncle Bob, that's terrible – it's terrible!' she cried.

'What's wrong at all?' Nelly said, and lifted the paper, but in her haste could not find what it was that had upset them.

'It's jail that fellow needs. And to think that last night I dreamt about thieves,' Bob went on, pacing the room. 'It's jail! If he were a son of mine I'd squeeze him as I'd squeeze a moth. I'd sweep him from about the place. Nothing but trouble and misfortune for me these days. A broken window, a dishonest brother, and now a thieving nephew – a lovely bit of material! It'll be hurled at me across the counter – and me a peace-loving, honest man!'

'Quit talking and show me where the place is,' Nelly kept repeating.

'It's there in black and white for everybody to see,' and Bob leaned over her shoulder and showed her the place, and she read how Frank with two other youths had stolen four bottles of whisky from the Mountain Inn and that Frank was fined and let off with a caution on the First Offenders' Act.

'I knew something was wrong when they didn't write,' Eileen cried. 'I knew it! And here am I away from all the trouble – enjoying myself – and that going on at home.'

'What kind of a monster are you to show her that?' Nelly turned on Bob. 'Have you no feeling in you at all? Not know when to speak and when to shut up? You that could go about the house for days and not utter one syllable.'

'If I didn't tell her some of the country people would. And they'd not do it as quietly as I did.'

'They'd have nature enough not to say it to a young girl's face!'

'All I get for my honesty is abuse,' and he backed towards the shop.

'There is kind honesty! There is ignorant honesty – it's that that you possess!' she said. 'Go on now to your retreat after putting a blight on the morning.' She put her arm around Eileen's shoulder. 'Don't distress yourself, Eileen girl. Don't be impatient with that which has already happened. If it were important news or scandalous news it wouldn't be stuck below the advertisements for second-hand bicycles. They were hard put to fill space when they inserted that trifle.'

'Oh, Aunt Nelly,' and she shook her head in despair, 'it will break father's heart. Frank, above all! God in Heaven what came over him to make him do a thing like that! He'll be disgraced and maybe dismissed from the university. And what will Philip think of us! We were well thought of at one time but now we seem to be breaking up.'

'Such nonsense! Things like that happen to all of us and we can't prevent them,' Nelly said. 'It's God's will and we must pray for strength to face up to them. Don't be lamenting your lot! You have much to be thankful for: you have a good father and a good mother, you have your health and your appearance – not everyone is as fortunate. And now that Frank has got into bad company and steals a few bottles of whisky you'd think the end of the world had come. I'll be ashamed of you if you don't dry those tears. Don't look again at that miserable rag of a paper,' and she lifted it out of Eileen's hands and burned it in the range. 'Finish your breakfast, Eileen.'

'I can't take another crumb. I'll go home today, Aunty, for each hour away from home would be a weary drag on me.'

She rose from the table and stood at the window, running her finger to and fro along the ledge. Through the trees there came the strokes of a wooden mallet, and she could see the canvas roof of the marquee shaking and billowing as it was being erected, and around it the green caravans shining in the sun.

Philip passed the window and Eileen withdrew with a start.

'That's Philip away past,' Nelly said. 'He'll be going to consult your uncle about that infernal window.'

Eileen ran for the stairs, and her aunt bade her stay where she was for she had done nothing to be ashamed of.

'I can't let him see me like this. He'd know that I was crying,' and she leaned over the banister rail, gazing down at her aunt with an expression of innocent penitence.

'He'll see you in all kinds of weather if I know anything,' Nelly said, determined to drag her away from any self-pitying mood, and she went to the door and spoke in to Philip and told him that Eileen and herself wanted to see him when he was ready. She went on with her work, clearing the breakfast dishes on to a tray, and singing loudly to herself as she washed them.

In about half an hour Philip knocked the door and came into the sitting-room. Nelly was there alone, and the sight of him, freshly shaved and flushed by Bob's unreasonable wranglings, aroused her old affection for him. But she did not take time to dwell on it; she checked it by impulsively rushing forward and grasping his hand with a joy that she forced into her greeting and compelled herself to share. 'Eileen told me all!' she said. 'I'm delighted! I'm delighted! You're getting a lovely girl, Philip. I feel as if it was myself that was getting married and not Eileen. You'll be very happy with her – I know you will!'

'Thank you, Nelly, thank you. I'll be on top of the world this morning if the new pane comes on the second train. I got a letter to say that my estimate has been accepted for the building of twelve labourers' cottages. I'm going to buy a lorry and go into the building trade in fine style. Where's Eileen till I tell her about my bit of luck?'

Nelly called up to her from the foot of the stairs. 'Eileen! Eilee-ee-en!' she called in a high joyful note. Eileen came down slowly and though she tried to get between Philip and the light from the window he noticed she had been crying.

'In the name of God did any of you sleep last night at all?' he laughed. 'Did your uncle keep you all on the go over that dream of his?'

'She's worried over Frank – he got himself into a spot of trouble,' Nelly said with slight gravity. 'But to look at Eileen you'd think the lad had committed murder and all the sins in the calendar. Himself and a few other boys went on a cheap spree – they stole a few bottles of whisky and this morning's paper reported it to fill up space.'

'I wish he had kept me a drop or two of it. I'm telling you it'd been more than welcome after the vision I saw at cock-crow this morning. Bob put the fear of God in me when he stuck his head in my bedroom window at the scrake of day,' and he laughed loudly, and then checked himself in case Bob would overhear him. He beckoned them to him in mock conspiracy, put his arms around their shoulders, and with many a grotesque grimace he told them in a half whisper of Bob's appearance at his window. But the whistle of the train from down the line drew them apart, and before its echoes had subsided Bob burst into the room. 'She's coming, Philip! She's coming! If it's not on her wire at once for immediate delivery. Hurry now like the decent man you are.'

Philip snatched his hat and ran, and Bob followed after him and took up his stand at the shop door, the leaf of his hat jutting out beyond the jamb. The train was in, the wet hiss of her steam muffling all other sounds and investing every movement in the village with exciting and concrete importance. Bob rubbed his hands: 'It'll be on her all right – it'll be on her. She's delaying more than usual. Handle with care! Handle with care! You can't throw a crate of glass about like a bundle of newspapers. Philip would see that they'd handle it with reverence. Easy does it! Take your time, boys, take your time. Leave her to me now – she's as safe and sound as an egg in a box of straw,' and in his mind he followed each careful movement of the unloading of a crate of glass.

The train whistled and moved off, and as its heavy sound whirred away in the distance each voice in the village fell about Bob's ears like a shout. The level-crossing gates were swung back into their place but no one as yet had come out of the station. 'It'd be better to go down and give Philip a hand,' Bob said to himself; he buttoned his coat, then, and was ready to step from the door when he saw his brother John, and Anne and Philip come slowly out from the station together. Bob backed into the shadow of the doorway, hurried behind the counter and tried to compose himself by sorting and arranging a bundle of stockings in their proper sizes. Time and again he gave a sharp, furtive glance at the window but there was no sign of them. It'd suit Philip better, he thought, to get ahead with the window instead of wasting the precious morning gossiping and floostering to no purpose. At last they reached the window where they halted, all talking at once, and Philip's voice loud above the rest in praise of his own part in the renovation. John, too, was commenting on its fresh and smart appearance and the greater light it must afford to the inside of the shop. Their voices fell – 'the peacock' was mentioned a few times; again their voices fell almost to a whisper and then Philip laughed loudly. Laughing at how the window was broken, Bob thought – they'd laugh less if they had to foot the bill.

Anne came through the open door and held out her hand. 'I'm glad to see you, Uncle Bob. And the new front is the last word. And look at the brightness it throws in here. But, Uncle Bob, you shouldn't have removed the peacock – it was unique in a way.'

'If I'd known you'd such an interest in it I'd have sent it up to your pupils – they could have had a good day's laugh to themselves.'

'But, Uncle, there was art in it.'

'There was the devil in it if you heed me,' he said tartly as Philip and John entered. Without greeting his brother he stared at Philip and said: 'Well?'

'It hasn't come,' Philip said.

'And are you going to stand moping there with your hands in your pockets like a retired gentleman? Send off the wire at once!' and he waved his hand with a curt dismissal.

'He has made a fine job of it,' John said. 'And you needn't worry about that crack – it could stand for many a long year as it is.'

'It'll not stand there another twenty-four hours if I have my way. I'm sick to death of that Doran. All he's good for is collecting his debts. I was the foolish man to pay him. I should have bided my time till I saw how his material weathered rain and storm.'

Eileen and Nelly came hurrying into the shop, and Eileen ran to Anne and then to her father.

'Upon my word you are well improved,' he said, making her stand out from him. 'Your uncle and aunt have been more than good to you.' Though he smiled she noticed that he was shrunken and pale and that his lower lip trembled as he spoke, and when she sought his eyes he glanced away from her, fearful of what she might read in them. He continued to talk to her with a forced brightness, endeavouring to disguise the grief-distracted feeling that Frank had caused. They moved into the sitting-room and he congratulated her on her engagement to Philip Doran. 'She didn't waste her time in the country,' he said to Nelly. 'Philip told us the great news coming up the street.'

Eileen blushed. 'There's nothing settled yet, father. And I'm not engaged to anyone.' She twisted the bangle on her wrist, and when Nelly and her father were seated on the settee she motioned to Anne with her eyes and they went off to the summer-house in the garden where Eileen immediately divulged what she had read in the morning's paper. The sharp excitement of the arrival and the unexpected meeting of Philip at the station, were at once submerged as Anne drew together from her mind an account of Frank's fall.

'It was a frightful blow, Eileen,' she said, 'and I feel that I could have prevented it if I had been honest and told father and mother the truth I had known about Frank.'

'What truth?' Eileen asked.

Anne shook her head and rested her brow on her hand. 'My mind, Eileen, is so fagged and dredged that I can't even think consecutively. Since the detective called at the house three weeks ago we've all been living in a kind of stupefied despair. He told father that Frank was caught with two other youths after they had broken a shop window and stolen a few bottles of whisky. Frank didn't do the stealing but he shared in the theft.'

'But sure Frank doesn't drink.'

'Father was worried thinking that Frank might be dismissed from the university if the theft were given publicity. But when he called at the secretary's office in the university he discovered – what Brendan and myself had already known – that Frank wasn't enrolled as a second medical at all.'

Anne raised her head, glancing at the river flowing in smooth but rapid peace. She paused, undecided what to reveal and what to conceal, wondering should she spare her sister what father had discovered in Frank's suitcase – a pawn ticket for a case of silver spoons, the silver spoons that had already been blamed on a dishonest charwoman. But the discomfited and harried expression in Eileen's eyes dissuaded her and she sat erect in order to control herself and to struggle against what her tongue would speak but not her mind.

'Since last Christmas Day,' she went on, 'I knew Frank

182

wasn't enrolled. On that day, in a fit of momentary anger, he told me, and I implored him in Heaven's name not to tell father and mother. In my foolishness I thought I could have protected them from some sorrow. Things we think are for another's good often turn out to be for their harm. The perversity of it sours me; it would have been better, much better, not to live day after day with the deceit and the lies, for they only breed and live upon themselves, drawing tighter the loop of confusion they carry with them. Father has got over it: "It took it all to bring home to me that Frank was not ordained for medicine or for study," he said last night. And he made the journey this morning to ask Uncle Bob to take Frank into the shop for a few months and then he could get him started in his own shop in town as a youth with experience.'

'Uncle Bob will never agree to it,' Eileen said. 'He went into a rage after reading about it in the paper.'

'If he doesn't we'll have to get over it. We can all outgrow it except Frank. It's Frank that I am sorry for. That misfortune, slight though it is, will follow him and people in anger will not let him forget it. And why, why he did it is beyond me. Why he spent his enrolment fees and why he took to drink. Father, above all, had not forced him to do medicine – that was Frank's own choice though he wouldn't admit it. But we'll not talk about it any more,' and she raised her head to the clothes swaying on the line, and their shadows narrowing and broadening on the grass. She went to the hedge and looked down at the boats and the water winding round their mooring poles. She breathed in the soft, slumberous air and asked Eileen to walk with her as far as the falls.

They walked slowly along the path and they talked mostly of Philip, talked without pausing so as to thrust from their minds the joyless presence of Frank's disgrace. On returning to the house they met Philip arriving with a telegram to say that the glass would be dispatched at once.

'There's nothing like sending a telegram, Philip,' Uncle

Bob said. 'A letter or a phone call wouldn't produce an immediate response. Always send a telegram if you want anything done.' He rubbed his hands and went in for his dinner. He ate more than usual and he even expressed regret that Eileen was going home this evening and would miss the bit of fun at the circus. Indeed he would have brought her himself to the circus if the window had been mended and her father hadn't arrived to take her home.

'Eileen can stay if she likes,' her father said. 'That's not what brought me to the country.'

Bob displayed no interest in the remark, and it was only after the girls and Aunt Nelly had gone off to visit Philip's sister that John gathered enough courage to approach him about Frank. He waited until there were no customers in the shop and going in quietly he once again spoke of the fine alteration, and then with embarrassment he explained how Frank had fallen in with bad company. Bob's interested silence misled him, and with confident candour he disclosed his plan for Frank's future and how he could get him appointed in his own shop in the city if only he had a few months or a half-year's experience in a country drapery store.

'You're idling your time if you think I'd have a blackguard like that about this place,' Bob said with an unexpected sharpness that startled his brother. 'It was in the paper this morning for everyone to read. There's a drop or two of D. J. in him, I'm thinking.'

'I wouldn't expect you to give him any wages. In fact I would give you a premium of fifty pounds if you'd take him. You could do a lot of good for the lad himself and for us all by agreeing to take him.'

'Take my advice and pack him off to Australia,' and he took down a narrow box from the shelf and attached price tickets to the ties he drew from it.

'He might go to the bad completely if he were away from home.'

'Wouldn't he be good riddance?' Bob said tersely.

John stared at him, casting upon him a look half of scorn, half pity. Living alone, he thought, must have led his mind into a dark mould of inhuman and callous feeling. He looked out of the window at the stretched awning shaking in the wind. 'You mightn't know it, Bob,' he said looking away from him, 'that a man's children are as close to him as the fingers of his own hand. I would rather Frank to be living where I could see him – even if the seeing of him brought despair – than he to be living away from me and maybe accusing me with hate in his heart for turning him off when he had only the sense of a youth and all a youth's extravagance. It would be wrong to shirk my responsibility towards him – wrong to get rid by any means of that which injures our respectability or causes us discomfort. Perhaps if D. J. had been left a share in the shop he might have been a different man today.'

Bob laughed, took down another box from a shelf and snipped the twine that tied it. 'I never heard the like of that in all my life – never. D. J. in a shop! Well, well, well – that's the best ever I heard. You're getting soft in the head, John. First it's Frank, and now it's D. J. Two lovely blackguards – a fine pair of bed-fellows.'

'You'll not take him in?'

'I declare to God I wouldn't have him standing at this counter for a single day – not for a single, solitary day. I'm a lover of peace and of honest dealing. I bother with no one and give no one any trouble. I want to be left alone.'

John walked out of the shop without a word, wandered about the country roads that he had known as a boy, and he walked quickly in order to quell the rush of fierce enmity that he felt at that moment towards his brother. Never at any time did he feel like striking him as he did then. But he mustn't think about it. He passed the cottage where D. J. lived but there was no one at the door or in the fields around it, and he walked on to the white schoolhouse and the river at its back where his old Master, Cullen, used to fish during school hours. The school was closed for the day and all the children gone home. Crows picked up crusts of bread from the playground, and under a hedge a thrush was rustling among scattered lunch-papers and shaking out the crumbs. It'd be a pleasant school for Anne to teach in, he thought; it was small enough and she could be her own boss and he wouldn't have to listen to Miss Mallon or her brother complaining to him eternally of her independent ways and of her new-fangled methods of teaching that would get her nowhere. He'd speak to Anne about the Monabeg school and she might be able to elbow her way in when the present old schoolmistress retires – the same old blade shouldn't have long to go for he was sure she was as old as himself. If she saw him now speeding along the road at this gallop she wouldn't believe it. Ah, there's nothing like a good walk for flattening out a raw-edged temper – nothing like it! He slowed down on reaching the old demesne wall and stopped to look at the rusty gates propped closed in the middle by the aid of a large boulder. He looked through the bars of the gate at the rabbits lying in the evening sun; they pricked their ears on hearing him at the gate, and then hopped off the weed-grown drive into the longer grass. Times had changed since he was a boy. The gate-keeper's lodge was empty, the diamond-paned windows broken here and there, and stuffed with sods of grass or old sacks to keep the draught off some sheltering tramp. In one corner slates had blown off the roof showing the framework underneath. It's pity, he thought, to see such a solidly built house going to rack and ruin. You could buy it for a song and it wouldn't take much to renovate it. It'd suit D. J. – they might be able to get him to settle in it after he gets the old age pension; it would be better than the workhouse, for that's surely to be the end of him if he continues the way he's going. He'd suggest that to Nelly, and maybe with Philip's help at renovating it they could settle him there for the rest of his days. He looked at his watch and saw that he had less than an hour to catch the train and taking off his hat he set back along the road at even a faster pace.

He reached the village with about six minutes to spare. Anne and Eileen were waiting for him and they passed into the shop in front of him, Aunt Nelly carrying Eileen's case. He could hear Eileen thanking her uncle for the lovely holiday and he held back till they had passed into the street. He approached his brother and for the last time asked him to take Frank into the shop even for a month – that's all he'd ask and he'd be for ever grateful to him. He was out of breath as he spoke. There was a strange hurried look on his face and it suddenly reminded Bob of Mrs. Bruce, the fork in her hand and her wild threatening fury. It all came back with a relentless, wrenching force and Bob raised his voice against it: 'No, no, no!' he shouted, and brought his fist down on top of a cardboard box and burst the lid. John passed into the street. People were hurrying to the circus and through the trees could be heard the harsh and inharmonious music and the rapturous cries of children as they curved aloft in the swing-boats. D. J. was standing at the newsagent's window and as John stretched out his hand in welcome D. J. shrugged his shoulders and said with expressive spite: 'On manoeuvres again for Bob's cash!' and before John could reply he turned on his heel and walked away from him. John made a few tentative steps to follow him but already the porter was swinging back the level-crossing gates and Anne had run out of the station to tell her father to hurry. He looked back but there was nothing to be seen in the village street except Bob with his long pole pushing back the awning into its place. The train slid into the station in powerful silence, and as Aunt Nelly bid them all goodbye she asked Eileen to come back again soon.

'She'll be back with her wedding trousseau,' Anne chaffed as she and Eileen leaned out of the window and waved their hands to Nelly.

On her way out from the station she met D. J. 'It's gone,'

he said. 'I should have spoken to Anne and Eileen – I hold no spite against the girls.'

'You should hold no ill will to the man that has befriended you so often.'

'He's a cute man the same John. You yourself will need to look sharp for he's after Bob's money.'

'He's out to do his best for his family and if you or Bob had that responsibility you'd be much better than you are. Bob is responsible to nothing only his shop and you think of no one except yourself.'

They walked together through the village street and sensing that he had peeved her he asked if she would go to the circus with him. She hesitated for a moment. 'All right,' she agreed. 'Wait here for a moment.'

She went into the shop. On the floor lay Bob, the pole against the stove. She ran to him. 'Bob,' she said. 'Bob!'

'There's something wrong with me,' he answered, scarcely able to breathe. He held his stomach. 'Something's happened – get Doctor O'Neill.'

'Will I get the priest?'

'I've little to confess,' and he closed his eyes, his head resting on the floor-boards of the shop.

She ran out and told D. J. to get the doctor. She ran to the barracks and asked them to phone for the priest for Bob Caffrey.

D. J. with long strides rushed out along the road to the doctor's, doing what he thought he'd never do: distressing himself for Bob's sake. The end has come, he thought, and he was surprised that he found no exhilaration, no feeling of joy in an end he had waited for so long; and as he rushed along he cursed for no reason the music of the fairground and the hum and stir of the excited carefree crowd. Turning on to the drive he remembered the wintry day when he had called secretly on the doctor to inquire about Bob's ailment and how on his way back from that visit he had encountered John and Bob on the snowy road. It seemed a long, long time ago – a long time to have to wait, and having waited so long what would be the end of it?

He knocked loudly at the doctor's door and had scarcely breath enough in his body to tell him what had really happened.

'He should have called on his Magheraglass doctor,' Doctor O'Neill said with a coldness that astonished D. J.

'For the love of God come on and attend him!' D. J. said. 'He's in a bad way! Nelly sent me!'

The doctor lifted a hat from the hallstand, took out his car, and drove into the village. He asked Nelly and a policeman to leave the shop till he examined the patient. He let up the new blind to let in more light and he bent over Bob who was lying on the floor.

'Ah! It's a bad haemorrhage,' he announced to Nelly. 'It's possible that it is a perforated ulcer. With your permission I'll drive him to St. Jude's Private Hospital – he'll be well attended there.'

The priest came as Nelly was getting on her hat and coat. Kneeling on the floor he heard his confession and then assisted him into the doctor's car, and with Bob's head resting on Nelly's arm the doctor drove off to the city. At a level crossing they had to wait, and as the train that was bearing John and his family rattled past Nelly looked through the window in an effort to catch a glimpse of Eileen or Anne, but she saw nothing only the blank blurred streak of windows and a flying shroud of smoke. And then silence flowed back, filling up the gaps and the hollows, and she could hear the ticking of the clock in the car and Bob's breathing, insistent with unknown fear.

The lights were being lit in the city when they reached it, and on returning to the village it was dark and silent with not even the glimmer of a light or a noise from the circus field. D. J. was waiting for Nelly at the side door as Doctor

O'Neill's car stopped, and after she had thanked the doctor and bade him good night D. J. joined her and they went into the house together. He poked up the range and filled the kettle while she sat on an armchair, taking off her hat, and sighing loudly to ease the heavy feeling of pain and fatigue that weighed upon her.

'The wick's too high in that lamp, D. J. – lower it a little or you'll crack the globe,' and she turned the hat in her hand as if admiring it for the first time. But she wasn't thinking of the hat or the hatpin that she kept pushing into the crown of it in an absent-minded way. Realizing what she was doing she left it on the table beside her and with her hands resting on her lap she related how Bob was taken from the car on a stretcher and how she had waited to see him into his bed in the hospital.

'A lovely room they have given him – comfortable and quiet and a pink eiderdown on the bed, hot and cold water, a lovely wardrobe for his clothes, and a statue of the Child of Prague on the mantelpiece. And, God forgive me, I could have laughed on seeing a cabinet gramophone that was in the corner.'

'But how was he when you left him?' D. J. said.

'I'm afraid he's done. He'll never get over it. Ah, if only he had stayed with Doctor O'Neill, if only he had heeded him long ago and gone up to town for the X-ray he mightn't be where he is now. But it's God's will and we needn't complain now at what wasn't done. It'll be a terrible blow to John. I'll have to phone him in the morning. I'd have called at the house this evening only I disliked delaying Doctor O'Neill or impose any more on his overkindness. What would we have done only for him?'

The kettle began to boil and as she wet the tea she asked D. J. to stay with her for a few days till she grew accustomed to the loneliness of the house.

'I'll gladly do that, Nelly – you can depend on me. The two

of us might be able to keep things going as usual till Bob himself comes out.'

'We might,' Nelly said wearily. 'We might.' And as she passed a cup of tea to him she tried not to notice the dirt that was on his hands. Surely he'll wash himself now that he's in a house where there's plenty of water and good clean soap.

CHAPTER FOURTEEN

IN the morning D. J. rose early and lit the fire. He shaved himself with a razor of Bob's and, on Nelly's advice, fitted himself out in a new shirt and tie. He swept out the shop, and coming upon the mouse-traps he brushed them all on to his shovel and tossed them in a heap in the yard. He prized up the lead half-crown that was nailed to the counter and put it in his pocket, and when Nelly called him for his breakfast he sat down at the table with an air of genteel refinement and explained how he intended to run the shop. She interjected an odd word or two of advice and warned him not to allow any customer credit until he had first consulted with her. He agreed to a suggestion that he would enter in a special note-book the details of his daily sales, for it was only by such method could she satisfy her own conscience and hope to satisfy Bob's by the time he was able to be up and around again. She, herself, would try to give a hand at the counter and keep things running as smoothly as Bob would wish.

After breakfast she phoned John at his shop and then phoned the hospital and was pleased to hear that Bob had had a comfortable night and that an X-ray examination would be made immediately. She would be informed later if an operation were necessary. Returning to the shop she found D. J. had taken up his stand behind the counter, and she was surprised at the grave and preoccupied look that he cast upon her. He was taking his job seriously, she told herself, and perhaps this measure of responsibility would transform him and entice him to co-operate with all of them.

D. J. had not long to wait for his first customer, an old woman who, after expressing her sorrow for Bob, ordered a yard of red flannel but on noticing the extravagant stretch of D. J.'s measurement she said: 'Och, D. J., you may as well give me two yards when you're at it. I'll always find some use for it.'

'There's nothing like taking it when it's freshly in stock. It's my own unvarnished opinion that the price of woollen goods will soar like a lark in the coming months,' and once again he unrolled the bale of flannel and liberally measured a yard on the brass rule attached to the counter.

'God bless that sweet stretch of yours. 'Tis a great pity you and Bob weren't partners. Now, now, I'm not saying an ill word about Bob. He was a man that never kept shoddy or dozed material – I can say that for him. And I can also say he's left the right man in charge.'

D. J.'s generosity soon spread throughout the countryside and those who remembered how he had pilfered the Railway Company's money were now willing to forget it. 'He was a changed man,' they all agreed. 'There wasn't a Caffrey like him for giving you a bit of discount. Even his own father couldn't hold a candle to him for decency.'

Nelly took over on occasions but, if she did, she attracted few customers and those who happened to come in when she was serving were not taken aback and they'd politely ask for some paltry article: a stud, a spool of thread, or a packet of pins; and on withdrawing from the shop they would dally about the village until such times as D. J. had once more taken command at the counter.

At night he would carry in the till-drawer and spill its contents on the table in front of Nelly and proceed then to enter into the special notebook the list of items he had sold in a day's sale.

'It's not that I don't trust you, D. J.,' she would say as she helped him to spell out the words he was laboriously writing down. 'It is that Bob would want me to render an account of every idle halfpenny that crossed or re-crossed the counter. You know the kind of man he is.'

'I do. And I think it would be better for all concerned that I was treated as a paid hand. I'll take my day's wages each evening. Bob would prefer that.'

'He'd prefer something else if I know anything,' Nelly would say. 'God knows how he'll take it. If I told him of the arrangements he wouldn't rest hand or foot in the hospital – he would be up and out if he could manage it. But he's a sick man and I am doing what is best for him and for us all.'

At the end of a week Bob was operated upon and on the third day after the operation Nelly set off to visit him. She would be able to tell him that Philip Doran had repaired the window – that would relieve his mind on that score; and she would be able to tell him that she was managing the shop as best she could. But about D. J. she was determined to keep her silence.

Before she arrived at the hospital Bob had been sleeping and on wakening he found a nurse standing beside the bed taking his pulse.

'How do you feel, Mister Caffrey?' she asked him, and placed her hand on his moist brow.

'I'm better, I'd like to go home.'

She smiled at him with professional dignity. 'Home! Well, it's good to hear you talk like that. But you need a long rest, Mister Caffrey, after that operation. You must give yourself a chance and not be yearning so soon for home.' She fixed the pink eiderdown around him and humming to herself crossed to the sunny window and looked down at the traffic moving on the road. 'It's a lovely day,' she said over her shoulder, and pushed up the window to let in the cool air. 'Anything you want, Mister Caffrey, just ring the bell,' and she tidied the things on his table.

'I'll not want much, Nurse; my needs are small,' he said with a forlorn look that roused her sympathy.

'Cheer up like a good man. We've given you the brightest room where you can get your fill of sunshine. We're doing our best for you — it's your brother's wish.'

'Hm!' he sighed and closed his eyes. He opened them again languidly. 'What's that buzz I hear? Is it in my ears?'

The nurse listened. 'That's the hum of the city you hear — you'll forget all about it as soon as you're able to take solid food again.'

'I was never a big feeder at any time.'

'You'll wonder what you can do in another few days. You'll be able to take some nice chicken soup.'

'Don't go to any trouble about me, Nurse. I don't want to give anyone any trouble. A light cup of tea will do me.'

'I wish all our patients were as easy to please as yourself,' and she smiled to him and walked backwards to the door just as Nelly knocked it and walked in. They exchanged a few words to one another and the nurse praised him as a lovely patient patient.

Nelly sat on a chair with her back to the window. He was thinner, his upper lip sunken, his eyes glazed, and clear beads of moisture oozing out on his brow. He was a done and broken man, she thought; and as a rush of warm protectiveness flooded her soul she opened her handbag on her lap, pretending to search for something till she had quelled the feeling that might betray her thoughts to him. But he didn't give her time to collect herself. He plied her with endless questions and didn't wait for her to answer them. 'Did that Doran fellow fix the window? . . . Are things going smoothly? . . . Hope D. J. is not pestering you? — keep him at arm's length . . . Don't be soft with him . . . Give no credit till I come out . . .' She, in turn, pleaded with him not to worry, not to fret, and that he would find everything to his satisfaction when he would come home in another fortnight.

'Another fortnight! Merciful God in Heaven! Who told you I'd be cooped up here for another fortnight? It's outrageous, it's a swindle – I'll be fit to go home in a day or two,' and he flexed the fingers of his right hand to show the power of his regaining strength. 'There's how I feel, Nelly. There's not a grain or tint of neuritis in that right hand of mine. It was the ulcer that was poisoning it and stiffening it and dirtying my clean blood. It's gone now and I'll be fit to go home in a couple of days.'

'Like a good man abide by what the doctor says. It was your disobedience on that point that brought you to this condition. Oh, many a time I say to myself, "If only Bob had listened to Dr. O'Neill from the first and travelled to town for the X-ray he mightn't be lying on his back away from his own fireside".'

'There's something in what you say. But you know as well as I do that it was D. J. who made me change my doctor.'

'Before ever D. J. returned to the country you were determined not to go next or near the X-ray machine.'

'It was D. J. that ruined my health,' he said with a rush of anger that worried her for his own sake. 'Don't I know what I'm talking about!'

'There, now, don't distress yourself over the head of that. Lie back on the pillow like a good man.'

'I'm propped up here like an Eastern prince. I can see everything without raising my head from the pillow. Look at the style of the bed would you. And look at the fruit on the silver dish – fruit that I never touch. And look at the thickness of that carpet—it could muffle the sound of a steam engine. What are you laughing at? It's no laughing matter. The longer I stay here the more I'll have to pay for the pleasure of looking at those things. It's an outrageous swindle if they intend to keep me here for another fortnight. Once I can get the weight of my foot under me I'll soon show them who's the boss.'

'What does it matter, Bob, if they kept you for two months as long as they send you home cured? If you get a relapse at home where are you?'

He stared at her with cold speculation and nodded his head with absolute disdain. He closed his eyes and she, herself, remained silent waiting for this raw-edged, impatient mood to pass from him. All the way in on the train she had kept thinking of him, expecting to find him broken by sickness and made generous-hearted by the nearness of death. And yet there he was with his mind unchanged, tight-packed and crusted with unnecessary worry and narrow contempt. Surely the doctor or the priest has politely asked him before this if he had had all his affairs in order. She had heard somewhere that that was the procedure in these hospitals before they put elderly men under the chloroform. There was one thing certain she could never have brought herself to ask him that question – from herself he would have taken it as a reproach, as a self-willed hope that she wanted rid of him. He was always difficult, and now if he takes it into his head to go home before his time nothing will stop him except, perhaps, the weakness that he must be feeling in his legs.

There was a polite knock at the door and John entered quietly and with him was Eileen with a bunch of carnations and Brendan with two library books under his arm. Bob still lay with his eyes closed and made no sign that he had heard that knock. They tiptoed across the floor and spoke in whispers to Nelly.

'Speak up all of you,' came a voice from the bed, 'and don't be like a band of conspirators. I'm not that far through that I can't take part in a bit of talk.'

'We thought you were asleep,' John apologized. 'Well, how do you feel today?'

'I'd feel much better if I were at home and away from this high-priced hotel. But nobody wants me at home, I can see that. I'd be too much bother at home if I had to lie in my bed for a day or two.'

'That's untrue and unjust,' Nelly said, hurt.

'We'd all help,' John put in. 'And there's Eileen and she'd go to the country this very minute if it were necessary.'

'I would indeed,' Eileen corroborated.

'Then why don't you bring me home?'

'Bob dear, you're not as fit as you think you are,' Nelly said. 'As soon as you'd try to walk you'd find your poor legs wouldn't support you. Have patience – you may be sure the doctor won't let you overstay your time.'

'You're a nice comfort I must say. All you bring me is a bag of annoyance.' He stared at Eileen and went on: 'If those flowers are for me you can cart them home again. What does a man like me want with flowers I ask you . . . And are those books for me?' and he shot a glance at Brendan. 'Didn't I tell you last week that I'm not a reader? It's plain to be seen that nobody heeds a word I say. And I was shoved into this private hospital without my leave or licence.'

Nelly got up from her chair. She couldn't listen to him any longer. Their presence was jarring him, and each word she spoke seemed to grind his worn-out nerves. He'd pick up all right if only he had the patience to give himself rest. Was the nurse sincere when she praised his patience or did she only say that to comfort her?

She leaned over the bed and put her hand on his moist brow, soothing it and telling him he'd be as fit as a fiddle soon if only he obeys the doctor.

'I'll drop in tomorrow,' John said from the door.

'And I'll be back at the end of the week,' Nelly said.

'I'll go home then,' Bob said.

'We'll see.' Nelly nodded and closed the door behind her with slow nervousness.

She went home with John for a cup of tea, and at the table they all agreed that he was a difficult patient and as difficult to manage as a spoilt child.

'To my knowledge he was never a whole day in bed in his life,' John said. 'And men like that are a problem when they're ill.'

'He has worn himself out,' Anne said, 'and the inactivity of lying in bed is new to him. You shouldn't cross him. Let him talk away and take his side in everything he suggests. Whatever you do don't cross him.'

Nelly suddenly put down her cup and let out an involuntary cry: 'If he hears that D. J. has charge of the shop it'll kill him. I don't know what to say, what to do, or how to think. My mind's in a pother. I seem to have become an old woman.'

'Nonsense, Nelly,' consoled Mrs. Caffrey, 'you have every article accounted for.'

'It's a thousand pities you didn't think of Frank at the time,' John said.

'You know how that would have turned out. D. J. would have tormented the life out of him, day and night. I did the right thing no matter what happens.'

'I wouldn't have gone without Uncle Bob's consent. I've some pride left in me,' Frank intervened with a boldness that made Aunt Nelly forget the disquiet of her own mind.

'All I can say is you'd have been a lucky boy to get a bit of experience in your uncle's shop,' his father said.

'I told you before, Father, that I don't believe I'd relish the drapery business. I'd like to be a purser on a trans-atlantic vessel.'

'You don't know what you want,' his father said crossly. 'You're as restless as your Uncle D. J. and mark my words you'll come to no good.'

To ward off a scene Anne laughed. 'Purser on an Atlantic liner! Sure the time we crossed to the Isle o' Man you were sea-sick going and worse coming back. You'd be safer with a good solid board under your feet.'

'Keep your insulting remarks for your quarrels with Miss Mallon. I don't need to be taught what to think,' Frank turned on her.

'That'll do, children, that'll do,' their mother said. 'Aunt Nelly has enough on her mind without listening to your senseless bickering. I'm sure she's surprised at you.'

But Aunt Nelly wasn't surprised at anything they said or did. The distraction had left her mind numbed and unresponsive, insensitive to flashes of anger, and she yearned only for rest, for sleep, for silence. When she arrived back in the village D. J. had the shop closed and he was sitting smoking in the kitchen, his day's takings in little cylindrical piles on the table, the notebook beside them with a pencil marking the place.

He saw how she flopped down on a chair when she came in, and without a word he rose, spread the cloth on the table, and made her a cup of tea. Deep down within him, she told herself, there was some good in him – all her life she had never known Bob to hand her a cup of tea and she dropping off her feet with fatigue.

'You're very kind D. J. to make that for me,' she said while she was taking the tea. 'You could have knocked me down with a feather as I came in that door, I was so exhausted.' And she spoke then of Bob and how the doctor had hoped to be able to send him home in another fortnight.

'The evening he lay on the floor of that shop I thought I'd never see him alive again,' D. J. said. 'Do you think the doctor's not sending him home to die? How does Bob himself look?'

'He's the colour of that wall and his neck, God save us, is as thin as your wrist. And as for talk – his tongue never ceased. And he was always a man of few words. His load of talk frightened me.'

'That's a result of the chloroform. I suppose he rambled in his mind like as if he were drunk.'

'He did not. He said he was going home and that no one would keep him there beyond his wish.'

'In that case he'll be home and my term of office will soon be at an end.'

'You needn't leave until I see him again at the end of this week. It's my own belief that he's not as well as he thinks he is.'

A change came over D. J. the next day. A fit of his old recklessness seized him; he desired excitement – to live the way he wanted to live, without restraint or deference to other people. In the evening he invited some of his friends to play cards with him after the shop was closed. He pulled down the blind and by the light of the oil-lamp they stood around the counter where D. J. dealt the cards. He allowed Johnny P.M. to come in as a spectator and since he was too small for his head to crane above the counter he pulled forward the small step-ladder so that he could sit on the top rung. They smoked and spat on the floor. They raised their voices in argument and Nelly stared in at them through the square of window space in the kitchen door.

'You're sister's peerin' at us,' they said to D. J. without raising their eyes from the cards in their hands.

'Let her peer away,' D. J. answered, slapping a card down on the counter. 'I'm boss here till my brother Bob returns. I'm boss.'

For the next four nights he invited them, and each night Neily protested and pleaded with him not to degrade the shop by turning it into a gambling school. She told him it would be better for him to go off and live with Johnny P.M. in his thatched house. He refused to go. She threatened to call in the police but that only made him worse. He got angry with her and said he had as much right to look after her brother's property as she had – and more right than she had for, after all, she was only a half-sister.

'Oh!' she cried. 'If only I'd known you were going to change like this I wouldn't have had you near me.'

'I may only have another week or less of it. You'll have Bob home then. I have kept the place honestly and you shouldn't complain of a game of cards. What is there in that?'

'What will Bob think of it if he gets to hear about it? And the spits on the floor that's enough to raise a plague. For the love of God have some respect for the place!'

But it was no good talking to him and she could turn to no one for help. She pined now for Bob's homecoming. She slept badly for she was afraid of a cigarette butt setting fire to the shop, and each night she arose from her bed with a candle in her hand and stealing downstairs she went into the shop where the mice rustled away from her and her own tilting shadow on the ceiling startled her. She groped around the cold stove with her fingers, rooting among the dead matches and butts and dust that had been swept under it; and then when her fears were allayed she would go to the pump for a drink of fresh water and stand for a moment in the cool night air and watch the stars twirling in the river. In bed she would take her beads in her hand and pray for strength to bear the sorrow she had brought upon herself by her own fault.

CHAPTER FIFTEEN

ON the following Saturday Nelly went off by an early train to visit Bob, and because there was a point-to-point race-meeting about eight miles from the village D. J. spent most of the morning in his shirt-sleeves at the door and gazed with impotent dissatisfaction at the lorries moving on the road towards the racecourse. It was a warm day and the dust rose up in gritty clouds from the road and in no time had blurred the shine on the door-scraper that Nelly had blackleaded the previous evening. Later, groups of cyclists passed through the village, and then traps and sidecars, and finally Daly from across the street closed his shop with scornful abandon and without as much as a nod to D. J. he mounted his bicycle and set off after the tail-end of the traffic. A motor car trailing a horse-box came next and as it slowed down to avoid the bumping at the level crossing the yellow head-cover on the horse seized D. J.'s forlorn attention and he withdrew sharply from the doorstep, pulled down the blind of the shop, and without a second's thought to what he was doing he wheeled Nelly's bicycle from the yard and set off with the intention of hurrying back before the last race.

He cycled along the road over the level crossing, his knees almost hitting the handlebars, his feet going round rapidly, and little or no speed coming from the bicycle. There was no substance in a lady's bicycle, he told himself, for a man might as well throw his leg over a broom-handle. Men in brakes laughed at him and kissed their fingers and shouted: 'Lanky Lizzie mind the dresser! . . . Get off that old gate and walk!' He smiled back at them good-naturedly and taking off his cap to bow to their ironic salutations the bicycle wobbled and he had to put his feet to the ground to avoid falling in the ditch. They went frantic with laughter and they beat the sides of the brake with their fists and one of them threw a few coppers on the road. 'The devil choke them for a lot of ignorant gurmudgins,' D. J. said to himself, and as his eyes watered with the dust he pedalled slowly and allowed the brake to get far ahead. He hung his cap on the lamp-bracket on the handlebars and as he drew near the course he had to dismount, and manoeuvring his bike among the hurrying throng he had to bear with mock indifference the corrosive abuse they hurled at him. Race-meetings, race-goers, and racecourses, he comforted himself, little any of them knew what a decent racecourse looked like – they wouldn't know one from a schoolgirls' hockey pitch!

He left his bicycle in the hay-shed of a farmhouse, dusted his clothes with the peak of his cap, and leisurely made his way over the fields to the course. Crippled men with canvas bags were holding out race-cards, shouting loudly, and waving them at the line of motor cars that were slowly passing. The smell of petrol, of oranges, and the warm smell of crushed grass filled D. J. with an exultation that he would not admit to himself. After all what was it but a makeshift of a course? — gaps broadened here and there in a farmer's field, a few bright red flags stuck on a hedge to mark the jumps, and an uphill finish on which no respectable owner would risk a pedigree horse.

With debonair elegance he bought a race-card, exasperating the excited seller by fumbling in one pocket, and then another before finally producing the shilling. He skirted the packed rows of motor cars and made his way to the parade ground where a few indifferent looking horses were grouped around the door of a tent which displayed a large card: JOCKEYS ONLY. The horses showed no nervousness and their grooms occasionally chatted to one another as they smoked cigarettes and spat out on the grass as if they were at a country fair.

The sun was strong and to escape from it D. J. entered a marquee, and sitting on an upturned box he drank a few bottles of flat porter. The shadows of the people on the sun-flushed canvas, the warm sweating grass, the hum of talk and the plunge of glasses into tubs of water drove him out again to the air where he sought for a stream to bathe his scalded, swollen feet. The drains in the shughs were dried up and he lay for a while in the shade of a hedge, and taking off his socks he covered his feet with cool dockin leaves and returned to the crowds as the bell was ringing for the first race. The bookies, standing beside their boards, went frantic then, shouting out the odds as they inserted them in chalk alongside the names of the horses, and then as quickly spat on their fingers to lower their prices when anyone ventured more than a quid on a particular horse. D. J. backed one, Falling Water, because the name appealed to him, and when the crowd shouted 'They're off!' and scrambled past him he stood calmly where he was, shading his eyes with the race-card. The course sloped away from him down to the edge of the lough which glittered with shoals of light, and the horses ran with vexatious slowness, hopped the jumps, the jockeys sitting erect as if they were out for the good of their health. He yawned and fanned himself with the card and noticing that each race was three laps of the course he sauntered to the marquee for another drink and emerged in time to see the finish – four or five winded horses staggering up the hill, the jockeys belabouring them with their whips, and urging them forward with such a frenzied plunging of their arms that it seemed at any moment they'd fly over the horses' heads and complete the rest of the journey on foot. D. J. observed it with as much scorn and boredom as he would a children's circus. In the interval between the first race and the next he sought out the shady hedge again and dozed there till the bell summoned him for the next race.

It was growing warmer; the bookies had taken off their coats, and over the hill there drifted from the car park the smell of petrol, of rubber, and sun-scorched leather. Three-card trick men were shuffling their cards on to the top of an open umbrella placed on the ground and were shouting: 'Find the lady, gentlemen! Find the lady for an even quid.' In another corner a trick-o'-the-loop man had his own fold-up table and D. J. noticed Philip Doran and a few men from the village gathered about it. He crushed his way beside Philip and saw to his dismay that he was placing the pencil in one of three loops that was formed in a doubled leather strap.

'Out again, Sir,' said the trickster, lifting Doran's pound note from the trestle table. 'It's all a bit of luck, Sir; mine now; yours the next time. You have to watch closely, gentlemen; it's all a matter of using your eyes. There's the leather strap,' and he placed the strap full length on the table. 'Now, I double it to make the first loop. You stick the pencil in that loop to be on the inside of the strap. Keep your eye on it. Fair is fair, chance is chance, your bread or mine – I must twist another loop in the strap, and then another. There you are, gentlemen, three loops like three eggs in a nest. An even pound to the gentleman that sticks the pencil in the right loop,' and he waved the pencil in the air.

Doran took a pound note from his pocket but D. J. plucked him by the sleeve. 'Keep your money – it'll help to buy Eileen the ring.'

'I know the right one, this time, D. J. I've lost five times and won once. My luck will turn.'

'It's a bloody fraud I tell you! Listen to me that knows a thing or two!'

Doran stretched out for the pencil but D. J. knocked it out of his hand.

'It's all in the luck of the game,' said the trickster to D. J. 'You're no sportsman. Take yourself to hell out of the road and leave room for sports.' As he spoke one of his confederates with a pink eyeshade over one eye seized the pencil and stuck it in one of the loops.'

'There you are, gentlemen, I lose this time,' and he glared at D. J. with narrow bloodshot eyes. 'Stand back there and leave room for sportsmen.'

'You'll not swindle friends of mine,' D. J. said back to him. 'Give them back their money.'

'The man's drunk,' said the trickster, and he appealed to the audience grouped round the table. 'What fraud could there be in the simple folding of a strap?' And once more he doubled the strap, made three loops in it, spreading his hands on the centre of the table so that everyone had a clear honest view. D. J. seized the pencil and threw down a pound on the table. The trickster had a few pound notes weighted down with a stone on the edge of the table and he took one and covered D. J.'s with it. D. J. put the pencil in one of the loops. 'Now,' he said, 'pull the two ends of the strap at once and none of your damned hunker-sliding.'

The trickster crouched forward and, talking at the same time, he tried to disengage one of the ends and reverse it round the coil but D. J. caught his wrist. 'Pull them together, you bloody hound. I'll have none of your twisting!' But the man wrenched himself free and D. J. lifted his bet. 'The bet's off,' he said and he pleaded for somebody to lend him a strap and he would show them how it was done. No one had a strap and D. J. took the tie from around his own collar and on the edge of the table he showed that even by only making one loop he could make the pencil be on the outside by manipulating the ends.

'It's a damned naked swindle,' Doran shouted.

'A bastard of a fraud!' said someone else and struck the table with his fist.

'They're off!' the crowd shouted and bustled to see the next race.

In the excitement someone up-ended the table, and as the stone and the trickster's pound notes fell to the ground Doran pounced on them and D. J. threw the trickster on top of his one-eyed confederate and as they struggled to their feet he and Doran made off to the edge of the crowd.

'Did you get all you lost?' D. J. asked him, and he had to sit down on the ground to control his laughter.

'I got four pounds of it,' Doran said, holding the money in his fist.

'You bloody fool, you deserved to lose every cent. I don't know what Eileen was thinking of when she agreed to marry a fool like you. You'll be a nice gom of a relation I must say,' and he rolled over on the grass laughing.

'Don't make an ass of yourself,' Doran said, riled. 'How'd I know it was a fraud? This is the first race-meeting I was ever at.'

'Race-meeting!' D. J. said, going into another fit. 'Race-meeting! – that's the best one ever I heard. You could get a lot of jack asses to run quicker. When you're married, Philip, we'll go to Aintree and see the Grand National, or go down to Baldoyle or Punchestown. It's a great life when you've a few quid to spend. Are you game?'

'I'm game for a good sharp bottle of stout if that's any news to you. Fix your tie like a respectable draper and get to your feet like a Christian.' He helped D. J. to his feet, and retiring to the marquee he made him demonstrate once more how to do the trick-o'-the-loop.

Philip drank his glass quickly. 'That'll quench the drought in me for an hour or two.'

'In the name of God don't let anyone hear you praise that for porter. There's no bite in it – you might as well drink the stale water in the lough. Eileen's getting a fine man of the world if you ask me,' and he laughed to himself, shaking his head and closing his eyes wearily.

'By the look of you you better not drink much more of it,' Philip said, impatient to be off. 'Are you coming to see the finish of this race?'

D. J. half-opened his eyes and stared stupidly at the froth slithering down the sides of his glass. 'Race! What race are you talking about? A lot of youngsters in their bare feet could run quicker.'

'I'm going if you're not,' and he bent over to him where he sat on an upturned box and spoke into his ear. 'I'm grateful to you, D. J. Do you hear that?'

'That's nothing,' D. J. said sleepily. 'Wouldn't anybody help a child like you?'

'Would you take a quid from me?'

'I've plenty of money. You insult me. You insult the drapery profession. Go on and enjoy your day and don't stand there making a fool of yourself.'

Doran left him, and as the crowds began to pour into the

marquee at the end of the race D. J. got to his feet unsteadily, and piloting himself past the car park he lay under the hedge with his cap over his face and fell asleep.

The hum of cars moving out from the course did not waken him, and soon there was nothing to be seen except the marquee with its fresh ropes, the bare trodden hill littered with bookies' tickets, crusts of bread, and tin-tops that glistened in the lowering sun. Along the hedge where he lay, three men, one with a pink eyeshade over his left eye, crouched towards him. They began to search his pockets. D. J. stirred, dragged the cap from his sleep-swollen face, and opened his eyes. He made to rise but one of them crashed a bottle on his head and something cracked against his knee. With a moan he rolled over on his face, blood from his head streaming on to the grass.

For over an hour he lay without a stir from him, and it was two men, sitting on top of a lorry-load of canvas and tent-poles, that noticed him as they were driving out from the field. He moaned but did not speak when they turned him over and saw the wound on his head, and his face and shirt steeped in blood. The driver hurried on to the main road to phone the hospital, and two of his men sat on the bank beside D. J. staring helplessly at him and chasing away the flies that crawled on the hardened blood on the grass. A great silence was settling over the fields, and before the mist of dew arose there appeared, on the brow of the hill where the sun was resting in the tree-tops, a group of barefooted children; and as they searched for pennies in the trodden grass their voices volleyed in the clear air. They flung tickets into the air, and blowing up paper bags they burst them with their fists and screamed with delight when the crows arose from the trees and flew off with wild cries. The two men sitting under the hedge looked across at them with apathetic interest. Then suddenly the children ceased their cries for into the field there came the unexpected sight of an ambulance. They raced to it, and with bundles of bookies' tickets in their hands they stared with stunned curiosity as a policeman emerged from the back of the ambulance and D. J. was lifted on to a stretcher, his cap lying on his chest.

The ambulance raced out of the field and on to the main road, and as it sped towards the nearest hospital it passed a taxi that was bringing Bob home, and in the back of it with him were Nelly and John and Eileen. Nelly's face was haggard, and as Bob lay back with a pillow under his head she kept wringing her hands and whispering to John if she should tell him now. She looked out of the window at the hedges choked with dust and at the landscape that was becoming more familiar. She turned once more to John.

'I can't wait any longer. It would be better to prepare him,' she whispered.

'Sh-sh! Let him sleep,' John whispered back to her and glanced at Bob.

'The suspense is killing me. I can't bear it any longer,' she sighed, and was stretching out her hand to shake Bob's shoulder when John gripped her wrist.

'Don't! Don't!' he said.

As yet she hadn't told Bob about D. J. When she had visited him in the morning he was sitting up in bed and had decided there and then that he wouldn't rest another night in the hospital. He was going home and that was all about it! The nurse tried to prevail upon him to stay but he shook his head stubbornly. The doctor told him curtly that he would take no responsibility for the decision. 'If you leave,' he said, 'you leave against my orders. All I ask is that you stay for another week – you'll be strong enough then for the journey.'

'I'll not stay another day,' Bob said back to him. 'My mind is made up. I'm breaking my heart here.' And he made Nelly engage a taxi to drive him home.

As she gazed out of the window of the taxi it all rose up before her with unrelenting force, and now as they approached the village the thought of D. J. standing at the shop door made her close her eyes to wrench away for a moment the tightened grief of the homecoming. 'Mother of God help us!' and she gave a cry that was drowned in the noise of a train that was passing the level crossing. The gates were closed, and as the porter swung them back to allow the car to pass, Bob opened his eyes. It jolted slowly over the rails and Eileen, who was sitting with the driver, showed him where to stop.

The blind in the shop was down. 'You did well to lower the blind when you were leaving,' Bob said. 'Of course you could have pulled out the awning and left the blind up if you'd wished.'

She said nothing but thought of D. J. and hoped he had gone to the races. They helped him out of the car and he stood looking at the old pump and its damp patch on the dusty road. 'I'll have a good cold drink from that this evening,' he said, and Nelly opened the side door, and as she and John assisted him into the house Eileen followed with his stick and pillow.

They placed him in an armchair and he asked Nelly to loosen the neckband of his shirt. 'Ah, it's grand to be back again,' he sighed, and raised his eyes to the lamp below the picture of the Sacred Heart. 'Is the light alive in it or is it the reflection from the window I see?'

'A draught has blown it out,' Nelly said, and she relit it and pushed the curtains far back to let in the summer evening light. She went about on tiptoe, taking off her coat, and speaking to John with whispers and signs that baffled him.

Bob's hand groped around the seat of the armchair and coming upon a playing card, the ace of spades, he turned it over, squeezed it in his fist and threw it in the fire grate. Beside him on top of the cabinet of the gramophone was a man's collar. He lifted it; it was greasy and soiled and of a size that wasn't his. He let it fall to the floor, and under a table opposite him he saw a pair of men's boots, one lying on its side where it had been shoved in there in a hurry. He pointed at them with his stick and asked whose they were. Nelly pretended not to hear him as she crouched before the fire and raked out the dead ashes. She turned her head and asked Eileen to spread a clean cloth on the table.

'It's a lovely evening, Bob,' John said from the window. 'The leaves on the trees are dying for a drop of rain.'

'Whose are the boots, Nelly?' Bob asked again, tapping his stick on the tiles of the floor.

'Your brother's.'

'D. J.'s?'

'Yes, D. J.'s.'

'Surely to God you hadn't him visiting here?' and his hand smoothed the arm of the chair.

She put a light to the fire and said nothing.

'Did he come here often?' he went on, afraid to ask what he didn't wish to hear – that he had stayed with her. He spoke again, and Nelly looked round at him, her lower lip trembling. In the armchair he looked small and crumpled and he a big man that used to be the very fill of it. Her heart ached with pity for him and she turned away her head to the fresh fire that was roaring in the range.

'Tell me, Nelly, did that playboy come often?'

'He did, Bob. He came often. I had no one to turn to for help at the time,' and she spread her hand to include John.

'What kind of help?'

'If you give me a minute or two I'll tell you all.'

'Tell me now.'

She explained that he had worked now and again in the shop but she had kept a strict eye on every penny and on every article that was sold. She appealed to him for the love of God to give her time and she'd show him the notebook and the amounts taken. But he raised himself up in his chair and as she and John rushed to assist him he brushed them aside and shuffled into the shop, supporting himself against the wall.

The yellow light from the drawn blind stunned him and two bluebottles, enclosed between the blind and the pane, hummed in the hot-gripped air. Groping his way along the edge of the counter he stooped into the window space, touched the blind, and it flew freely from his hand and swirled madly on its roller.

'Bob,' Nelly pleaded with him, 'wait till you get a cup of tea and I'll tell you all.'

'Calm yourself like a good man,' John said, 'or you'll do yourself harm.'

He didn't seem to hear them. With a soulless stare his eyes ranged round the shelves as if he were in a strange, unaccustomed place. Nothing was in its proper order; a bale of tweed lay on the counter; boxes that he had numbered and arranged in rotation were pushed together with seeming irate irreverence.

'God,' he said, 'all I've lived for to be made a mockery of!' On the counter he spied the bright circle of space and the rusted hole from the nail where he had fastened the lead half-crown. 'He has robbed me!' he said. 'The curse of God on him for a meddler!'

'Hush, Bob, don't say the like of that!' Nelly cried with tears in her eyes. 'I tell you again that I've every penny accounted for.'

'The signs of his thievery are everywhere. Look at the till-drawer lying open and empty!' he said, struggling round to the back of the counter. He lifted up the lid of his desk, took out his entry-book, and on seeing D. J.'s handwriting scrawled on leaf after leaf he flung it on the floor with disgust.

Nelly stooped and lifted it. 'That's not the book I'm referring to. I have it locked in my drawer upstairs.'

He did not seem to hear or see her, for he was glaring at a few flattened butts of cigarettes on the floor and at his stove that was scored with the strikings of a match. 'My lovely place! A randybooze he has made of it! And me the very core of orderliness and honesty! Oh, why didn't you tell me he was here? Why did you keep it from me?' and he squeezed his forehead with his hand and leaned on the counter to rest. 'I'm not fit for the like of this. Everything is breaking up.'

Nelly put her hand on his shoulder. 'Come back to your chair and rest yourself. Come on,' and her voice was gentle and comforting.

He raised his head, and there was a moist mark on the counter from his breath. The sweat gleamed on his forehead. He stared at John. 'It was you did this on me, I know that now,' he said. 'You're responsible. You always had a softness for that thief.'

'As God's my judge he had nothing to do with it,' Nelly intervened.

'Don't anger me, woman. From the very first it was John shoved D. J. down here to get rid of him. Do you think I forget the snowy day D. J. followed me to the door after he'd been up to see Doctor O'Neill on my account? You knew all about that, John!' and he shook his head with grim mockery. 'And now you've twisted him into my lovely place.'

'It's untrue,' John said. 'I had nothing to do with it.'

'You're a liar!' and he raised his stick in the air but it struck the lamp over his head and the oil jabbled on the bale of grey tweed on the counter.

'The grace of God is absent from this house this day,' Nelly said. 'There's no sense in it when a sick man is bent on destroying himself.'

'It's absent from the thieves that's gathered about me,' he said, and seeing the stains spreading across the tweed he raised his voice and threw the stick from him. 'But I'll put an end to the whole gang of you! I'll finish all your twists . . . Eileen, Eileen,' he called out in haste. She came running from the door at the kitchen, her eyes streaming with tears. 'Run over to the sergeant,' he said to her, 'and tell him to step over here and witness my will. You'll do the other witness . . . Go on when you're bid.'

'Go on, Eileen,' her father said to her as she stood irresolute.

He rummaged in his desk for a sheet of paper and coming on a block of his own bill-heads he tore one off and turned over the unprinted side. He dipped a pen in the ink-bottle that was sitting without its cork. He wrote: 'I, Robert Caffrey, on this twenty-second day of' – but the pen scratched, and on the downstrokes the wings of the nib parted making two thin parallel lines. He flung it from him and it stuck in the floor and quivered like a dart. 'He has destroyed the very pen on me!' He breathed with quick short gasps.

John unclipped his fountain pen from his pocket and handed it to him without a word.

Whether it was at the sign of this cool gesture or his own anger at not being persuaded to desist but the instant he took the fountain pen on his palm he struck it hard against the edge of the counter where it splintered and splashed on his hand. He closed his eyes, then, at what he had done. 'Forgive me,' he said, and stretching himself to his full height in an attempt to gather his strength something in his mind seemed to dissolve, his thoughts loosened and fell away from him like black garments falling one by one from a line above his head, and as his hand slid from the counter John caught him as he was sinking to the floor.

With difficulty they dragged him through the narrow passage between the counter and the wall and placed him in the armchair where he lay with his arms limp, his head hanging on his breast. Eileen came running into the house. 'The sergeant's at his tea and he'll . . .' but the rest of her words caught in her throat.

'Take the bicycle, Eileen,' Nelly said, 'and go for Doctor O'Neill. I don't like the look of your uncle.'

John bent over him and opened his waistcoat. He felt the

feeble beats of his brother's heart. 'Get the priest, Nelly. He's far through.'

Eileen tapped the window. 'The bicycle's not there. I'll run on as I am.'

Nelly went to phone for the priest, and hurrying back she found John crouched over his brother, and without speaking she went on her knees as she heard him recite the Act of Contrition in his ear: 'Oh, my God, I am very sorry for having offended Thee because Thou art so good and I will never sin again.' Over and over again he repeated it and then turning to Nelly he said: 'May God have mercy on his soul this night!' He got up and stood at the window, and through the tears in his eyes he saw the parched trees eased by the falling dew and saw a barefooted boy walking away from the pump with a bucket of water that swayed and splashed on the dusty road. Eileen came running back from Doctor O'Neill's, her fair hair rising and falling on her shoulders.

'He's not at home,' she said out of breath.

No one answered her. Her father stood at the window and did not turn round, and then seeing Nelly on her knees she knew that her Uncle Bob was dead.

'Say a prayer for him, Eileen,' Nelly said. 'He has died without the priest. I'm to blame for it all.'

'It's God's will,' John said. 'There's no one to blame. You never stinted yourself, Nelly. You never spared yourself in the way you served him. You stayed with him and worked for him when many another would have gone off and left him in the hands of a housekeeper.'

'I know, I know. But I mustn't take credit for what I couldn't help. I would have married if the chance had come my way.' She wiped her tears with her handkerchief and said quietly to Eileen: 'Run down to Philip's and ask Martha if she'd come up and help me.'

The kettle boiled over and hissed on the range, and outside the crows settled down in the tree-tops and women passed and repassed the window on their way to the pump for buckets of water. They called loudly and pleasantly to one another, and then seeing the priest hurry past them into the Caffreys they grew silent and gathered at their doors, glancing at the dark shop till the stars came into the sky and it was time to put the children to bed. And then on hearing of Bob's death they returned to their doors again and stood about upon the road, gossiping quietly.

Out of respect for Bob the public house closed down and men gathered in knots. Johnny P.M. slouched among them, his head cocked to the side like an old watchdog's. The three policemen leaned against the barrack window-sill, their hands in their pockets their heads bare and tunics unbuttoned against the cool summer night. Daly was out at his door, two cats brushing against his legs, and one up on his wife's shoulder and purring against her neck.

The men agreed it was D. J. who had killed Bob and that it was a pity that Nelly hadn't had more sense than allow a rogue like that to run the shop.

'That's not what you were saying when you played cards with him to all hours of the night,' the women defended.

'If we did play with him,' the men answered, 'we never won as much as a brass farthing. We should have known the kind of travelled rogue he was. He had the cards marked for he could always deal out a good hand for himself.'

The postman smiled at this for he had seen D. J. at the day's races gambling and drinking. 'Hm, when rogues expose rogues it's time the cuckoo built her own nest,' he said, and went on to relate how he had seen D. J. expose the trick-o'-the-loop man. They laughed and then ceased abruptly, remembering that a death had taken place a stone's throw from where they stood. They glanced over at the shop and saw the lighted window upstairs and shadows passing across the drawn blind. They spoke in hushed voices, then, and the women drew away from them while the lights from their open doors stretched out in the night and a breeze, flurrying in the dark trees and rasping a piece of dry paper on the road, gathered them closer in a warm and sheltering intimacy. Mrs. Bruce was among them but she said not a word, for she was recalling to her mind the day she had threatened to put a curse on Bob because he had insulted one of her children about 'disgraced money'. It's well she didn't put a curse upon him, she sighed to herself, it's well she didn't. May God have mercy on him! Through the open door at her back she heard the children laughing and play-acting in their bedroom. 'Would you listen to that brood of mine,' she said to the neighbours, 'and Bob Caffrey just dead.' She went into the house and up the stairs to the children. 'Go to sleep at once,' she shouted at them. 'Go to sleep or I'll give you a good welt or two with the weight of my hand. That's a way to be carrying on and Bob Caffrey lying dead in his bed a few doors away from you. You're worse than a pack of heathens. You should be out on your knees saying a prayer for his soul. Didn't you torment the life out of the poor man when he was alive – chalking names on his shutters and firing gravel at his window? You're a disgrace. Do you want to send me to my grave in the same way? Go to sleep and not another word out of you this night!' The children pulled the clothes over their heads, fearful that if they opened their eyes they'd see the man they had tormented bending over them with his white hair and shaking a yellow fist at them. Their mother whisked downstairs again and joined the group on the roadway.

'To think that he's gone now,' a woman was saying, 'and didn't live to enjoy his new window and his bit of canvas that chokes out the glare of the sun.'

'He should have left it the way it was. The old peacock did nobody any harm. He shouldn't have meddled with it – a man of his years. But we needn't talk – we've all done foolish things at some time or other. It'd suit us better to quit talking and go and get ourselves ready for the wake.'

'That's right,' they all agreed. The group of women was breaking up when they heard the phone ring in the barracks and saw the sergeant hurry in from the window-sill to answer it.

'Wasn't it well the sergeant wasn't in bed and had to get out to answer that phone?' a woman remarked.

'If he had it'd be the first bit of work he did this day,' another answered her. And once more the women bunched together and with arms folded they complained about how hard-wrought their own husbands were when one compared them with the fat lazy life of the police. They halted their talk and all turned their heads to the lighted barracks, for the sergeant was coming out in haste buttoning his tunic and striding across the road to the Caffreys. Returning again he spoke to Daly and to the dark group of men. D. J.'s name was mentioned, and the women pressed forward to hear. The sergeant was telling everyone that D. J. was lying unconscious in the hospital. He was picked up near the racecourse, he was saying, his head opened by the blow from a bottle and his kneecap broken or displaced. The hospital authorities weren't sure of his identity but in his pocket was a business letter addressed to Robert Caffrey, High Class Draper, Monabeg.

Who else could it be but poor D. J.? the women spoke among themselves. It was D. J. all right. No one had seen him return from the races and no one except D. J. could have a letter like that in his pocket. God's pity on poor Nelly this mortal night! Sorrows are like flies they never come singly! And poor D. J., what was he but a homeless fly-away of a man who was decent when he'd anything to give? Look at the fine length of a yard he'd give you when you called to buy a bit of material.

The policemen withdrew from the gossiping groups and closed the barracks door. Daly went in to get ready for the wake. Freight wagons rumbled into the station and far away came the lowing of cattle moving on the road. The group of women broke up and soon there was no light in the village except the signal lights at the station and the lighted window in the Caffreys'.

CHAPTER SIXTEEN

DURING the two nights of the wake Nelly obtained no sleep, and now in the chapel as she knelt in black behind the coffin and in the same seat as John and his family her eyes ached and her nerve-stunned mind wandered from the words in the missal and from the movements of the priest on the altar as he offered a requiem Mass for the repose of Bob's soul. A long sleeve of sunlight stretched through one of the windows, and outside in the graveyard a wren singing alone repeated its little song with sweet and confident insistency. The song with its unusual clarity arrested her mind but as it was repeated and repeated with the same marked intervals of silence it gradually merged with sounds that are no longer heard, and her mind once more struggled involuntarily with the ravaged thought of Bob's unhappy death and with her own self-accusation of being responsible for it. She closed her eyes in an attempt to shake the thought from her but it arose before her with as terrible a reality as the colour of the coffin that rested in front of her, and gnawing as it did with such remorselessness she sought in Bob's last 'Forgive me' something to anoint the doubts and scruples that grappled her. And how often, she thought, had she sat with him in the same chapel and in this very seat, close to the altar as he had always wished, and listened to a Missioner as he preached about dark lanes and lonely roads and boys and girls that follow hideous occasions of sin. It was strange that those were the only sermons that he ever discussed with her and she remembered once how after one of those sermons he had said to her at the gate: 'Man alive but that was a grand preacher! He fairly gave it to you tonight – that'll put the dancing out of your head for a while,' and he had smiled with satisfaction at the subdued youths who stood about upon the road smoking their cigarettes. But if sermons of that kind had no effect on a man whose sense of sin had shrunk to one commandment hadn't he ears as well as the rest of us to hear the Epistles that were read aloud from that very altar Sunday after Sunday? But she mustn't accuse him! She, herself, was no better than she should be! And here she was allowing her thoughts to scatter and not paying heed to what she should be doing.

She raised her eyes to the priest vested in black, turned a few pages in her missal and once more applied herself to feeling the language that she was reading. The wren was singing again. Thank God it was a lovely day! Many had left the hay-making to attend the funeral. They were good neighbours when all was said and done. And the help they gave her at the wake she'd never forget that. And the way Dr. O'Neill took out his car and drove herself and John to see poor D. J. – and the comfort he gave them saying all the time that he'd pull through. No, she'd never forget that kindness! And Philip Doran arranging everything with the undertakers and his sister staying behind in the house to have a good meal ready for the visitors when they'd come back from the funeral. Yes, love is the fulfilling of the law . . . Whilst we have time let us work good to all men . . . Bear you one another's burdens . . . Where there is anger and rivalry there you will find disorder . . . Bless and curse not . . . The lukewarm, neither cold nor hot, I will begin to vomit thee out of my youth. . . .

Her missal dropped on the floor. Christ, O God, what was she doing! She stooped to pick up the book and raising herself again she felt the blood pounding in her forehead and through the tears in her eyes she saw the candles reflected in the varnished sides of the coffin and saw the priest leaving the altar. She bowed her head and endeavoured to shut out all the fragments of epistles and gospels that were accusing herself and Bob and all of them. She hadn't done enough for him – that was true! She didn't go out of her way to understand him! She had failed him; she had crossed him; she had hastened his death.

The priest came out again and stood beside the coffin to give the Absolution of the Dead. He sprinkled holy water on the coffin and some of it splashed on Nelly's hand.

'Let us pray,' he read aloud. 'Absolve we beseech thee, O Lord, the soul of thy servant Robert from every bond of sin that he may be raised up in the glory of the resurrection and live amongst thy saints and elect. . . .'

John got up from his knees and passed out to the aisle. Frank and Brendan followed him. For a moment he stood looking at the row of kneeling people until Philip Doran came up and whispered to him. Presently they lifted the coffin, Frank and Brendan shouldering it in front, and John and Philip at the back. They walked slowly down the aisle, out through the sunlit door, and over to the grave where the fresh clay lay drying in the warm sun.

They grouped themselves round the grave, and when the dry ropes had lowered the coffin the priest shovelled clay on top of it saying: 'Remember man that thou art dust and unto dust thou shalt return.'

Nelly pressed a handkerchief to her eyes and bowed her head. There was dust everywhere – on the gravediggers' clothes, on the road, in the cracks of the floor-boards of the shop and under the stove, and in the ornamental grooves of the pump. Everything dust and maybe a soul damned.

Neighbours were shaking hands with her and with John and taking their departure, and soon there was no one left in the graveyard except the chief mourners and those who had come from the city. They stayed till the top sods were rolled back and beaten down on the mound of clay, and kneeling once more to say a prayer for Bob's soul they drove back to the village in the motor cars that were waiting for them on the road.

In the house Philip's sister had all the blinds raised except the blind in the shop. The windows were open and the curtains wavering in the pleasant draught of air.

'It's a lovely bit of countryside,' said Mr. Mallon as he stood at one of the windows with a glass of whisky which John had given him.

'Beautiful and fresh!' Brendan's boss confirmed, fingering his watch impatiently, and wondering how his assistants would get on in the library with two of the staff absent. Something was sure to go wrong, he thought – those good-for-nothing girls would never think of having a look into the Reading Room and chasing out the snoring old tramps. If he didn't get back in time they might lock up and maybe leave one of them behind.

'Will you take a nip, Mr. Dunne? It'll stimulate your appetite,' John was asking him, handing him a glass and tilting the bottle towards him.

'A thimbleful, Mr. Caffrey. Must get back. Short staffed.'

'It was very kind of you to come, Mr. Dunne. And it was kind of you to come, too, Mr. Mallon.'

'Don't mention it,' Mr. Mallon said. 'The school's on vacation at the moment. It was no trouble for me to come,' and he just checked himself in time from saying it was a pleasure.

'Lovely countryside, indeed,' Mr. Dunne said, drinking his whisky in one gulp and patting his lips with his handkerchief. 'People read much? No time, I suppose. Harvesting and what not – eh?'

The girls pushed past them as they went to and fro from the table with chairs and plates and John ushered them out of the road to the back of the house till they'd see a view of the river. They sat in the little summer-house in the back garden and looked over the hedge at the river flowing slowly and clearly because of the dry spell of weather.

'This is where I intend to retire to,' John said. 'I only wish, men, you had the time, we could take a sail down the river as far as the Island. Maybe you'd wait for the last train?'

'Not now, Mr. Caffrey,' the librarian said. 'Must get back. Only girls in charge.'

John said again that he was very grateful to him for coming.

'Out of respect for Brendan I came. Fine boy. Will go far. Will step into my shoes,' and he took out his watch and made a few tentative steps towards the house, and at that moment Eileen called from the window: 'Dinner is ready, gentlemen.'

They went in and as Nelly was placing them round the table Mrs. Caffrey put her arms around her and pushed her into a seat. 'Sit down and rest yourself, Nelly, like a good girl. Let Anne and Eileen do the running to and fro with the dishes.'

The librarian was finished first and he kept fingering his watch and looking over his shoulder at the window. 'Train always up to the mark, Mr. Caffrey?' he said.

'They're not too particular about here. Ten or fifteen minutes late is nothing unusual,' John said. 'But she'll not leave without you. The station-master would see to that. He'd hold her up for a few minutes if I sent him word. But you needn't fear, you'll hear her whistling a good five minutes before she comes leaping in.'

When the dessert was served Eileen prepared a tray with cups and saucers for coffee. Mr. Dunne eyed her, annoyed at the way she would turn round from the tray and join in the table conversation. He could bear it no longer and he stood up and said: 'You'll pardon me, ladies and gentlemen. I don't take coffee. I'll step down to station. Make sure all is right.' He bowed himself from the room. John whispered something to Brendan. Brendan shook hands with his Aunt Nelly, bid the Dorans goodbye, and followed after Mr. Dunne.

They drank the coffee slowly, smoked cigarettes, and when

223

they heard the whistle of the train John rose from the table with Mr. Mallon and walked to the station with him to see him off. On returning to the house he saw Frank going off with Philip and he was glad of that – he could ask for no better company than that. Anne and Eileen and their mother were cleaning the dishes, and seeing that himself and Nelly were alone they went out together to the quiet of the summer-house to discuss what they'd do with Bob's affairs. Nothing, they agreed, could be finally settled until D. J.'s recovery but in the meantime Frank was to be given entire charge of the shop. And if D. J. was willing they arranged to buy the lodge for him and Nelly, and have it renovated and made fit enough for anyone to settle down in in comfort.

'I trust in God that he'll have sense and live with me,' Nelly said, 'for if he gets over his injuries he'll never be fit for much gallivanting about. And the house is lovely – you can see the chapel and the graveyard from one of the bedrooms.' She sighed heavily, and after a few minutes she said: 'We could all be very happy here: Eileen married and maybe Anne take the little school when the schoolmistress retires. There'd be no loneliness in the place again. God grant that D. J. will agree.'

'If he doesn't he might force us to sell the shop and let it pass into the hands of some stranger. In any case we'll have to have it valued and his share given to him. I don't know how to approach him on that matter – he misunderstands everything I say to him. But first and foremost I'll have to tell him soon about Bob's death. He may get to hear it from some stranger or maybe pick up a stray newspaper and come across the obituary notice – you'd never know what twist he would put then on our silence.'

'It was the doctor's orders,' Nelly said. 'Let a week or so elapse before you tell him – those were his words when I phoned the hospital this morning. But I'll leave that to you, John, for when he'd see me entering the ward in black he'd guess immediately what had happened.'

And so a week afterwards when the stitches had been removed from D. J.'s head John decided to break the news to him of Bob's death. He arrived at the hospital in the morning, and on entering the ward with its four beds at each side he caught sight of D. J. with his shaven head bare of bandages and his fractured leg strung up by pulleys on a wooden frame.

'I'm still on the gallows,' he greeted John, 'and there's as many stitches in my head as there is in the backbone of a herring. The nurse brought me a mirror and the sight of myself gave me the shock of my life.'

'It's a blessing of God you weren't killed outright.'

D. J. pulled up each sleeve of his pyjamas in turn, stared at his bony arms, and then raised his eyes in a smile. 'Lazarus come forth and he came fifth and was disqualified – that was always your joke for a man with no flesh on him.'

'You've mended since I saw you last.'

'I'm mending with somebody else's blood in me. I've had a few transfusions already and I don't know who the hell I'll be when I rise up from my confinement.'

'What does the doctor think about the old leg?'

'He tells me I'll never have two legs again. I'll always have three – the third one will be a good stout stick. And that reminds me – when you're down in the country again tell Johnny P.M. to mark a few good thorns for me. But if he sees a good one tell him to cut it right away. Do you ever remark that when you're watching a good stout thorn growing there's not one old fella but maybe a dozen watching it too? That's the reason he should cut it. Maybe he should cut two for I'm sure Bob could be doing with one when he comes home. How is he?'

'God rest him, D. J.; he's dead and buried,' John said, and after a pause he explained that he or Nelly would have told him sooner only the doctor forbade them. 'He got a stroke the evening he came back from the hospital and he died in his chair before the priest arrived.'

'May God be merciful to him! He wasn't the bloody rake

P

that I was. I've been lying here doing nothing but going over the past and the past has gone over me. I don't know where the years have run but they've flew past like a school of steeplechasers.' He fingered the thin skin on the scar on his head and looked at his brother. 'Did he made a will?'

'We found no trace of one in his drawers and there's no word of one from any quarter. We'll settle everything justly when you're fit to come out and discuss it with Nelly and myself.'

'Life is cruel,' said D. J. 'To think I'll have a bit of money and maybe not be fit to enjoy it. I don't know what possessed me to go to that hole-in-a-corner of a race-meeting. Who's in charge of the shop now?'

'Frank! It was the best arrangement we could make. Nelly will tell you all. She'll be in one of these days to see you,' said John, and he rose from the edge of the bed and lifted his hat.

'And what do you intend to do with me?'

'What do you intend to do with yourself?'

'I'll think that out. But don't make too many arrangements – I have a big say now.'

'That's understood, D. J. You need not worry on that score. But wouldn't it be a crime if we let the business slip out of the family name?'

'I don't know if that would cause me an extra heartbeat,' D. J. said, and raised himself up on the pillow.

John asked him if he wanted anything in the line of books or papers or fruit and he'd have Brendan or one of the girls bring them out to him.

'I can't read. The blows the bloody tinkers gave me have affected the sight. I'll need a good pair of spectacles – that'll be the first item on the agenda.'

'I'll have to go now, D. J.,' John said, and stretched out his hand. D. J. gripped it tightly and in that clasp John felt a oneness with him that he had always yearned for.

'You'll not forget about that thorn stick and tell Johnny P.M. to dress it nicely for me. And don't forget to have him brought in to see me.'

'I'll not. And if there's anything special you want just drop a card to Nelly at the shop for she'll be the next to visit you.'

At the door of the ward John turned and waved his hand to him. D. J. waved back, and resting on the pillows with his hands under his head he rejoiced in the contentment that the unexpected security had brought him.

CHAPTER SEVENTEEN

NELLY came to see him and with her came Eileen and Philip Doran. They found D. J. bent over a newspaper spread out on the bed and reading the sporting column with the aid of a rough-edged magnifying glass that an old man had lent him. So engrossed was he in the paper that he didn't see them until Eileen took an apple from a bag of fruit and rolled it on top of the newspaper.

'Oh, oh, this is a surprise,' D. J. said, blinking at them. 'And Philip and Eileen! And my game leg still hung up like a goose in a Christmas window. This is a nice pickle the pair of you got me into,' he laughed. 'Aw, if I'd minded my own business and not helped a mug like yourself I'd be out striding the country roads this fine weather.'

'It'll not be long now till you're up and about,' Nelly said.

'Aye, but I'll be propped up with a stick. I suppose there'll be a bonfire blazing for me in the village street on the day I come back. Has nobody written a song on how I exposed the trick-o'-the-loop? – they've written songs on less important events than that.'

'They're too busy getting ready for the harvest,' Philip said.

'Well, I've started to write one myself. By all appearances,

Philip, you'll not give me much help for I'm sure you're too busy coortin, these fine nights. When are we to have the big day?'

'We can't have that, Uncle, till you're ready to sing for us at the wedding,' Eileen said.

'I'd need something to cover this pate of mine first – I'd be a scarecrow among the guests,' and he reached out to the little table, lifted an enamel mug, and balanced it upside down on top of his head. 'Would I be all right wearing that?'

Nelly laughed till the tears came into her eyes. 'We'll be put out of the ward, D. J., if you don't stop the capering.'

'And now for the little song I was telling you about,' and putting his hand under the pillow he drew forth a folded-up sheet of notepaper. 'It's not finished yet, but I'll read what there is of it.' He cleared his throat, called them closer to him and began:

One bright summer morning as the birds they did sing
There was Point-to-Point races at the Lough's eastern ring;
There were horses of all kinds – black, brown, and grey,
And trick-o'-the-loop men thick in the fray.
There were boys from the bogs, and boys from the shore,
Shopboys and builders and greenhorns galore.
And there was D. J. Caffrey who biked out for the day,
And Daly and peelers without extra pay.

'That's as far as I've got,' he said, folding up the paper with care, 'but when it's finished and I put a rollicking air to it I'll give it its first public performance on the day you're married.'

'Nobody could do it better,' Philip said, 'but I hope you'll let me down easy.'

D. J. tapped his forehead and winked a cunning eye. 'You never can tell what's in store for you in that attic of mine.' He turned then to Nelly. She looked very thin in black and he told her she was failed away to scrapins and that she should take a good rest and go somewhere for a change.

'I'm getting plenty of rest these days,' she said. 'Anne is down on her holidays and she and Eileen bring my breakfast up to bed every morning. And as for the change I'm thinking of buying the lodge to live in. Philip is going to do it up from top to bottom. Would you care to come and live in it with me?'

'The lodge! In the name of God what possessed you to think of that for a dwelling! The diamond-paned windows would remind you of the workhouse, and coming to the door in the morning and seeing nothing but the rusty spikes of the big gate – Pooh, you might as well be in a jail!'

'A lick of white paint would soon scatter the rust. And if that wouldn't please you we could have the gates removed altogether.'

'And the trees shuffling at night,' D. J. said, and shrugged his shoulders as if he were cold. 'The place would give me the bloody creeps. And sure nobody would walk out there on a winter's night for a game of cards.'

'We all would,' Eileen said. 'Wouldn't we, Philip?'

'You wouldn't think of living with Johnny P.M. surely!' Nelly said.

'Who said I was going to live with Johnny P.M.?' he answered her sharply. 'I didn't say it!' and he leaned away from her.

'Well, I thought I'd be the best person to look after you,' Nelly said. 'You'll need somebody to cook for you, and maybe somebody to help you in and out of bed.'

'I'll have a stick but I'm damned if I'll let anybody make an invalid out of me.'

'You'll have to be sensible, D. J. You'd not have far to walk to Mass of a Sunday. And there's Philip will make it as fit to live in as a palace.'

'I'll do that all right. I'll see that the very best of stuff goes into it,' Philip said.

'I'm afraid you're buying the cage before you've caught the bird,' D. J. said coldly. 'I've my own plans and I don't want

anyone arranging or pre-arranging my affairs until I'm out of
this. Do you hear that – the lot of you? And you can tell that
to your father, Eileen.'

His face grew solemn. Nelly looked at him and then at the
old man in the next bed and back to D. J. again. She was afraid
to ask him what his plans were, and in the silence she drew
forth her handkerchief, blew her nose, and looked at Eileen
and Philip, hoping they would say something that would drag
his mind back to a lighter mood. But it was D. J. who spoke. 'I
wonder, Philip, would it be too much to ask you to bring my
old friend Johnny P.M. out to see me. I would take it as a great
favour if you'd do that for me.'

'Certainly,' Philip said.

'I'll see that it's done,' Nelly said. 'You can depend on that.
Is there anything else we could do for you?'

'Not a happorth,' he said.

They got up to take their leave and they left fruit and cake
on his little table, and Philip gave him a large box of cigarettes.
He thanked them and said that they had gone to too much
trouble entirely, and as they left the ward he called Nelly back
and asked her for the loan of a pound or two as he would like
now and again to send a few shillings out to back a horse. It
was the only comfort he had left and it would make the daily
paper more interesting for him, and he assured her he would
pay her back every shilling as soon as Bob's estate was wound
up. She opened her handbag and gave it to him and advised
him not to be foolish.

'A few shillings wouldn't make anyone foolish,' he said, and
thanked her. 'And see that Johnny is sent out soon.'

'I'll take a walk out there tomorrow and I'll explain to him
that you want to see him.'

She left him, and the following day she took the key of the
lodge and set out to visit it and to call on Johnny on her way.
Anne came with her for she had arranged to call at the school
which her father had boasted would suit her down to the

ground. On approaching the school they heard the drone of the children, and Anne stood for a few minutes at the gate talking loudly to Nelly, so as to warn the schoolmistress and give her time to get her classes in the best of order and on their best behaviour. They walked slowly to the door and knocked. After a few minutes they knocked again and it was opened immediately by the junior assistant who taught the infants at that end of the room. She welcomed them into the school-room. There was an unnatural silence, and none of the forty children looked around as the schoolmistress walked forward to greet her guests. Some of the children were writing on copy books, some grouped around a table on which was a flower-pot and a coloured ball that they had to draw, and at the top of the room near the teacher's desk seven of the bigger children, boys and girls, stood in a semi-circle with reading books in their hands.

'Silence, children, and continue at your work,' said the teacher in a pleasant voice; and with a ruler in her hand she pointed to this group and now to that, showing how skilfully she had them all employed: some at arithmetic, some at draw-ing, some composition, and others reading. Anne expressed her astonishment and told her that she herself found it difficult to manage even one class.

'It's experience,' the teacher said, 'though at times I feel that a man is needed to get the best out of the bigger boys. They grow surly and you haven't to take any notice of it.'

She lifted a composition from a child here and there and handed them to Anne.

'The handwriting is beautiful,' Anne said. 'You would never get the like of that from city children.'

'I wouldn't take slovenly work from them. I would keep them in after school-time and make them write it over again,' said the teacher. 'And do you know: twenty years after a pupil would leave this school I'd know their handwriting among a thousand?'

Poor Bob knew a lot about it too, thought Nelly, for he was never done rubbing their scribbles off the old shutters.

Anne glanced at a composition on 'Haymaking':

> Summer is the time for making hay. If you made it in bad weather the cows would not eat it. If we did not make hay the cows would starve in the winter time for they would have no fodder. They would have nothing to eat and then we would not get any milk or butter. We would have to import these things from other countries like Canada, Australia, Denmark, etc. . . .

'What do you think of it?' the teacher asked.

'The etcetera is very disarming.'

'That's a little dodge of mine,' said the teacher proudly. 'When they can't remember lists of names I tell them to put etc.'

She was handed other books to read. They were all of the same pattern and she realized that whether you wrote compositions in low school or high school the same impersonal and commentative approach prevailed; there was no personal immersion in the material and no consequent respect for individual differences. They were all written without feeling, without poetry – teaching children to be general and not particular, alive but not living: expressing everything but their true selves.

'I'm sure this is a good girl,' Nelly said, patting the little girl who had brought Bob the 'defaced money'.

'She is, Miss Caffrey, but she wasn't good today. She ruined her frock with blackberries and to look at her tongue you'd think she had swallowed a copying ink pencil.'

The bigger boys and girls laughed and the teacher tapped her ruler on the desk to call them to order. She got them to read, and afterwards Anne thanked her for showing her the workings of the school, and when they were out on the road that led to the lodge Nelly asked her if she'd like to be in charge of a school like that.'

'I would not, Aunt Nelly. I could never control all those classes.'

'You could learn how to do it. And look at the freedom you could have. You would be independent and you could live with me in the lodge if you wished. We could make it into a lovely little home.'

'I couldn't think of it, Aunt Nelly. I'd rather stay in the town.'

'Maybe you've a boy there?'

Anne laughed.

'In that case I won't press you. I hadn't heard.'

'It's nothing serious of course. But there is somebody I'm fond of.'

They reached the big gate and Nelly pushed away with her toe the stone that propped it closed, and with difficulty they swung the gate across the gravel. About them the trees were on the turn, spiky chestnuts lay on the paths, and some withered leaves rested on the tops of nettles at the side of the house. They opened the door and their voices echoed in the chilly air of the empty house, and the trees outside cast a mellow light through the diamond-paned windows. In the room that was the parlour bits of oilcloth clung to the nail-heads on the floor and in the sooty fireplace was a mildewed boot and an old clay pipe. 'The old tramps will have to find some other doss now,' said Nelly as they made their way upstairs where cobwebs clung to their faces and sleepy flies dozed on the walls.

'This will be my room, Anne,' and she opened one of the windows and looked out on the fields and trees that extended in a rise in front of them. 'You can see the chapel and the graveyard from here. Oh, if only D. J. will come with me. I could go to Mass every morning and visit the grave. Do you think he will come?'

'He will,' Anne said to please her.

'Your Uncle D. J. can be very headstrong and you'd never

know what he'd do. But if he doesn't come I couldn't live here my lone. I'd hate to leave the country now that Eileen will be coming to settle down in it and your father and mother coming to live in the shop. Please God, D. J. won't make any difficulties! Look how happy he could be here. We could have a little garden and we could cut down the trees that's dripping and putting a green scum on the slates, and we could paint the doors and windows a bright green and polish the verdigris off the brass knocker.'

They made their way downstairs and into the kitchen that was bright and airy; it had a porcelain sink that to Nelly's surprise had not one speck of iron rust.

'Look how dry it is, Anne. There isn't a spot of damp on the tiles. Working here would be a great pleasure.'

They came out then, and closing the door sharply its boom disturbed the dozens of rabbits that were feeding on the grass-grown drive. 'D. J. will have to get a gun. We could never keep a garden with those playboys about. It's a pity I didn't mention that when I was speaking to him. I'll tell Johnny P.M. to mention it to him.'

On their way back she called to see Johnny about his visit to the hospital. They saw him standing at his door but as Nelly was making her way up the lonin that led to his house he went inside and barred the door. She went to the window, tapped at it, and called out who she was and what she wanted. He opened the door then and brought her in and she noticed at once the coloured pictures of racehorses that were pasted to the walls. She explained that it was D. J. who told her to call as he wanted him to come to see him; Philip Doran would give him a lift in in his lorry and take him back again; and if he'd call at the shop in the morning her nephew would fit him out with a new suit.

'Will you go, Johnny?'

'I will, Miss Caffrey. I'll be down in the morning.'

She shook hands with him and gave him a few shillings to

buy tobacco. He walked with her to the door and raising his
stick he pointed to the thatched roof where a few blades of corn
had sprouted. 'There's a poor yield in my harvest the year,' he
said. 'The boys is always asking me is my harvest saved.
That's the way they make fun of me! But me and D. J. will
come into our own, Miss Caffrey – that's what he wants me for.'

'I'm sure it is,' she said. 'D. J. will be good to you.'

'I fairly miss him out of the house,' he said. 'I miss his songs
in the evening.'

'He'll be back soon, Johnny. You'll not forget about the
morning?'

'Is it Johnny P.M.? You need have no fear, Miss Caffrey –
I'll walk down as soon as the sun thinks of rising.'

In the morning he was standing at the shop door before the
sun had time to dry the dew from the slates. The early train
came in and went out again. The postman cycled by with his
letters. Daly opened up his shop and chased the cats out of the
window, and a half an hour later the blind went up in the
Caffreys' but the window was too misty to see who stirred
about inside. Presently the door opened, and Johnny saw a
pale young man come out with a foot-scraper in one hand and
a brush in the other.

'Are you the man that Miss Caffrey told to call?' Frank asked
him. Johnny nodded and followed Frank inside, and Frank
stooping over the stove put a light to it and turned up the
wicks. 'That'll not be long taking the chill out of the air,' he
said, and rubbed his hands briskly together. 'Take a seat like a
good man,' and he fingered his chin thoughtfully. 'We'll start
with boots first – any particular kind that you'd fancy?'

'If it'd be all the same to you, young fella, I'd like a Sunday
boot.'

'I can give you that in black or brown,' said Frank, and as he
stood on a small step ladder to take down his boxes of boots he
told Johnny to take off his old ones.

He fitted him out with socks and boots but Johnny being

short in the legs and long in the body he had difficulty in attiring him in a suit and he had to compromise by giving him the trousers of one suit and the coat and vest of another.

'I'm grand now,' said Johnny.

'You've everything except a hat.'

'I cut the rope at that. The hat I have will do me – I'm as fond of it as I am of my pipe and my stick.'

Frank tried to convince him that the old hat robbed the good look of the suit but Johnny shook his head, and on going outside to wait for Doran Nelly called him for a bite of breakfast. She had already sent the girls away from the kitchen to ease his embarrassment, and as he drank his tea with the spoon in his cup she herself went off to the scullery coming to the table now and again to refill his cup and to cut more bread for him, and when Doran drove up in the lorry Johnny was sitting in the armchair where Bob had died and was saying over and over again to Anne and Eileen that he'd have married long ago if he'd known that there were girls in the village as kind as Nelly Caffrey.

Philip drove him to the hospital, escorted him to the ward and told D. J. that he'd be back within half an hour.

'Well, Johnny, my lad,' D. J. said to him when they were left alone. 'It's a heartsome sight to see an old friend again.' He passed no remark on the suit nor did Johnny. Johnny stared around him, his eye travelling slowly from bed to bed, from floor to ceiling, halting at last on the wooden frame that held up D. J.'s leg. He began to laugh. 'It's like a weaver's loom,' he said, and laughed again. 'It's like an old loom with broken threads.' His eyes rested on D. J.'s shaven head and D. J. smiled at him. 'Well, what do you see there?'

'I see a poor harvest,' Johnny said, 'a poor harvest and the cut from a scythe.'

'It was a bottle the buggers cut me with,' D. J. said.

'So I heard.'

'Do the lads talk much about me?' D. J. asked, and raised

himself up against the pillows. 'Do they talk much about me?' he asked again with impatient eagerness.

'They do. They say you killed Bob.'

'Who said I killed him?'

'They all said it the night Bob died. They said you were a rogue and that you marked the cards. And they said something about a cuckoo that'd build a nest of its own.'

D. J. lay back on the pillows. 'So that's the dirt and scum I had about me. I'm beginning to see them for the first time. When you're down they'll keep you down!' And he remembered the evening he was drunk and they tied a towel to his tail. 'I'm finished with them. They're no fit company for a travelled man.' He remained silent for a long time.

'Are you going to take me to live in the shop?' Johnny asked. 'There's a nice young fella in it now – is that your helper?'

'That's a son of John's,' D. J. said. He smoothed the scar on his head. 'The shop is for him, Johnny, but I'll be in a house close to yours and you'll go for my newspaper in the mornings and you'll ramble over to see me in the evenings for a smoke and a sing-song. I'll cold shoulder the village spawn! Ignorance is a curse,' he said to himself. 'They laughed themselves sick when Bob broke his window.'

He put his hand under the pillow, drew out the piece of paper with his song on it and tore it in fragments, and when Philip came back for Johnny he handed him a note to deliver to Nelly.

'And Doran,' he said, 'when you're fixing the lodge I want you to take the big gates to hell out of the road and to cut down all the trees that darken the windows. Do you hear that? It must be ready to live in when I step out of this. At the outside I'll give you three weeks.'

'You said that for all the world like old Bob,' Philip said to him. 'I'll start the men on it right away.'

'Johnny, here, will keep an eye on you,' D. J. said and winked at Philip.

'I'll do that, D. J. You can trust me. I can see all that goes on from my own doorstep,' Johnny said, and on bidding him goodbye D. J. gave him a tin of tobacco that Brendan had sent to him. 'When you get off the lorry, Johnny, tell Nelly that Philip has a letter for her – he's apt to forget if Eileen's anywhere around.'

On their way back in the lorry Johnny didn't utter a word. He pretended to doze, and as his stick kept tapping to the vibration of the engine he rhymed to himself: 'Philip Doran has a letter for Nelly Caffrey!' The lorry stopped at the pump at the side of the house, and as Johnny climbed out backwards from the high seat he asked Philip to be a decent man and allow him to deliver the letter.

Nelly opened the letter at the door, and running back into the house she called out to Anne and Eileen that their Uncle D. J. was coming to live with her in the lodge. She ran into the shop and told Frank, and hurrying out to the post office she phoned her brother John.

'D. J.'s coming to the lodge,' she said out of breath. 'He's coming. Get him to sign an agreement about the shop.'

'I will not,' John said back to her over the phone. 'I know him too well not to do that – the sight of an agreement form might send him back on his tracks. We'll let the bird sit.' He told her, then, of the furniture he could spare her from the house in town, and that in another four weeks or so he would retire to Monabeg and leave the house in town to Brendan and Anne. He placed down the receiver and clapping his hands he went to his two assistants and told them that in a short while they would be getting promotion.

And the evening that D. J. was to leave the hospital he and Mary went for him in a taxi, and in order to avoid passing through the village D. J. made them take another route. They drove up to the lodge door, the wheels of the car cutting the freshly raked gravel and crushing the fallen leaves. Inside a fire was blazing, the table set for tea, and Anne and Eileen arrayed in new frocks. Nelly helped him to an armchair but on placing a boss near it for his leg he knocked it away with his stick and told her not to make an invalid out of him.

After the tea Frank and Philip came in. They had been out shooting on the lough and they brought him a pair of wild duck.

'You'll give us a song, Uncle D. J.?' Mary asked him.

'My voice is gone,' he said. 'Let Nelly there wind up the gramophone.'

'It's you we want to hear,' Eileen coaxed. 'Go on, Uncle D. J.'

'Give's your own song about the Point-to-Point races,' Philip put in. 'The bit you read us in the hospital was damned good. Go on, D. J., give us that.'

'What song is that?' Frank asked. 'I never heard it.'

'No, nor you'll never hear it from me,' D. J. said.

'Give it to us and none of your codding,' Philip persisted.

'Can't you leave the man alone,' Nelly said, 'and let him sing whatever he likes, himself?'

'Here, here,' they said, and clapped their hands gently to encourage D. J.

He thought for a minute, and sitting on the armchair with his hands folded on his lap he closed his eyes and began to sing 'The Last Rose of Summer.' His brother John looked across at him, thinking of the last time he had heard him sing that song – in the snow with his cap stretched out like a beggar.